The Lost Queen of Crocker County

a Novel

ELIZABETH LEIKNES

sourcebooks

Published by Sourcebooks Landmark, an imprint of Sourcebooks, Inc.
P.O. Box 4410, Naperville, Illinois 60567-4410
(630) 961-3900
Fax: (630) 961-2168
sourcebooks.com

Library of Congress Cataloging-in-Publication Data
Names: Leiknes, Elizabeth, author.
Title: The lost queen of Crocker County : a novel / Elizabeth Leiknes.
Description: Naperville, Illinois : Sourcebooks Landmark, [2018]
Identifiers: LCCN 2017040811 | (softcover : acid-free paper)
Subjects: LCSH: City and town life--Fiction. | Homecoming--Fiction.
Classification: LCC PS3612.E35884 L67 2018 | DDC 813/.6--dc23 LC
record available at https://lccn.loc.gov/2017040811

Printed and bound in the United States of America.
VP 10 9 8 7 6 5 4 3 2 1

For my husband, John

"Follow your bliss, and the universe will open doors where there were only walls."

—Joseph Campbell

PROLOGUE

A FAINT BUT UNDENIABLE EAR of corn lived on my left calf. I was born with it, a six-and-a-half-inch birthmark filled with alternating light-dark-light-dark pigmentation, which created a pattern that can only be described as corncob-like.

"It won't come off, Mama," I said, scrubbing.

Mama was having none of it. "Now, we've talked about this, Janie Marie Willow. This is a part of you." She touched my shoulder and sat down next to me and Strawberry Shortcake on my bed. "This is who you are."

"But the kids at school call me Corncob." I scrubbed some more, the hot washcloth rubbing my skin raw.

Mama took the rag from my hand and looked at my leg. "You know what they call birthmarks in Italy?"

I just squinted at her.

"*Voglia*. And in Spanish, *deseo*." Mama patted my leg. "But no matter the language, Janie, the translation of the word 'birthmark' always means the same thing—'wish.'" She tucked my blond hair behind my ear. "A birthmark is a mother's secret wish for her child," she said, smiling. "Your daddy and I wanted you so badly, and you are marked with that love." She traced her index finger around my birthmark. "You are our hope. Our dream."

But why mark me with corn? I was already surrounded by it. Did Mama think I was going to somehow run out?

She kissed my forehead like a mother does, walked over to my bedroom door, and said one last thing before going downstairs to make supper. "Never forget where you come from, Janie Willow. It's the surest way to get lost in this world."

No way. I would always be surrounded by cornfields, because I was never going to leave. This was home. This was where I belonged.

I glanced up at the picture hanging on my bedroom wall, a framed poster with the word *Iowa* spelled out in bold block letters at the top. The center of the poster featured Des Moines and the state capital building surrounded by other midwestern fare—a John Deere combine, grain silos, farmhouses dotting the hills, a fiery sun disappearing into endless cornfields—but my favorite part of the picture, the part I would remember for the rest of my life, was the miniscule depiction of the rest of the world. On the outskirts of the poster, small versions of larger-than-life world landmarks—the Statue of Liberty, the Eiffel Tower, the Acropolis—jutted out like mere cartoon afterthoughts, leaving my truth in the middle of the poster, in the middle of the heartland: Iowa was the center of the world.

CHAPTER ONE

Present Day

I'M IN A DARK room with James Bond again.

The interloping morning sun tries to peek through my thick office blinds. To be clear, I'm on a couch and Mr. Bond is on a projection screen, but we are sharing something together. This scene, the one I watch more than I should, is both the best and the worst of life, a scene that saves me from my daylight.

A tuxedoed Bond smiles at his newlywed wife in her gown, white chiffon scarf blowing in the wind. They talk of a sunny future while the Aston Martin, adorned with pink and white wedding roses, hums down the ocean-side highway. Bond pulls to the side of the road to remove the flowers from the hood and kiss her. Just then, his arch enemy drives by and sprays the car with machine gun bullets before it continues down the road. James Bond remains unscathed, as he does, but not Tracy—no, not Tracy.

The broken Bond holds his slain bride and kisses her dress. When he speaks, I speak. "She's simply resting," he tells the policeman, and my chest tightens as fate plays out on screen. I pause when Bond pauses. His past is too much to run from. It is his fault and he knows it. Like I always do, I let him carry the guilt. "There's no hurry now," he says. "We have all the time in the world."

I close my eyes while the credits creep by.

"Jane, are you done yet?" And then knocking.

Damn.

In a practiced maneuver, I turn off the projector, turn on the lights, open the blinds, and let in the harsh LA sunshine. I sit down in my father's old oak desk, a sturdy reminder of where I come from. I look out the window at the clear view of the Hollywood hills in the distance. Humanity exists, somewhere, ten floors down, but the closest I can get to it are the faces staring at me when I swivel my chair back around to see four framed movie posters— *Moonraker*, *Big Fish*, *Magnolia*, *The Wizard of Oz*—hanging on my office wall.

I glance over at the fifth movie poster resting on the floor, propped up against the wall in the corner of my office. A birthday gift from my parents five years ago. Every time I try to hang it up, I can't. Some stories need to be earned, and I am not worthy of this one. Maybe someday I will be able to watch that film again, hear the proverbial ringing bell and the stars talking to one another, sorting out the logistics of a lost soul. But for now, when loneliness wears me down, I look at them, Jimmy Stewart and Donna Reed, smiling, grateful, surrounded by children and love, and I am struck by the impossibility of a second chance at life.

Sidney knocks again.

"Coming," I stall. I put James Bond back in his DVD case, erasing all traces of nostalgia, an unsavory notion in the world of critics. By now, the whole city is reading what I think of Hollywood's recent indie-breakout-film-turned-Oscar-buzzworthy hit, *The Hole of Schmidt*, an in-depth drama about a man and his hole.

I finally let in Sidney Parker, my editor for the last ten years. He walks into my office sporting jet lag and a serious tan, even for LA. The trepidation over what he might have missed while he was gone shows on his face. He's come back from vacation on a Friday in anticipation of my latest assignment. He takes the newspaper tucked under his arm and places it, along with a to-go coffee cup, on my desk. When he stretches out his arms, I go in for a welcome-home hug, but I know what he wants. He wants to know that it's all going to be okay. All editors force small talk, pretend to be casual, but what they really want to know, to hear, is that you've not only met a deadline, but that you've done so without making enemies in Hollywood, the epicenter of all things movies.

"So...finished? In the paper today, right?" Sidney says, brow raised, a smile pending the right answer. "Tell me you didn't call the most anticipated film of the year a piece of crap or something." His almost-smile fades, replaced by panic. "Jane?"

"Not exactly."

When I wrote the review last week, my diction changed with each breath. At first, I'd typed *uninspired*, then backspaced, typed *soulless*, backspaced again, then whispered to no one, "It is what it is," and retyped the harsh truth: *excrement*. But the words ended up evolving, sentence by sentence, becoming more accurate, really. So accurate, in fact, they became the title of my review. Incessant revision is a habit I've inherited from my father, who has always believed nothing is ever a final draft, even one's words. I save the act of reviewing, reliving, and revising to the only place it works: on the page.

Sidney buries his face in his hands. He stands before me in his tweed-for-Friday vest, always expensive and always tailored, looking a bit like a deranged Gregory Peck prepared to kill his beloved mockingbird who sometimes sings songs he doesn't like. He runs his hand over his dark hair, a gesture that tells me he doesn't know what to do next. Sid has an affinity for anything classic and prefers the good old-fashioned newspaper print to the ever-ready online world, so when he opens the newspaper rather than grab his phone, I'm not surprised.

I try not to cringe as he rifles through the paper, page by page, toward the film reviews. He stops. His finger traces an invisible line from Cinegirl's caricature in the top left of the page to the headline title of my review.

Wait for it.

"'What a Schmidt Hole'?" he screams. He shakes the newspaper at me. "'What a Schmidt Hole'?" he screams again, like he doesn't believe his own voice. "I'm only gone six days and I come home to this shit storm?"

"Schmidt storm," I correct him, feeling out the revision as the words hang in the air.

"You called the most anticipated film of the year a piece of crap."

"Excrement, actually," I say, "and then Schmidt Hole, but never—"

"Listen, Jane." Sidney takes a breath, tries to calm himself. "Remember?" he says as he points to the Gotham Award hanging on my wall. "Let me remind you what they said about you. 'Jane Willow's prose'"—his hands frame an imaginary headline—"'straddles both auteur and blockbuster films…her writing is startling, explosive, sophisticated.'" Sidney softens. "Cinegirl is the most widely read… Would it kill you to throw Nick a bone?"

"I don't write for Nick, or any other director, Sid. He'll get over it. I loved his last film." I swipe my bangs away from my face. "I just really hate this one."

I really do hate this film. I don't tell Sidney that it reminds me of the giant hole in my life. I don't tell him that I hate that this Schmidt character thinks he can dig his way to redemption. I don't tell him that I hate this film because it has the audacity to find hope amid dismal circumstances.

I glance at the framed picture of my parents placed on the farthest corner of my desk. My dad, the only lawyer in my hometown of True City, Iowa, was considered our unofficial judge by popular opinion and can smell the faintest hint of horse crap long before the closing argument. He has English and law degrees from the University of Iowa, but his no-nonsense sensibility makes him well loved by his coffee-shop friends, some who didn't even graduate high school. I begin to mimic my dad's voice, which captures Bobby Knight's intensity, a convincing tone booming from each word. "People want the truth, kid. You're a bullshit detector…" I say, just like Dad says all the time. "You get that from me."

Sidney, who has listened to stories about my dad over the years, leans forward in his chair, probably his way of acknowledging my hereditary predisposition for detecting excrement. "But this is an art house film, Jane." Speaking of bullshit, I smell it as Sidney continues. "It's got some really cutting-edge scenes, like…"

"Like the nine-minute scene featuring"—I drum roll on my

7

desk with two pencils—"the many nuances of dirt! Very avant-garde. And *Hole of Schmidt*? Really?"

"It's a double meaning. *Whole* of Schmidt. I think." He gestures a rough outline of a person and then shrugs. A shrug from Sidney means defeat. "The whole man. You know..."

I do know. When I'm watching movies, talking about movies, thinking about movies, I feel whole. I'm no expert on life, but I know movies. They are sacred to me. Once, when I got into an intellectual scuffle with a who's-who producer, I ended up having to see a therapist because the owner of the *Times*, Sid's boss's boss, demanded that a professional try to diagnose why I didn't "play well with others." The therapist said I was clinically fine but socially detached, likely from some sort of emotional trauma, which shut the big-times up for a while. What all of these idiots don't know is that I don't see life like them, through simple, rudimentary visual cues. I see everything like a cinematographer in perpetual record mode, comparing each image to scenes from films I hold dear. The problem is, real life never holds up.

"He's digging a hole to end world hunger, Sid." I throw up my hands. "World hunger should never be in the same sentence as a man's hole."

"So, you didn't feel even a little—"

"I felt hungry, Sid!" I snorted. "Alert the morality police. I felt hungry in a movie about world hunger." I raised my pointer finger. "Okay, first of all, it was forty-five minutes too long, and second"—I raised another finger—"it somehow managed to be a heartless film about a heartrending topic." I raised only my third, middle finger in the universal fuck-off position. "It was a self-indulgent, masturba-tory romp, and Nick Wrightman should strangle himself with his own film. God knows there should be loads of it on the cutting-room floor, because he'll never work again."

"You're kind of scary when you talk," Sid said.

I pucker my lips into a pout, but deep down I know I'm right. Nick Wrightman will never work again—he's used up his chance. I used to believe in second chances. But that was Before. The Before Jane thought about things like that, believed in things like that. I'm After Jane, linguistically tidy but caustic and jaded, like an honest, brazen film review. Eloquent yet unforgivable.

"No, Jane, I mean it," Sidney says, demanding eye contact. "In print, you're formidable, but when you speak…you destroy people."

I wait a beat and say, "Get the sand out of your vagina, Sidney Poitier Parker."

Sidney's parents, third-generation Los Angelenos who loved their city and who loved movies, named Sidney after one of the greatest actors of their time. When I want to ask Sidney to catch a bite to eat, I ask in my most convincing tone, "Guess who's coming to dinner?" He always says yes, because that's what self-appointed father figures do.

In my assessment, the most accurate reduction of a person's personality is finding out their favorite movie. If someone asks Sid what his favorite movie is, he'll say *Citizen Kane* because it's a respectable answer for an editor of serious film criticism, but Sid's real, secret favorite movie is *Butch Cassidy and the Sundance Kid*. I happen to know this. I also happen to know that deep down, he is a lovable outlaw masquerading in the City of Angels, secretly defying his destiny. Heart over art sometimes. We all have our secrets.

Instead of a rebuttal, Sidney looks up on the wall at the framed first-run edition of my weekly column, Cinegirl, featuring a cartoon-drawing likeness of me: Bridget Bardot meets Debbie Harry, my pronounced upturned nose further exaggerated. I wonder if Sidney is comparing us, me and Cinegirl, with our sixties-inspired mascara and wild hair. The only difference between us is Cinegirl's perma-smile and seemingly perky attitude.

In my least perky voice, I say, "Hey, let's call Nick, tell him his movie's a piece of crap, and then order pizza. There's a marathon showing of *The Texas Chainsaw Massacre*. It'll cheer us up."

Sidney's eyes widen. "Who *are* you?"

I greet him like I greet everyone: Bond style. "Willow," I say, hand outstretched. "Jane Willow."

"No, seriously, what happened to you as a child?" Sidney's brow furrows. "Mean imaginary friend? Lead paint? I thought midwesterners were polite."

I nod. "Pathologically polite. Something in the corn, maybe." I pause, glance up at my wall of accomplishment, proof of solid midwestern work ethic, and think of my mother. "Every bedtime, my mother made me repeat her down-home mantra: Work hard. Be nice."

Sidney takes that in. "Well, one out of two isn't bad."

I walk to the window and stare out at the hilly, Los Angeles sprawl. "Look, Sid, America doesn't care that I was a film studies major. They don't care that I know that the awful nine-minute dirt scene employed nonsynchronous sound and that the denouement was one big deus ex machina. They don't care that one of the perks of Cinegirl's remarkable popularity is this beautiful office. They don't care that I say inappropriate things at inappropriate times. They don't care what I look like, and they sure as hell don't care if I'm socially pleasant. My guess is they have better things to do than ponder the motivations of a film critic."

I turn to him. "They love me because I tell them the truth. Like the Master." I point at my shrine to film critic legend Pauline Kael on my desk, which includes a small sign—*WWPKS* (What Would Pauline Kael Say)—propped up on a miniature easel, along with a classic photo of the famous, late film critic draped in a writerly scarf. "Now, she was a woman with balls."

Sidney nods, uncrosses his legs, and focuses his attention on the photo of my parents. Sidney knows it's home I'm avoiding, not my parents, but nevertheless, I tread lightly.

"My parents were just here two months ago, Sid. I took them to Grauman's Chinese Theater, even let them sleep in my bed. They can fly here whenever they want."

My parents are getting older, and I should try harder to see them. It's difficult for them to travel, even if Dad does have his own plane—Hawkeye, his single-engine dream. But they'll have to come to me. I don't go home. Ever. I can't.

"And I haven't told you the news." I put my shoulders back, proud, and turn toward Sidney to see his face. "I'm planning a surprise trip for them—five-star treatment." I pause. "Red-carpet treatment."

"Really." Sidney sits up a little straighter.

"Yes. My dates for the Oscars—Mom and Pop. I'll have to tell Mom that she can't wear her housecoat and cardigan, and Dad will probably give several A-listers unsolicited legal advice." I take a deep breath in preparation for the real news. "But the tickets to the Oscars is the small surprise, Sid. This is the big surprise."

I pull up a photo on my phone from the Century 21 website of a townhome in the heart of Studio City with a *Sold* banner. "No more Iowa winters for Mom and Pop," .I say, showing him my parents' new home away from home. "What it really means is that they can come to me rather than me going to see them, that I can see them whenever I want instead of once a year."

Sid stares for a moment, and his voice breaks a little when he says, "So this is what you've been saving for." He doesn't look up, just keeps staring at the photo. "Well, that's really something."

When he finally looks up, he sees me scowling at some sort of children's party invitation on the top of my mail pile. It is adorned with a big, pink heart. When I pick it up, he says, "Ah, you really do have a heart, Jane Willow."

"Shut up, Sid," I say, cringing at the thought of attending a kid's party.

"And it's gone again." Sid nods and leans against my desk.

The pink-hearted envelope features balloons, and the inside invitation has a birthday cake with seven candles.

> To: Ms. Jane Willow
> From: María Pacheco
> What: Felicia's Birthday Party
> When: Saturday, 11 a.m.

My assistant, Maria, has also attached a Post-it Note to the bottom of the invitation. *Please know this will be totally lame…nothing like your usual fancy events…money's tight lately. Anyway, for some reason, Felicia wants you to come. Don't feel obligated.*

I stare at the note, lingering on "for some reason." Three small words can pack quite a punch. Maria probably thinks I don't know Felicia exists. I've never bothered to tell Maria that sometimes, when Maria's sitter gets flaky and she brings Felicia to the office with her, Felicia and I hang out. When she's supposed to be in the conference room coloring until she dies of boredom, I sneak her into my office and teach her things every little girl needs to know, like why it's imperative that producers stop overusing gerunds in movie titles. *Finding Forrester, Drowning Mona, Being John Malkovich*—okay, I really do love that one—but come on already, and I teach Felicia the harsh truth: people who don't know their favorite movie when asked are just plain dumb. When she tells me she thinks *Frozen* is silly and how she loves animals even more than she loves cupcakes, we watch *Born Free* together, and I introduce her to the "other" Elsa. Lions are her favorite.

"Have you told your parents about the house yet?" Sid asks.

"I'm gonna call them tonight," I say. "Mom's gonna cry"—I smile—"and Dad's gonna tell me I spent too goddamned much money, but then he'll tell all of his friends about it and be secretly proud."

Sid gazes out the window. "Why do you never go there?" He pauses before he says the next word. "Home."

My stomach twists and knots up.

Ah, home. We leave home to truly know it. If that isn't a load of crap. I left home because I needed to forget who I was. To me, this is as clear as a midwestern sky full of the brightest stars in space. Truth is, I tried so many times to go home. Whenever I got close to going back, got brave enough to confront my past, a new movie emerged, new characters' arcs that came full circle without me having to. Eventually, today became tomorrow, tomorrow became someday, and someday never came.

Answering the question isn't an option.

It's time to bring him out, the spy who loves me in my dreams, so I say, "We have all the time in the world."

Sidney has one last question. "Was that *On Her Majesty's Secret Service* playing in here earlier?"

I shrug his question away.

"You say you're all about truth, Jane, but..." He stopped. "Secrets are dangerous things."

"Okay." I nod with purpose. "You want the truth?" I blurt, then I soften. "Truth: I tear up when Wilson floats away in *Castaway*. David Lynch films put me to sleep better than Ambien. And I love James Bond films because my dad and I... They remind me of happy times." I look out the window, a break from the truth.

"Jane." Sidney lowers his head. "I shouldn't have—"

"No, you're right. My past is complicated." The truth begins to unravel. I head in a different direction. "Sid, you grew up here." I stretch my arms toward the window. "It's exciting here. Botox gone wrong, fashionable cults, Mercury in retrograde, Steven Soderbergh at Whole Foods. Life here is one big, fantastical Tim Burton movie. We live in a city that nobody wants to leave." Fred Allen was right. Hollywood is a place where people from Iowa mistake one another for stars.

I sigh. "Life in Iowa is a rom-com cliché. Predictable dialogue. Incessant talk about the weather. Slurpees. Bad casseroles. Crying in sentimental movies, and using 'cute' as a definitive, stand-alone film critique. It's abysmal. And don't even get me started on the overwrought, over-referenced *It's not heaven, it's Iowa* bullshit. Middling movie. Middling, saccharine, vapid drivel—they're just fields, trust me; I've detasseled them. No dreams, no heaven. You think it's some storybook landscape that can heal with its good old-fashioned horse sense, but there are as many broken people there as there are in your city of broken dreams."

Time stops where I come from, I want to say. *No twist ending there,* I want to say. And let's face it, we're all holding out for the twist. Even though the secret I bear is evidence of the contrary, I say, "Nothing happens there."

Before Sidney can respond, my phone rings. "Willow," I say. "Jane Willow." I smile at Sidney. "Is this Cheryl from Century 21? All the paperwork's ready. I just have to fax—" I stop to listen. It isn't a woman's voice. I smile again. "Who is this? Did my parents put you up to this?" I cover the mouthpiece and playfully whisper to Sidney, "Apparently my parents are dead, Sid, so I'll finally be planning a trip home."

For a moment, I smile wide.

And then I drop the phone on the floor.

CHAPTER TWO

*S*IDNEY'S FACE LOSES ALL expression for a moment and then worry settles in his brow as he picks the phone off the floor and hands it to me.

The policeman on the phone is still talking, but all I can hear is what he said just seconds ago.

Plane crash.

My whole body goes numb. "Uh-huh," I say, barely audible, followed by "I understand." But I don't understand. Not really. I only heard the words: *Plane crash. Dad at the helm. They were together.*

"Yes. No," I choke out. I clench my hand, my nails digging deep into my own flesh. "I understand."

The truth seeps through to my insides, and my body betrays me. My posture sinks into submission. My vision is blurred with emotions so foreign, I have to reintroduce myself to them.

Shock. *Nice to meet you.* Anger. *How are you? Pissed off, I presume.* Loss. *It's been a while.*

The policeman's kind voice softens as he tells me how he had known my parents. How everyone knew them. How as police chief he looked up to my dad. How True City would feel this loss. How they were real gems.

I drift between present and past. I stare hard at the clock, willing it to slow. But it doesn't listen. The second hand moves in a perfect cadence, a mean metronome reminding me of what was, what will never be again.

Time does not stop. It keeps *tick-tick-ticking* away from things that should've been: heartfelt phone calls, refused trips home, red-carpet dreams.

"Was it my dad's fault?" I clear my throat and squeeze the phone to calm my trembling hand. "Was there anything he could've done?" I can tell Sidney thinks this question is odd, but making things right, proper revision, would have been important to Dad.

The policeman on the phone tells me there'd been an engine malfunction, and as I often do, I say the worst thing possible. "Thank God. If he hadn't done everything he could to right that plane, that would've killed him."

Sidney closes his eyes for a few seconds, then opens them, as if to blink away my unfortunate phrasing.

I search for the right words.

Words are not permanent.

"He believed in making things right." I swallow away the lump in my throat.

I hang up the phone, stare, in shock.

"My dad," I finally say, unable to look at Sidney. "He thought life was one giant rough draft." My voice breaks, and I try to disguise a hiccup-breath, the kind of breath one takes midsob.

"Jane." Sidney rises to his feet, walks to where I stand, touches my shoulder.

I look out the window, avoid my own reflection, and think of Dad's words. "He'd say, 'We all screw up at some point. Try not to let it be you. But if it is you...'" I turn to Sidney, as if always-sunny Los Angeles were unworthy of my father's words. "'That is to say, if it is you, if you screw up, just make it right, kid.'"

But how can I make anything right? My parents are dead. I can hear my father's voice, as if we are both sitting on the porch together again, searching for the right words.

Dead.

Deceased.

That is to say, gone.

A full-body chill takes hold, a harsh reminder that I may never be warm again. Sidney's questions keep coming. *What can I do to help? Do you want me to have Maria clear your schedule? Are you okay?*

I can't answer a single one.

Instead, flashbacks arrive with haunting speed, faster than any director could ever storyboard. No time to recover. Mom and Dad holding my hand as we walk into *Star Wars*, my first time in a theater. Mom singing "Madam Librarian" while watching *The Music Man*. Fresh watermelon picnics under the big willow tree. Dad taking the training wheels off. Restoring the Aston Martin. Mom laying out patterns for Bond Girl–inspired prom dresses.

Cornfields and unconditional love...everywhere.

Sidney reminds me this is real. "This is... God, I'm so sorry, Jane. I don't even know what to say."

"I know."

Sid reluctantly leaves after I convince him I need a moment, and the second he does, the tears unleash.

This.

This is the moment I've dreaded my whole life, the moment I thought wouldn't come for another twenty years. They will go to their graves not knowing what happened to me, what I did, why I couldn't come home for all these years, what kind of person I really am. For this, I am grateful. They deserve at least that.

But they will also go to their graves never knowing the truth, never knowing that because I am weak, because I couldn't bear to face what I'd done, I let the magnitude of my secret and my shame outshine my love for them, and for that I will never forgive myself. Who could?

I should say something to someone, but my words are not my own. I am somewhere else, with someone else's words. I close my eyes and imagine us together one last time. My parents and I take off, flying through the air in Dad's single-engine dream. Dad clears his throat to temper his vulnerability and tells Mom, "Darlin', you're outta this world." She knows this is his version of "I love you," and she prefers it. She avoids looking at the impossibly blue sky ahead and at the tiny squares of land below, and instead looks at Dad.

This imaginary flight with my parents is the biggest montage of my life, and the screenplay in my mind writes itself, flowing out of me with the beauty of a perfect, backward glance.

I write how the sky had been their playground, how two people, husband and wife for forty years, courted each other in the clouds. I write how the big, blue Iowa sky—the only place Dad would ever sing—was their heaven. On the ground, they were servants to the ordinary, but up there? Up there they were ambassadors to the moon.

But if I think about what they saw in the last minutes before they died, if I think about how they loved it when the cornfields caught the golden sunlight of their crisp, autumn Iowa sky, I will have to remember other things.

I sniff away the moment, the day, everything that hurts, and look around my office at the life I've created for myself. The language of it all overwhelms me. Words. Words everywhere. For a woman who judges people by their actions, the irony is right there, right there in the pile of papers on my desk, in the framed awards on my wall, in a decade's worth of reviews—a barren wasteland of words is what remains—a bittersweet consolation to a parentless child.

I feel the bitter part come through. It is yesterday. And the day before that. Any day that isn't today. Any day in my past. Any day when a girl could bury a secret part of herself in a soil so rich, so fertile, it's hard to imagine anything unable to survive there.

But that was yesterday. And today is today. So I will push the inevitable onto tomorrow.

After all, there is all the time in the world.

And tomorrow, I will finally go home.

CHAPTER THREE

I SLUMP INTO MY RECYCLED bamboo chair at the Crossroads Café, the least crowded restaurant on my way home from work. Sid had begged me to come to his house, to drink away my sorrow with him, but I am finally going home tomorrow, and I have work to do.

A young, gum-chomping waitress fueled by organic food and blind optimism bounces over to my table, her extra-small T-shirt proudly displaying a button that reads *Real food has mud, not blood.*

Her voice smiles. "And how are *you* today?"

I muster a nod. *My parents are dead*, I want to say, but she seems really, really happy.

"Hi, I'm Clara," comes out in a singsong cadence. "I'll be helping you today," she says with a wide smile and teeth so white it hurts my eyes.

You can't help me.

"Can I get you started with an alkaline water or a shot of wheatgrass or maybe—"

"Bourbon." True bourbon is made from at least fifty-one percent corn, and since I'm heading back home where endless cornfields blanket the horizon, maybe this will help me acclimate.

"Aw," she says with an apologetic pout. "We don't serve alcohol here. Rough day?"

When I don't answer, she nervously glances up at the poster hanging next to my booth, and with my eyes, I dare her to try to cheer me up and invoke its message: *Give Peas a Chance.*

Do it, Clara. I've got nothing to lose.

There are no follow-up questions, because she doesn't really want to know how I am. Nobody out here does. Not really.

I am suddenly aware that I am far away from my home, that I have been far away for a long time, and I've never been so alone. Two other sets of silverware stare back at me, two-for-one meal specials scream out in loud fonts, and laughter from happy tables for two, three, and four fills the room.

I imagine if Mom and Dad were here. How Mom would tell Clara the waitress that she has lovely blue eyes and ask her if she got them from her mother, and how she'd listen for an answer, really listen without interrupting, like people here do just so they can talk about themselves. And then Dad would say, "Jesus Christ, Mary. Ya can't ask a thing like that. Maybe her mother's dead!" That last part, the morbid stuff-you-shouldn't-say-out-loud part, would somehow be louder than the rest of the sentence and attract a roomful of disapproving glares. But that wouldn't matter, you see, because somehow, Clara would find this all charming, and before Dad could finish his free iced tea refill, they all would've exchanged numbers, and she would have plans to stay on our farm on her way out East. She would love my parents because they are as real and bright as a giant, Iowa harvest moon.

Were. Were real. Were bright.

My eyes well up, and I turn toward the peaceful peas on the wall so nobody will see.

Clara wants to take my order, wants to get as far away from me as possible, whichever comes first. "What can I start you off with?"

I sniffle my almost-tears away like they're summer allergies, and before I can order a sensible low-carb garden salad, some long-ago craving unearths itself, and I suddenly feel the urge to feed it.

"I'll take a steak," I say, and after hearing my mother's reminder about manners in my head, add, "please."

"Super! Do you want the charred tofu, the seitan steak, or the sautéed mushroom steak?" Clara says as she points to a menu photo of a colossal mushroom the size of California held hostage between two gluten-free buns.

"A real steak." And then I whisper, "Made from an animal," like we're involved in some sort of carnivorous espionage. "And some mashed potatoes, with, like, a stick of butter," I add, my grief-induced state temporarily forcing me to be someone I used to be.

The look of horror on Clara's face says she can't decide what's worse, bovine homicide or a week's worth of carbs in one dollop of potatoes, the latest item to be vilified in the land of no-fun food.

When Clara returns fifteen minutes later with the best she could do—sweet potato fries and a veggie burger between two sad pieces of lettuce—I am struck by a new realization: perhaps my surly attitude isn't so much because I'm a total bitch, but that I've been chronically deprived of carbohydrates for years and have subsequently depleted my brain of serotonin and all things happy.

A skittish and covert Clara places the bill on the table and starts to turn away. "Wait. Here," I say, calling her back. Along with the bill, I give her a hundred-dollar tip, my apology for being a pain in the ass. When she softens, stops to give me a smile, I feel an undeniable longing for some sort of humanity, like this scene needs a more meaningful, cinematic resolution. So I ask her the only question that really matters.

I wait until our eyes lock and then with a smile ask, "Hey, what's your favorite movie?"

Clara readjusts a half-full glass of water perched on two dirty plates. She grins, confused. "What?"

"Your favorite movie, what is it?" I repeat, now noticing her name tag that reads: *Clara D.*

She stops, painfully in thought, but then loses her focus and glances out the window. A convertible on the street outside hums by, blaring Randy Newman's "I Love LA." Clara ponders for a few more seconds, and I prepare for the moment I've been waiting for, when a movie unites two random people scurrying through this thing called life.

"I don't watch movies," she says and darts away.

Now I am left alone to talk about movies all I want. All day. To nobody.

So there it is. A moment of clarity with Clara D.

I look down at the small bag sticking out of my purse, holding the DVD I've just bought Felicia for her birthday. I had planned on dropping it at the office in the morning for my perfect plan. No party. No people. No problem.

Hey, Happy Birthday, Felicia. Sorry I chose not to spend time with you on your special day. Here's a movie instead!

Must revise. Right now.

"Thank you, Clara D.," I say to myself and dial the number of my first of three accomplices.

"Sean," I say. "It's Jane Willow. You owe me a favor."

The next day I wake up, pack for my short trip home, and swallow away the lump in my throat that forms every time I look for texts from my parents.

But there is one thing I need to do, want to do, before I leave.

When I show up on the tree-lined street in Burbank, the whole affair looks less like a birthday party and more like a neighborhood barbecue. Seven pink balloons are tethered to the mailbox out front, and a small *Happy Birthday* sign sticks out of the tiny lawn. *Felicia* is written in with a black Sharpie.

Neighbors mill about, mingling amongst the aroma of meat on the grill and Maria's beautiful flower garden lining the sidewalk leading up to the small, modest home. Before I even have a chance to ring the doorbell, Felicia bounds out the front door and hugs me around the waist.

"I knew you'd come!" she says. "I'm really sorry about your mommy and daddy," she adds, taking my hand like a child does, followed by a heartfelt moment of solidarity. "I hate airplanes."

Maria is close behind and greets me like one greets her boss who has come to her daughter's birthday party when she should be planning a funeral.

"Jane..." She stops in front of me, trying to conceal her shock, partly that I showed up at all, but mostly that I showed up after yesterday's news. "How are you... I can't believe you..."

"You only turn seven once, right?" I say, handing her Felicia's gift—*Born Free* on Blu-ray and a Blu-ray player in case they didn't have one. I urge them to open it later, and tell Felicia to go have fun. We all walk to the backyard together, and sometime between my first and second trip to the adult beverage station (a must at any birthday party if you want return guests the following year) it happens.

It begins with the sweet part, the procession of caterers in baking smocks carrying tray after tray of cupcakes, each adorned with *Felicia* written in fancy-chocolate-cursive goodness. They walk past the small card table strewn with a few mismatched paper plates and napkins and unfold a large industrial table. They attract some attention from the partygoers as they begin to stack the cupcakes on a four-foot-tall wire frame in the shape of a giant number seven. Store-bought cupcakes will probably not taste as good as Maria's homemade sheet cake, but it is quite a sight—a giant mountain of Felicias, larger than life, ready to take on the world with love and luck on her side.

Before Maria can make her way over to the caterers to ask who sent them, if there's been some mistake, the real show begins. Two trucks, both with the LA Zoo sign and logo on the side, pull into the side driveway that leads to the backyard. Sean's nephew, the animal caretaker and outreach program director who brings his animals to the late-night talk shows, steps out of the truck. He and three other handlers wave to the partygoers, now brimming with excitement, and completely ignore me as instructed. One handler carries a giant blue-and-gold macaw on his forearm, while another mingles with the guests, showing off a baby orangutan who is clinging to her like a baby clings to its mother.

Then comes the best part, the climactic scene when Felicia, holding her own mother's hand, sees the cinematic moment of the day: Sean's nephew holding the newest addition to the LA Zoo family of cats—a baby lion cub.

"Mama, it's Elsa!" Felicia belts out, but then softens, careful not to scare the baby animal.

By now the crowd is overflowing with oohs and aahs, and I can't take my eyes off Felicia, who is beaming with wonder. "Do you guys know Elsa?" she says to the crowd. "She's from *Born Free*. That's my favorite movie!"

Every good woman knows her favorite movie. "Atta girl," I whisper to no one.

I almost don't notice a slow-moving cloud as it blocks the sun for a moment, because the scene here is so euphoric. I take one last close-up shot of Felicia, petting her Elsa, and look for my exit.

As I sneak out amid the bustling excitement, I hear Maria pleading with one of the animal handlers. "No, seriously, who set this up?" I can hear a slight fear in her question, a concern about the cost, so I call Sean's nephew over to the side of the house, out of view.

"Remember what I said, right? She won this, courtesy of the LA Zoo Outreach Program… God knows my donation should keep it up and running for quite some time."

He smiles. "Whatever you say, Ms. Willow—I hear you're a real ball breaker."

I shrug. "Hey, don't let anyone get mauled today, all right? I don't wanna see this end up on *Dateline.*"

I drive away from Burbank toward the unknown, my long trip home a long shot in a finished scene, and as the wind blows through my hair, I feel the weight of being free.

CHAPTER FOUR

*J*T'S BEEN THREE DAYS, eight hours, four minutes, and twelve seconds since I lost my whole family at the age of thirty-six.

A plane would've gotten me to Iowa too fast, left me with two days to spend in True City before my parents' funeral, so I take the long way home and drive. Any time one drives across the full length of Nebraska, it's considered the long way home, regardless of where home is, but my mode of transport and gift from my father—a fully restored 1964 Aston Martin DB5 painted in the quintessential *Goldfinger* Silver Birch, color code ICI 2829—makes me feel like the road is endless, no destination. The engine's purr soothes, numbs, anesthetizes.

This car, this sweet, sweet car, is the stuff of boyhood fantasies. Every time, and I mean every time I drive it, I am reminded of this. The envious looks, the long stares—most of them assuming that a woman couldn't possibly appreciate the magnificence of such a rare automotive gem, but they underestimate my own childhood fantasies fueled by images of Bond's DB5 racing down dark alleys, owning the rolling countryside. What the envious onlookers don't know is that after Bond marathons with Dad, I would imagine Q debriefing me about my very own modified Aston Martin, complete with revolving number plate, left- and right-mounted machine guns, and my personal favorite—the ejector seat. In seventh-grade math, while Mr. McCallister wrote algebraic equations on the board, I was somewhere else, racing through a tree-lined road, five car lengths ahead of the bad guys, moving fast toward a clandestine getaway with my finger on the smokescreen button—imagining the day when Dad's masterpiece would be complete.

And now, twenty years later, even though it doesn't have air-conditioning or power steering, I am still driving the dream. I actually prefer the amount of muscle needed to control this car, how you feel everything, the slight pull to the left, the oppressive heat when life gets sticky. I love that unlike other legendary cars—the Lamborghini, the Corvette, the Porsche—that say *board shorts* and *flip-flops*, the Aston Martin says *immaculate tailored suit*. Driving an Aston Martin is like spending stolen moments with an unattainable lover, and unlike most of the actors I meet, it does not disappoint in the flesh. When you first see that sleek shape, the elongated front and shorter back, it gives the illusion of hope, that you have more ahead of you than what you've left behind. Yes, that profile makes you think you can do anything. And when the all-aluminum-triple-carb-fed 4.0-liter straight-six roars for a second, then settles into a polite idle, you know you are ready to chase the horizon.

Right now, I'm not chasing anything. I'm inching my way through Nebraska—the state the never ends. I grew up surrounded by corn and have subconsciously looked for fields my whole life, but the cornfields outside of North Platte, Nebraska, blanket the land like mere frauds—weaker, shorter than Iowa corn. Knee-high by the Fourth of July. That's the saying, but this corn is barely waist high, and it is late August. Every field I pass, from Kearney to Grand Island, unsettles me, perhaps a precursor of what awaits me. What words would my father choose to describe my current state?

Orphaned.

Solo.

That is to say, alone.

Close to where Nebraska ends and Iowa begins, the landscape comes alive. Flat land gives birth to peaceful almost-hills and happy, cartoon-like trees jut out of nowhere like little warnings of what's to come. It's the calm before the storm. A deceiving easiness. It's Cary Grant thinking he's going for a stroll in the cornfield, only to be attacked by a malevolent crop duster. It's Jack Dawson serenely drawing Rose right before the iceberg hits. It's Quint, Brody, and Hooper throwin' back whiskey while their fate circles below.

I focus on the immediate road, not what lies ahead. But despite my attempts to keep my focus shallow, my eyes remain wide open with the ugly truth: my former self, Before Jane, left me a long time ago; the current me, After Jane, abandoned my own parents, the very parents who taught me to take care of those I love.

My chest tightens. I switch focus so I can breathe again.

Depth of field. An important tool in a director's bag of camera tricks designed to manipulate a viewer's emotions. *Citizen Kane*'s deep-focus shots flashed in my mind and across Interstate 80 as I fight hard to avoid what comes into focus next.

Welcome to Iowa: A Place to Grow.

Jesus. Even the signs here are preachy.

With blurred cornfields deep in the background, the highway sign, signature green with white reflective lettering, comes into sharp focus, letting me know exactly where I have landed.

The full-blown rolling hills announce themselves within seconds of crossing the state line, as if to give a tentative hello to the stranger I am. I hear Mother sing how the hills are alive with the sound of music. The hills are one more thing I have forgotten. So green. Impossibly green. Like someone has taken the black-and-white childhood I remember and colorized it, angering the purists who believe the past should be left untouched.

It is jarring to see a place that is so dead to me teem with such life. I touch the metal bangle I always wear on my left hand, this time letting my fingers go straight to the inside inscription. At first, I try to ignore the pronounced emptiness that has taken residence in my core, but then I let myself feel it: all ache, no mercy.

I need to regroup, and what better place to get my bearings than an I-80 truck stop? I pull into the Sapp Brothers truck stop, a beacon in the Midwest known for the enormous water tower they've rejiggered into a giant, vintage pot of coffee. Inside there will be no trace of Los Angeles. No juice bar, no wheatgrass shots, no chai lattes, just pure midwestern fare: Funyuns, Hostess cherry pies, Slurpees.

A handful of people who are fueling up their semis, pickup trucks, and sensible sedans stare at me as I walk past them. Their eyes widen when they see my Aston Martin, the shiny, out-of-place foreigner devoid of dust or humility. I see their eyebrows lift as they take me in. My blond hair in loose pigtails, my definitely-not-from-here outfit: frayed, cutoff jean shorts, black go-go boots, and a faux-fur shrug draped over a fitted T-shirt featuring the original *Jaws* movie poster circa 1977.

As I approach the convenience store entrance, a local trucker quickens his lumbering pace to open the door for me.

"Thank you." I flash a brief smile and walk in.

The trucker smiles back, gives me a nod upward, the signature midwestern farmer's nod. "Sure, kitten."

I've been in my home state for under three minutes and have already been addressed as a helpless baby animal. Something deep inside me stirs, then wakes up, forces my shoulders back. I stop, turn around, and step in front of him. "Kitten? Really?" I wait a beat, prepare to just walk away, but when the words surface, I'm unable to stop them. "I prefer pussy," I say, way too loud, and as the words hang in the thick Iowa air, I realize that although I meant to emasculate this guy, I've somehow declared that I'm a lesbian. Loudly. Before I can clarify, a man in a leather jacket walks past, giving my emphatic lesbianism an enthusiastic thumbs-up, while a mother glares and puts her hands over her little boy's ears.

The trucker evolves from startled to pissy. I can't decide if he's angry because he thinks I might play for the other team or because I'm blocking the way to his next dose of donuts. His too-small tank top, which reads *I wish my girlfriend was as dirty as my truck*, stretches over his sizable beer belly, then tucks into his jeans. "Your mother know you talk like that?"

"Does your girlfriend know you call other women 'kitten'?" But now something else in me comes loose. My shoulders fall, my voice softens. "And yes, my mother knows I talk like this, but it doesn't matter. Nothing matters anymore. She's dead."

Recently dead.

Freshly dead.

That is to say, not able to be my moral compass anymore.

Before I can stop myself, honesty leaks out of me until I'm standing in a puddle of truth. "I can't believe she's gone."

The truck driver gently lifts up his hands, like he's going to try to fix what he's broken. "Aw, hell, sweet"—but he revises—"ma'am. I'm real sorry."

I smile, sniff away his apology.

The two of us—a couple of sorry midwesterners—walk into the gas station convenience store together and revert to the midwestern default conversation: weather.

After a pregnant pause, he says, "Looks like it's gonna rain."

"Yep," I say.

"We sure need it," the trucker says, and it all comes back to me. Midwesterners love to speak as if they are the land itself, like the land needs a spokesperson. My memory starts to come into soft focus somewhere between the Little Debbie snack cakes and the carousel display of dueling Iowa Hawkeye and Iowa State Cyclones key chains, and just when the trucker and I find common, Iowa ground, we part ways.

I make my way past the beverage coolers, and a woman hovers next to me, swaying her body in order to rock the small baby nestled in the Baby Bjorn strapped to her chest. Although the baby is quiet, the woman makes no attempt to hide her own whimpering as she stares, wide-eyed, at a small gas station television set hanging from the corner ceiling. She shakes her head, mouthing Superman's "No, no, no, no, no!" as he sees his beloved Lois Lane, lifeless among the fallen boulders.

"Sorry," the woman whispers to me. "This part. Always. Gets me."

The woman wears her postpartum mania like an oozing, melodramatic badge of honor, giving us all a silent warning to tread lightly around her irrational behavior. I turn to bolt in the opposite direction, but to my horror, she touches my shoulder in some sort of cinematic solidarity, and I freeze.

"I'm in a hurry," I lie and try to pull away, but she's having none of it. She takes my hand. In LA, this would be some version of assault, but in Iowa, it's neighborly. The Slurpee machine slurps, and a steady stream of beeps continue as new customers enter the store, but the woman keeps her eyes on Superman.

She continues to mouth the words as she watches the screen, and we hear Jor-El echo from the past, telling Kal-El that it's forbidden.

Then, as if the woman's seeing it for the very first time, she nods at me. "But he's gonna do it anyway." She beams. "He's gonna turn back time to save her."

For a moment, she lets go of my hand to conduct a silent mini clap. This is my chance to walk away. I'm free to go, and I know I should before this hormonally challenged woman calls this classic, Academy Award–winning film "cute" or "sweet" and shames Richard Donner's legacy.

I take my eyes off the screen, prepare to leave. But then it happens. I hear the trumpets, the theme song that, for just a moment, makes heroes of us all. Now comes the full-bellied orchestra, the collective sounds of courage itself taking flight, dripping with possibility, strings and horns marrying their unlikely overtures, coupled with the iconic image of Superman, flying fist first, like an angry bullet, moving the Earth for love.

More customers enter, more Slurpees get slurped while Superman reunites with the five-minutes-ago Lois Lane, who is now safe in her car, not knowing the unfathomable act of love that saved her. When Superman looks at Lois, the woman he's just saved, and simply says "Hi," the woman next to me falls apart.

She begins waving her tears away like they might somehow dry up if she works hard enough. But they don't. I am tempted to console her, but that would mean we have something in common, and I don't want to admit I have anything in common with someone who cries in truck stops. What I really want to say is that deep down, in a place I keep protected from the world, I know exactly why *Superman* moves her to tears. From the Rockwellian scenes depicting Americana at its best to the moments when the impossible becomes possible, this movie reminds us of an undeniable truth: love can move the world.

This is what movies do—they remind us not of what we think, but of what we feel. Forget about other so-called lame American pastimes. No one has ever reevaluated their life while listening to Coltrane or had an epiphany while awaiting the conclusion of the ninth inning. Admit it. Jazz is annoying. Baseball is boring. But movies? Movies tell us who we are. Who we want to be. Hollywood, with all its shallow, out-of-touch shortcomings, is one more reason that this is the greatest country on Earth.

I want to tell this woman what I love about this movie. How I always choke up when Jor-El and his wife, even in the face of death, tell their only son they will never leave him. How he will carry them inside of him all the days of his life.

I want to tell this woman that her daughter's sweet, warm baby smell is wafting up, making me dizzy with jealousy. What's it like to have someone to love, to take care of, to move the world for?

What's it like to feel another you, whose heart is beating just inches from your own?

I suddenly want to tell my parents that I know how much they loved me, that I will carry them with me all the days of my life.

I want to tell this woman how lucky she is that she'll never have to rely on second chances that don't exist outside of Hollywood. I want to tell her that I'm a shitty person, and for the first time in my life, I want to confess why.

Instead, I blurt, "Your boobs are enormous." I feel Sidney's horrified glance, four states away.

The woman, laughing now, shakes her head. "I know, right? I could feed Dubuque with these things," and rests a hand on her heaving, lactating cleavage spilling out all sides of the baby carrier.

"She's beautiful," I say, sneaking a peek at the sleeping, fine-featured face nestled safely near her mother, her everyday hero. The woman's husband walks up, and when he sees his postpartum wife's been crying—again—offers her his Slurpee, says they have to go.

"Good luck," I say to her as her very own Superman wipes her leftover tears and they fly away.

A lonely sadness sweeps over me. Without warning, some long-ago instinct unearths itself from dormancy, and I find myself doing something no self-respecting, health-conscious Los Angeleno would ever do. I grab a diabetes-sized container, featuring a psychedelic spiral graphic, and like a good midwesterner, follow the directions on the see-through machine. *Pull.* And when I pull down the big red lever, it begins to flow. The slush is a color not known in nature, a turquoise-blue with a green undertone, sort of like the ocean if the ocean was dangerously close to a toxic waste dump. I begin to rotate my cup so the sugar-slop falls into it in consistent rings, little revolutions meant for someone who is preparing to come full circle.

I sip my Slurpee, the Midwest's answer to the smoothie, let the cold punish me all the way down.

"That's a dollar forty-three," the clerk says when I approach the counter.

My God, I forgot everything's practically free here. I add Funyuns, a Hostess cherry pie, and because I'm clearly experiencing some sort of psychotic break, a prepackaged barbecue sandwich.

Scan. Beep. Scan. Beep. Scan. Beep. "That'll be four dollars and eighty-seven cents."

I shake my head. In LA, I'd need two twenties to cover this meal that would feed an entire Pilates gym for a week.

The clerk has the *Des Moines Register* open to the syndicated Cinegirl column. He takes my money and opens the till but keeps reading. "I love this chick." He laughs, pointing to my cartoon likeness. "She said *Hole of Schmidt* was a steamy pile of crap!"

Is going from kitten to chick a lateral move or a demotion? I lean over to look at the newspaper for effect. "Oh, I don't think she said 'crap.'" I point to paragraph two. "See? Just 'excrement.'" His addition of *steamy* is a nice touch, though.

He looks down at Cinegirl, then back up at me. I think about how long of a pregnant pause I'll put between *Willow* and *Jane Willow* when I introduce myself. I prepare for him to say, "Oh my God, it's you—America's favorite film critic," maybe even call me what the *Chicago Tribune* once called me: "the female Roger Ebert."

But instead, he puts my change in my outstretched hand and points to my upper lip, where toxic-blue Slurpee has accumulated.

I wonder if my idol, Pauleen Kael, got recognized when she went to convenience stores. I wonder if her sharp tongue had ever tasted a Slurpee.

I wipe my lip, collect my fifteen-hundred calories, walk toward the door with no identity and even less pride. Welcome home.

Willow. Jane Willow.

Revise.

Parentless, Childless, Single Woman with Slurpee.

With the suddenness of a midwestern storm, the whole convenience store seems inconveniently hopeless. I glance back up at the television set. Fox News has replaced *Superman*. Two truckers argue about the weather. The Slurpee machine glugs and sputters, exhausted. I switch my focus to a bossy neon sign on the wall in the shape of the Hawkeye state, flashing a message I don't want to see: *All roads lead to Iowa.*

What a Schmidt Hole.

CHAPTER FIVE

1986

"T HAT IS TO SAY"—I watched my father search for the right phrasing—"no, you may not be a Bond Girl for Halloween, Janie." He smiled, looking like a ruddy-faced Bobby Knight post-victory. "You're nine, for Chrissakes."

As his words settled, I stood up straighter, tried to look older—a difficult task in my Smurfs pajama-gown. I recited Holly Goodhead's fictional résumé. "She's a doctor, you know, Daddy. A space scientist."

He glanced up from his current project—a gift from an old law school buddy: a broken, rusty, inoperable 1964 Aston Martin DB5, the unpolished "before" picture of someone's well-designed dream. His life's motto—everything's a work in progress—in the form of an aged hunk of metal.

Old Spice cologne wafted through the garage as my father rolled around on the under-car creeper, its small wheels squeaking with intent. The headlights looked up as if to convince me of what it once was, to remind me of nature's most miraculous law: all things return to their natural state eventually, no matter the journey.

"Hand me that suction cup," he said and pointed to his countertop of tools. "I'm gonna show you how to get a dent out, kid."

I handed him the suction cup. Excited by the notion of a second chance, I made another plea for a Bond Girl Halloween.

Instead of answering, he placed my hand on top of his. Together, we popped out a big dent in the front-left quarter panel. He opened the driver-side door, offered his hand, and helped me step into the empty shell of a car—no engine, no gearbox, no seats.

"It's kind of a junker, Dad," I said, surveying the empty, soulless car and sitting down on a small stool.

"Believe so," Dad said.

"You think so, too?" I asked, thinking he meant that he also believed it was underwhelming. "Well, we could fix it by—"

"No, Janie," he corrected me. "Not 'I believe it is so' but *believe so*. As in, if you believe in something enough, it will happen. Nothing nonchalant about 'believe so,' no matter how you slice it. It's brilliant, see, depending on how you use it, when you use, and where you use it. '*Believe* so. Believe *so*.' See the difference? You have to pick what syllables you'll stress, just like you'll have to pick what moments you emphasize in your life, Janie. Understand?" he said, closing the door. "Now, is this car amazing or what?"

I smiled. "Believe so." I closed my eyes, released my ponytail, shook out my hair, and let the imaginary wind blow. It was like I'd stepped into a movie. I considered a camera angle I'd seen when Dad watched *Moonraker*, positioned my profile for optimal light exposure, and recited random lines as they flashed in my mind.

I opened my eyes and yelled to an invisible Mr. Bond with the fervor of a first-rate villain.

Dad had now taken his eyes off the Aston Martin, replacing one dream by focusing on another. He looked at me, his only child. "Someday this will be yours, Janie." He patted the almost-car. I didn't recognize the look in his eyes but sensed I should listen. "Wherever you land, you'll land there in style."

I stopped driving the car that was going nowhere. "Land? I'm not going to land anywhere. I'm going to live here forever," I said, betrayed by the very idea of Crocker County, the only home I'd ever known. Who would have wanted to leave the place that birthed John Wayne, Ann Landers, Gopher from *Love Boat*, and Captain James Tiberius Kirk? And even on a bad day, at least Iowa wasn't Nebraska. Nebraska was unforgivable. Everyone knew that.

Things happened in Iowa. Buddy Holly died in Clear Lake. The world's biggest strawberry was grown in Strawberry Point. Jesse James picked Iowa for his first moving-train robbery. That had to mean something.

"Daddy, did you know that Iowa is the only state that begins with two vowels?" I folded my arms for effect. "And Superman's from Iowa."

"He's from Kansas," Dad said, now inspecting yet another dent. "There's a big world out there, Janie."

Maybe there was. That I didn't deny, but I could learn all about it. From right here. At home.

"Are we done yet?" I asked, knowing that for my father, nothing was ever really done.

"Only meat can be done. Tasks are finished." His lawyerly tone grated on me. "A little hard work never killed anyone, Janie." He perked up and looked over at the radio, its staticky oldies station filling the garage. "Speaking of death." He looked at me and made a declaration that played out like a final crescendo. "At my funeral someday, this is the song I want, Janie," he said, foot tapping the garage floor with the beat.

"Daddy! That's sad." I tried to control a pout.

He smiled. "But *this* isn't," he said, snapped his fingers, and belted along with the chorus.

Something about him flying, singing till the end of time, as if one lifetime would never be enough. For love, I think. Keeping time with the song, my father's fingers now began to tap the Aston Martin, the dream that, unlike us mere mortals, would live forever.

I noticed my father glance toward the garage door. He would never admit it, but I knew he was looking for Mother. On the rare occasion he wasn't with her, it was like he was always waiting for her to walk through the door, waiting to say what he always said when he saw her. *Outta this world.*

In a matter-of-fact tone, he told me that he knew he would go first. The men always went before the women. Then came his favorite four words. "That is to say," he said, leaning into the very phrase that breathed life into his personal truth: nothing is permanent. "That is to say, no need for anyone to be sad, Janie."

That is to say, the song would be for his widow. Mother.

That evening, Dad and I sat on the wraparound porch of our Iowa farmhouse and watched a crescent moon illuminate a tiny patch of sky. It was the stars that had us both searching. Against a backdrop as black as the fertile soil below, stars adorned our sky with an authority, a purpose to be pondered. They were the kind of stars that meant business. How could we attempt to describe stars so bright, so clear, that it seemed they belonged to just the two of us? "Bright," he'd first said, rocking slowly, and then, "Clear." But he stopped rocking when he found the right word. "Ours," he said, comfortable with its perfection, his smile offsetting his gruff voice. Then my father said something that settled into me: "Finding the right word after a long journey of diligent searching feels like…home."

CHAPTER SIX

*T*HE MORNING SUN SCREAMS through the windshield, makes me the object of an unforgiving spotlight as I drive past the Crocker County road sign, and then finally, True City, population 782. Home.

A jury of 782 people (no, I didn't say 7,000) wait to pass judgment. The Aston Martin slows and I am already eager to leave, to get the hell out of here and back to LA. My silver bangle, now hot from the sun, flames into my skin. Reminders everywhere. My past pops up in Sam Peckinpah-inspired slow-motion frames. I think of the first time I ever watched *The Wild Bunch*, relishing in Peckinpah's violent yet artistic scenes, slowing down for ultimate tension. But as my own past now comes into focus, I wish I had a fast-forward button.

First comes the view of my high school, which from the hilltop leading into True City looks like three tiny rectangles. After another mile comes Charlotte's farm, my childhood home away from home that sits at the base of the sledding hill. Finally, nestled in the valley, is my home, marked by the largest willow tree in the county.

A quarter mile from town, I see a farmer walking in the ditch, surveying the perimeter of his land. His image reminds me of Iowa's unofficial slogan: Idiots Out Walking Around. After untying a large metal gate leading to his field, he lets it swing open wide and gives me a farmer's nod, a barely-there lift of the chin.

When he motions me to pull over, I conduct a temper tantrum in my head. No, my name's not Sweetie. No, I don't want to talk about the weather, or why my plates don't say Crocker County, or how your little grandson can drive the combine.

I slow the car and try to hide my aversion to the always-relentless midwestern friendliness. The barrier between us disappears when I roll down the window. The man in the Carhartt bib overalls ambles over to my driver-side window, leans in. He smells of manure, instant coffee, and hard work.

"Welcome home, Janie Willow."

We exchange stares. I sit up straight. How does he know me when I don't know him? The only familiar thing about him is his Clint Eastwood-ness—tall build, straight shoulders, slight squint, almost-angry whisper in his voice. Not the Make-My-Day-Punk Eastwood, more Josey Wales.

"It's…Jane now." I pause. "Jane"—my secret agent introduction losing steam here in God's country—"Jane Willow."

"Janie, I was real sorry to hear the news. Good people, your folks." As if out of reverence, the farmer removes his soiled John Deere hat.

The wind picks up, whistles through a nearby grove. A chill runs through me, leaving me exposed, off-center.

"They did a lot for me…for everyone here." The man holds his head high, higher than I thought a man wearing muddy overalls could. He glances toward True City's two giant grain elevators standing like proud beacons of hope. I try to look away, but I know it's time I look, really look at them—monuments named after my parents, the two people True City considered to be the backbone of their small, humble town.

"Jack" stands on the left, the bigger of the two—although both elevators were the biggest in the country when they were first built—and "Mary" stands on the right, the perfect companion to her mighty mate; that is to say, her man of steel. I watch the two of them stretch into the sky, into another world. *Outta this world.*

"Well, might get some rain," the farmer says, and forces my gaze to land back on him. "Clouds comin' in."

There it is. Meteorology once again at the forefront of conversation.

The farmer stares at me with a slow, quiet intensity, the type people in Los Angeles have no patience to perform. After three or four full, loaded seconds of him taking in the impractical heels on my boots and the faux-fur shrug around my neck that could surely strangle a person on a hay baler, he answered a question I didn't ask out loud.

"Everyone knows you."

I nod. "From Cine—"

"We remember people here." His voice, stern and confident, makes me almost apologize. I now realize he has no idea about Cinegirl or about who I've become. He only knows the part of me I've abandoned.

Before Jane.

As After Jane in Los Angeles, I create blockbusters and bombs with my words. But here I am, Jack and Mary Willow's only daughter, who never came to visit. The shittiness of it all forces my barbecue sandwich into my throat.

"You're the Crocker County Corn Queen." His stare, deep and knowing, cuts through me, like he knows this and so much more.

He extends his hand through the open window. When my hand touches his calloused skin, something shoots through me, something equal parts happiness and sorrow. I study him, look for evidence of our connectedness, but see nothing.

In my haze, I imagine writing my way out of this.

Once upon a time, I saw a farmer wave at me and I kept driving. I lived happily ever after. The end.

But if this is a fairy tale and I am the narrator, this man is a gatekeeper, the character who catalogs people's entrances and exits in and out of a land called True City.

"It's good to be home," I lie.

He looks at me like a parent about to deliver wisdom, and I brace myself. "Your true home, Janie, always opens its door. It always forgives." Then he lets out a quiet affirmation. "Romans 5 something, I think... He loves us at our darkest."

I put the car in drive and give him a goodbye look. He glances at the darkening sky.

"There's a storm a-brewin', Janie Willow." With this, a sharp gust of wind erupts; this time, it's like an announcement. When he stretches out his arm, the lower half swings hinged at his elbow joint, like a farmhouse door opening with ease. A welcoming gesture perhaps—entrance back into a land he guards.

But then I notice his finger point toward the passenger door as

I pull away. I accelerate until the sight of his overalls fade. When I look in my passenger-side mirror, I see the shoulder strap of my purse hanging outside the car, flapping and tethered, flying proud, stupid, and aimless through the air.

Once again, I revise. The idiots are obviously driving around.

What is it about the air here? More oxygen, maybe? I can't comment on the science, the chemistry, with accuracy; but with every breath I'm feeling annoyingly dizzy, like the air itself is urging me to take stock of my life. Seems a bit pushy, if you ask me. All of my achievements from the last eighteen years fade a bit in this strange, thick air. Strong and simple particles shake my memory loose, try to have their way with me, but they do not know who they're dealing with.

The farmer's gate disappears into the fold of a small hill, and I endure another mile of unsettling inhalation. Memories flood my mind. I am ready to call Sid, tell him I've contracted some sort of flu that's affecting my ability to act rationally. Everything around me has slowed down, flashing in deliberate, familiar images—giant red barns that reach toward the clouds, metal mailboxes with neatly painted *Andersons* and *Smiths*, bales of hay piled with the precision of someone who takes pride in small things.

When I pass the Browns' farm, the wind picks up, causing Mrs. Brown's rooster weather vane on her machine shed to go temporarily berserk, its red tin arrow landing in my direction when I glance up. The chest-high corn sways at first, dances, really, and I try to dismiss how enchanting the wind looks whipping through the corn rows, stalk by stalk bowing slightly as I drive by, like the land itself recognizes me as one of its own.

A half mile down, I turn left in an autopilot maneuver, and although I want to change course and alleviate the twinge of pain deep inside me, a gravitational pull fights against it. I drive right to it, defying all good sense and disobeying my rule of never looking back. The car idles for a moment at the beginning of the turnoff, the beginning of so much, but within seconds I am face-to-face with it. Face to tree rather.

I get out of the car, and when I walk across the ditch to confront what I've been avoiding for eighteen years, I feel the sky give way. Just one drop at first, then too many to count. As usual, I once again bring rain. With each step, I feel the heaviness of it—the oldest willow tree in Crocker County—tower over me. Strong branches sprout thousands of leaves, now shimmering in the wind, but my gaze falls on the showstopper—its trunk—too big to hug even if I'd wanted to. I imagine the root system so widespread by now it must have its own life, and I am compelled to take off my boots. My feet tingle with what lies buried below, with what happened here, but when the tingle becomes an ache, I abandon it and leave it behind.

I get back in the car as the rain subsides and follow the path—a long lane that leads to a white farmhouse planted firmly at its end. It was my grandfather's farm, given to my dad even though he chose not to be a farmer. Although I've driven down this lane hundreds, thousands of times way back when, now it seems like all roads have led to this one. I sit in the driver's seat and stare at the house, the only home I've ever known. It is my home. And it isn't.

My memory has betrayed me. The wraparound porch—the

same one I hated as a girl because the tiny wooden slats were a nightmare to paint—now looks less like the barrier I remembered and more like an invitation. One could do so many things while on that porch—watch a sunrise, watch a sunset, watch a daughter grow.

Without thinking, I wait for my parents to walk out, slam the screen door, planks creaking beneath their feet. But all I hear is the rope rubbing against the rubber tire as the wind makes it twirl from the giant willow tree. The rope frayed its way to breaking several times over the years, but Dad replaced the rope, put it back up every time in hopes there would be reason to have it. That is to say, he'd hoped to be a grandfather someday.

I carry my hollowness with me as I put one foot in front of the other, climb the porch steps, and search for the courage to walk past the two empty rocking chairs, freshly painted barn red. I open the front door, which I know will be unlocked—the very idea of locking a door seemed unneighborly here—and I am home.

My clothes still damp with rainwater, I step across the worn door jam and cross yet another invisible threshold. I watch my eighteen-year-old self walk past me and venture out into the world. I try to recall if I'd waved goodbye to my parents on my final exit, but when I glance behind, I see a young girl not looking back.

I walk into the living room, sit down in one of the two gray-corduroy La-Z-Boy recliners, his and hers. I'm in Mom's. Her weekend cardigan, the lavender one with the missing button and a rumpled tissue peeking out one pocket, is draped over the arm-chair and smells like her lilac perfume. I breathe it in, try to hold it inside me.

I know what's in the DVD player without having to look. It's what my mother fell asleep to every night—her all-time favorite film, and according to her, the best musical ever made. Most critics would say it's no *West Side Story*, no *Guys and Dolls*, that the Iowa native Meredith Willson was neither Rodgers nor Hammerstein, but Mom thought *The Music Man* was in a league all its own. She thought it was better, because when we watched it, she said *we* were better.

Like a bittersweet reminder, I glance at the floor-to-ceiling bookshelves on the north wall of the living room. My father built them when Mom's reading habit began to take over the house. Madam Librarian, he'd call her when she gave a book more attention than him. I can still see her reading face, weathered from a full life, yet according to my father, the prettiest face in Crocker County. That was Mary Willow: midwestern as a pot luck, a woman who owned dozens of cardigans—practically perfect for every temperature.

Before I can resume play, find out the last scene of *The Music Man* Mom had watched for the very last time, I realize something so right, so pure that it hits me with the weight and precision of a truth found out too late: Dad was Mom's Harold Hill.

My eyes well up as I redefine the father I thought I knew, revise my memory of him. In his fantasies, he was James Bond, but in reality, he was exactly what a grounded, pragmatic midwestern girl wanted—someone to make her feel out of this world. Someone to fly with, to make her believe in dreams.

Believe so, kid, Dad would say, channeling the moxie required for unbridled hope—the kind of hope that practical people bet against. *Believe so*, he'd say, for when Mom, when we all, needed it most.

Something calls me to my bedroom, so I climb the wooden

stairs, prompting a creak on step three and a bigger creak on step seven, like always, and when I open my bedroom door, I am breathless. I have stepped into my childhood.

Everything. The. Same.

My framed poster of Iowa, my center of the world. My oh-so-high-school red-and-black comforter that replaced my little-girl Strawberry Shortcake set. The wallpaper border that looks like a film reel. My wall of movie posters: *The Shining, Ghostbusters, Raging Bull, Back to the Future*. My small bookshelf full of little-girl things—Nancy Drew, Laura Ingalls Wilder—and my tall bookshelf representing my teenage obsessions—my Ian Fleming collection, a Christmas gift from Dad, in order from my favorite to least favorite, *From Russia with Love* first, *Live and Let Die* last. My heart flutters a little when I see my '64 Corgi toy car, an Aston Martin replica complete with ejector seat, missiles, and the signature Silver Birch paint job.

On the top shelf is all things movies. Not the types of heavy film-theory books I read in grad school, but the fun ones meant for someone newly fallen for film: *How to Read a Film*, Cavell's *The World Viewed*, and of course, my shrine to my then-and-now idol, Pauline Kael. When other mothers had been buying their daughters Judy Blume books, mine was buying me the semantic stylings of the legendary film critic Ms. Kael: *I Lost It at the Movies, Kiss Kiss Bang Bang, Raising Kane, When the Lights Go Down*. I had them all and knew every word.

By now, the heart of True City is putting on their funeral attire, getting ready to pay their respects to my parents, and it's almost time for me to go. It is. But I'm not ready to leave. Not yet. I need to remember another time, so I sit down on my bed and sink into a long-ago summertime evening. Mother is tucking me in. She buttons her cardigan, then pushes open the wooden bedroom window, swollen with humidity, lets the rickracked curtains dance as the finally cool breeze joins us in our nighttime ritual.

Outside this bedroom window, the daytime sun blazes, but not in this dreamscape I'm in. Here the lights are off. Iowa starlight floods through the window. I wait for Mother to take her spot on my bedspread's worn red-and-black quilt square. Right on cue, a gentle tuck of my hair behind my ear, the ritual begins. "Janie, what do we always do?"

"Work hard. Be nice."

Then I recall the sweet voice that once helped me drift into sleep. Shirley Jones had nothing on my mother, though. "Goodnight, My Someone" was a tune she sang to me hundreds of times. She sings me good night.

Her voice pours over me.

She tells me dreams are my own.

Drifting, I whisper, "Am I your someone…or is it Daddy?" Quieter. "It's okay if it's Daddy."

"That old coot?"

I let out a sleepy laugh. "Mommy, are there really dreams up there?"

Mother speaks like an authority on all things celestial. "I'm sure of it."

I shut my eyes, take in a child-deep, relaxing breath. Half-asleep. "Do you have a dream, Mommy?"

"Sure do," she whispers, and smiles as she watches her greatest dream breathe in and out, a cadence so beautiful it could make a mother thank her stars.

CHAPTER SEVEN

*T*HE CLOCK IN THE kitchen reads a quarter to *Time to bury your parents.*

I've changed into proper mourning attire, a black Betsey Johnson shift dress and modest heels. I've made several phone calls to make sure what I have planned for the funeral is on schedule. It's time to go, but my body moves in slow motion, each step, each movement a deliberate stall tactic to put off the inevitable. I inch around Mother's lemony-clean farmhouse kitchen, the perfect set kitchen for a film starring a nurturing protagonist whose job it is to love.

I take in all that Mother has made here—breakfast, lunch, dinner, peace, I hope. What do I make, besides enemies? I scour my memory for the last time I actually created something of my own, but can't remember when. Truth be told, I make criticism, plot it out scene by scene, and then have the audacity to wonder why the audience doesn't want an encore showing.

Everything on the counter is neatly in its place, tidy with pride, a midwesterner's prerequisite for leaving the house. *You never know*, Mom would say. When I open the refrigerator, it too is organized with purpose—milk close to the front, veggies nestled sensibly in the crisper, and now I see it: my favorite. "Heaven in a casserole dish," I say out loud to no one, knowing that in Los Angeles this would be an impossible metaphor, an oxymoron even, given their prejudice against overcooked, rectangular food.

But this dish, Mother's scalloped corn casserole, transcends, makes you feel like you might, in fact, have died and gone to heaven. She always made it before she and Dad went flying, so they'd come home to a finished dinner. Died and gone to heaven casserole. The irony hits me when I see the untouched casserole, no pieces gone, uneaten by those who have already died and gone to heaven.

Mother used to make it for me when she sensed I needed it— when *discotheque* knocked me out of the spelling bee, when E.T. went home, and later when, unbeknownst to Mom, the Before Jane turned into After Jane—and here it is now, when I need it the most.

I lift the oblong Pyrex dish out of the fridge and place it on the kitchen table. After peeling back the plastic wrap and breathing in the sweet and salty goodness in perfect proportion, I sit down at the kitchen table and serve myself a big square. It was as good cold as hot, and I let my fork pierce the golden-brown and crusty top, then buttery corn bread crumbs and saltine crackers, and right when I'm struck by the layers I'd forgotten about, I reach the soft middle. The main feature. The heart.

The flavors awaken in my mouth. Paprika, farm-fresh eggs, a dash of pepper, a pinch of sugar. And corn. Of course, corn—both creamed and whole kernel, straight from the field. But today the corn is not the star. I think of Mother, beautiful and golden, and swallow the last bite.

I put the remaining casserole in Tupperware, walk into the breezeway, and open the deep freezer. Might as well save it for someone else. What greets me when I open the lid takes my breath away.

Stacks and stacks of labeled containers full of the same thing. I don't have to open them to know. Scalloped corn casserole perfectly preserved for the chance that Mary Willow's only child might come home. I look through the labels, which date back two years to the last time I had mentioned I might make a visit.

JUNE. Summer's coming.

My busy time, Mom. Summer movie previews.

JULY. Go to the parade?

Sorry, Dad. Deadline for War Horse. *Can't make Spielberg wait!*

OCTOBER. Corn Festival.

Preparing speech for American Film Critics Award ceremony.

NOVEMBER. Thanksgiving.

UCLA guest speaker.

DECEMBER. Christmas.

Best of holiday movies top-ten list.

JANUARY. New Year's.

Getting ready for Sundance Film Festival.

FEBRUARY. Dad's birthday.

Oscars wrap-up.

MARCH. Dad's retirement party.

I'm out of excuses, but the thought of being back there makes me short of breath.

APRIL. My birthday.

Hell no. This would mean looking back, confronting the secret that paralyzes me from living my life.

MAY. Mom's birthday.

This is what shame does. It makes you miss your mother's birthday, and there's no excuse for that.

I let the freezer lid fall shut, slump onto the linoleum floor, and for the first time in years, cry. An indescribable chill seeps into my bones as I sit shivering on the cold, hard floor. When I notice the coatrack by the breezeway door, I force myself up, walk to it, and grab what hangs from the brass hooks—four of Mother's cardigans.

I put on the first one, slate-gray with pearly, iridescent buttons. The scent of fresh-cut lilacs wafts through the air, and I pretend it's confirmation that she's here with me. When that doesn't seem enough, I put on the second, baby-girl pink with frayed wristbands, then a third, sunshine-yellow, buttery enough to melt in your mouth. Not willing to leave any part of her behind, I put on the last one, blue as a cloudless sky.

I tug on all of the layers, all I have left of my mother tightly wrapped around my cold self, and dream of how warm Mother had been. She is here. I hear her. *Of all the babies in this whole wide world, I got you. You. The best one.* And then in utilitarian fashion, she tempers the compliment with some practical midwestern common sense. *Now put on a cardigan. You never know what the weather will be like.*

You know, you really don't.

CHAPTER EIGHT

*E*VEN THOUGH I'M WEARING four layers of my mother, I am still cold. Eighteen years cold. When you are consumed by shame, there's not a lot of room for warmth. I can't seem to peel myself up off the linoleum floor, and with the deep freezer full of yesterday's abandoned dreams staring back at me, I cling to the phrase that justifies my truth: it is what it is.

This phrase, this small, fatalistic dose of succinct syntax is cliché-tastic. Given its lameness, it should be a writer's kryptonite, but for me, it represents a truth most people can't accept: there are no second chances.

Your wife left you for her personal trainer named Rocco?

It is what it is.

Cute little Fluffy's got feline leukemia?

It is what it is.

You squandered your kid's college fund at Caesar's Palace?

It is what it is.

We are our decisions, and sometimes those decisions are really,

really crappy. Lean into the shame and let it punish you until you forget, and then do it all over again the next day.

I begin to look for the movies I've sent my parents as stocking stuffers each Christmas. First I check the entertainment center—no, the neighbors might see them there. Maybe they're hidden in the curio with all of Mom's Christmas village collectibles and Hummel statues—nope, not there either. Finally, I check Mom's beloved bookshelves Dad made for her—it's the perfect spot, really, for contraband, if you're Mary Willow. In her eyes, books were the antidote to all bad things: ignorance, boredom, complacency. Ironically, I feel the same way about film, but for Mom, words on a page were justified in a way scenes in a movie were not.

Sure enough, when I go to the center shelf I see *Great Expectations*, *Gilead*, and *A Prayer for Owen Meany* sticking out a little farther than the rest. Like a literary lightning bolt of clarity, I realize these novels' story lines are her unspoken dreams for me—allowing love to fuel redemption; finding beauty in the ordinary, even a cornfield in the glow of an Iowa sunset; and getting the ultimate gift of an answered prayer: life and destiny colliding when you least expect it.

I dismantle the mini wall of books, and I am greeted by a stack of familiar friends: *The Virgin Suicides*, *The Usual Suspects*, *American Psycho*, *Reservoir Dogs*. I grab the one on the top, the first movie I ever sent my parents in the hopes that we could someday discuss its cinematic merits, and I pop it in the VHS player.

It resumes to its last stopping point, and when I see what that stopping point was—subsequently my parents' breaking point—now blaring at high volume because my parents' hearing was never great, I begin to laugh, and I cannot stop. A naked serial killer named Buffalo Bill is wearing a blond wig and lipstick and dancing around the creepiest basement ever recorded on film.

This is where the day, the hour, the current tragedy that is my life, catches up with me.

Thoughts of my parents, nestled into their La-Z-Boys on a Saturday night, getting through the majority of *Silence of the Lambs*, only to call it quits so close to the end. In my grief-induced haze, I can't decide which is more astounding: that I actually had the audacity to send them such a film, or that they almost finished it for me.

I am still nervously laughing out loud at the extended serial-killer dance sequence and the absurdity of it all when I hear something.

"Janie?" a voice yells over Buffalo Bill's dance music. Startled, I turn around to see four casserole-holding women looking past me, horrified at the sight on the screen—naked Buffalo Bill writhing about in all his serial-killer glory, now with his man parts tucked neatly out of sight. In a panic, I fumble for the remote, but accidentally hit the volume button instead of pause, just in time for Buffalo Bill, at full volume, to drop a couple of f-words and utter one of the most disturbing lines of dialogue in all of cinematic history.

They are frozen in horror, the mother-women who have come a calling because that's what small-town neighbors do when tragedy strikes. At the early inklings of death, their very DNA demands first the baking and then the delivering of the perfect casserole that sums up their customized condolences. One of them carrying an oblong Pyrex dish draped in a hand-crocheted dish towel uses her free hand to cover her mouth. Another woman with a fancy zip-up covered casserole-to-go dish stares at the screen wide-eyed like it's the scene of a bad Highway 71 accident from which she can't avert her eyes. The other two cling to their green bean and tater tot casseroles, protecting them like they're children in the presence of unsightly evil.

I finally manage to hit the pause button, and now the silence is deafening.

"The door was open," Green Bean Casserole says apologetically.

In a schizophrenic series of reactions, I first let out an awkward laugh, accompanied by a defense of my parents. "This is not Mom and Dad's—they hated this type of thing," is where I start, but then as the disapproving stares soften into something closer to pity, I am overcome with emotion and begin to tear up. "When I'm stressed, movies comfort me," I say to the God-fearing bakers of Crocker County. "Movies are like a warm blanket, you know, really comforting," I add as we all stare at the paused screen image of a serial killer frozen in his naked, maniacal rage.

"Beautiful day," sings out Tater-tot Casserole, and I've never been so happy to hear a weather-related declaration. "Let's get this food into the deep freezer. We don't want to be late to the service."

I sigh. Oh God. Not the deep freezer.

I tell the casserole ladies a heartfelt thank you and tell them I'll see them at the funeral home. There's a stop I need to make on the way. After a three-minute drive down the blacktop, and two right turns into True City, they call to me like two giant beacons of hope.

As a kid, I learned the facts behind Jack and Mary, our massive grain silos. The residents of True City decided to name them after Mom and Dad for one reason: in 1973, after Dad had received an Elks award for founding the True City Historical Society (designed to torture grade school children with lessons about True City's

66

history), Dad had joked, "Hell, gentlemen, if you really want to show your gratitude, name those new behemoth silos after me and my lovely wife." So they did.

But as I approach them now, all I see are my parents, larger than life, reaching for the sky, commemorated by people who knew them best.

I pull the Aston Martin up as close as I can before getting out and walking toward them.

When I see the expanse of what lies at the base of the two towering silos, my heart feels the weight of them, and I struggle to stay on my feet. I stop to take it in, but there's so much, I'm forced to rotate my head to see it all.

Love. Everywhere.

Everywhere I look I see love. It's a temporary graveyard of love. Dozens after dozens after dozens of tributes to my parents. It looks like every member of True City has brought something. I step over a practical offering of a jumbo box of Kleenex. Then a mini shrine of Mom's favorite: lilacs bundled in recycled ribbon. I make my way farther through the living memorial to see Dad's famous gavel with a note attached:

> Gavel for sale: Never used. Jack Willow
> liked to yell in his courtroom instead!
> Miss you already, Jack.

Amid the rocks and gravel there are spots of tenacious blades of grass determined to get through, sprouting up in between offerings of Irish whiskey from the Elks Club and a hand-sewn quilt from the Ladies Auxiliary. Someone has painted a watercolor of our giant willow tree and put it in a homemade frame of twigs and branches. The Boy Scouts have left a rope with some sort of fancy knot tied in it and a note written in crayon, thanking Dad for being the best scout leader in Crocker County. An honorary certificate from the True City Public Library is taped on Mom's silo, declaring that Mary Willow holds the record for the most books checked out in a lifetime.

Those that couldn't make it to the house to drop off food have left disposable containers—no sense losing a perfectly good pan—containing True City favorites like Scotcheroos, sheet-cake brownies, chocolate chip cookie bars, and the ultimate sign of despair, Jell-O salad. They all line the base of both silos like a little sidewalk of grief and sustenance. No doubt, a designated member of True City will retrieve them later tonight and bring them to the house. Waste is not an option. Perfectly practical for every occasion. Mom would approve.

Propped up at the base of the silo ladder jutting out of the cement is one of Mom's wooden spoons, with a note from someone named Martha, saying that even though it's been five weeks since the church bake sale, she is finally returning it to the best baker in True City.

It's true. Mom is…was…the best baker in True City, and probably in all of Crocker County. She was also a raging perfectionist, so baking wasn't her only exceptional skill. She sewed better than everyone else, her garden was enviable, she was more well-read, and she was a fabulous dancer. I used to hate how good she was at everything, as if she did it on purpose, and some of the ladies in True City would get frustrated with her irritating perfection too. "Mary Willow, practically perfect," I heard Mrs. Anderson snicker when Mom brought a four-tier red-white-and-blue cake, sprinkled with rose petals from her garden, to the Fourth of July veterans' fundraiser.

Dad was certainly not without his faults. "Walking Encyclopedia" they'd call him when Dad would go on some tangent about something he'd recently learned, or when he'd cite evidence for why he was right. Somewhere between Exhibit A and Exhibit B, the men at the coffee shop would lose patience, and sometimes even storm out before pie was served. Problem was, despite their eye rolling and huffing, Dad was almost always right, which was annoying. I knew that from years of firsthand experience.

And both Mom and Dad had a penchant for being blind optimists, which could be tiresome. They each disguised it differently—Mom shrouded her idealism in careful silence and hard work, while Dad buried his underneath gruff, red-herring comments like "Hell, it'll probably crash and burn," but every last person in True City knew that if something needed to be done, Jack and Mary would get it done, because they believed anything was possible.

If I didn't already know this, someone reminded me. Two feet to my left, someone had used various rocks and pebbles to spell out *Believe so.* Everyone in True City knew this phrase. Dad had used it everywhere: graduation speeches, coffee shop get-togethers, funerals, anywhere he'd sensed the slightest hint of doubt. There was a buffer of space around the words, as if Dad's mantra deserved the reverence, as if *he* deserved the reverence.

So here I stand before Jack Know-It-All and Practically-Perfect Mary Willow, stretching to the heavens, holding a million bushels of grain and a million different wishes at the same time, and for me today—and let's face it, probably forever—their flaws are buried deep beneath the soybeans, deep beneath the corn, immortalized by the power of love. Of all of the emotions I'm supposed to feel— respect for their character, gratitude for their full lives, remorse for my ignorant and selfish teenage ways—I only feel one thing.

I miss my mom and dad.

CHAPTER NINE

ANE. HOW ARE YOU?" Sid sounds afraid to ask. The staticky cell reception reminds me how far away he is.

For starters, I am a horrible person, I consider saying. Being here reminds me of everything in my life that I've screwed up. And oh yeah, I just witnessed the culmination of my sad, twisted life in the form of dozens of casseroles, frozen in time, stacked up like guilty little corpses in my mother's deep freezer.

"I'm awesome," I say, one hand on the wheel. "On my way to my parents' funeral." Even my sarcasm sounds defeated, so Sid doesn't dare comment on it.

"You have fifty-seven messages from Nick."

I wait a beat, take in some thick, humbling Iowa air until my head feels light. "Is Nick having a Schmidty day? Cuz *I'm* having a Schmidty day, Sid!" I say, revving up. I know I'm reminiscent of the lunatic version of Clark Griswold when he takes Walley World hostage, and I don't care. This is what crazy sounds like on a cell phone. In five minutes, I'll be face-to-face with my past, with people who will want to hug the Before Jane as she says her final goodbye to her parents. I want to vomit.

I begin nodding to nobody. "Yep. A super, super-duper Schmidty day! To be accurate, Sid, I feel like a piece of Schmidt, and as far as I'm concerned, Nick Wrightman can eat Schmidt and die!"

Five long seconds of silence go by before Sid says, "Good talk." More silence.

I can't stand the quiet. "Do you think there's hope for me, Sid?"

"It is what it is, right?" he says, mocking.

"That's my line."

One second, two seconds, three seconds. "Do *you* think there's hope for you, Jane?"

No, I don't. I'm a hopeless mess.

I try not to make the accent too much. "I wish I could quit—"

"You're going *Brokeback Mountain* on me right now? You really need to stop doing that, Jane, talking in film dialogue when you don't want to answer questions. Seriously. You're an award-winning writer, for God's sakes. It's the only thing you do that's cliché. Makes you sound pedestrian."

I almost give Sid an obscure line from *Midnight Cowboy* in response to me being pedestrian, but then I remember I'm on the verge of burying my parents, and suddenly, something in me breaks. I pass the Petersons' barn, see True City ahead, getting larger, closer. "You still there?" I squeak out, trying to control the ugly cry that's forming without my consent.

"I'm here, Jane." He sounds like a father torn between scolding and consoling.

"Sid?" I say, too exhausted to keep my guard up anymore. "I think you might be my only friend."

"I am." He sounds confident. "I have access to your Facebook profile. Nobody likes you."

I laugh, which is his intent, and I am grateful for it. For him.

"You're welcome," he says.

"I didn't say thank you."

"No, but you should have." Now he's scolding. "You should say thank you to people more often. While you're at it, live a little. Go on a date, for the love of God."

I think of how my last date ended in an argument before dessert was even served. (What kind of moron calls *Casablanca* dumb just because he thinks I'll be impressed with his putting down a mainstream movie?) I change the subject to an inaccuracy that I need to correct. "I don't really want Nick Wrightman to die." I may be a bitch, but I'm not a killer. "And since you gave me some advice, here's some for you. You should probably tell me to fuck off more often."

"I like how you're thinking." His voice is gentle, careful to find the right tone.

"Thank you," I say, trying out my new phrase. "I gotta go, Sid."

"Yes, you do. Hey, Jane?" He takes the kind of well-placed pause that an editor would take, and while striking the perfect balance between shocking distraction and unconditional love, sweetly says, "Fuck off."

CHAPTER TEN

*E*VERYONE KNOWS I'M HERE. Already. This is how it is in small midwestern towns. They sense an out-of-towner like they sense an insincere apology or a store-bought cake. I drive down Main Street, past Sweet's Bakery, Carol's Diner, and I see passersby looking at me, the car, whispering. Before I reach the post office, a young girl flags me down, motions for me to pull over.

"You're on your way to Happy, aren't you?" a little girl says when I roll down the window.

On my way to happy? I'm soon to be on my way to forlorn, shamed, heartbroken, but definitely not happy.

"Happy," the little girl says to me again, "from Happy Days Funeral Home."

"Right." I shake my head. In my haze, I'd forgotten that, against all logic, Happy is the funeral director's name at Happy Days, True City's one and only funeral home. I'd talked with him on the phone yesterday when we wrapped up plans for the funeral. When I'd inquired about the ironic name of the funeral home, he'd answered, in a strange, childlike way, "It's named after my daddy, Happy Senior. Good thing it's not named after Uncle. His name is Lucky."

He was right. Lucky's Funeral Home is just mean. Even by my standards.

"End of Main Street, right?" I ask the girl and point toward my destination.

The girl nods and begins to run away.

"Hey," I call after the girl, but when she turns around, I can only stare and wonder how she knows me.

The girl glances north at the Jack and Mary grain silos towering into the heavens. Her eyes widen. "You're *that* Corn Queen." She smiles in awe, then scurries away, and I remember something Mom and Dad told me a few years back. Each year now, before the new Crocker County Corn Queen is crowned, the MC pays tribute to the most famous Corn Queen in the history of the Crocker County Corn Festival: me. It is this version of me, a legend that has gained steam through time and imagination, that the little girls of True City know.

I drive away wearing the girl's comment like a heavy, awkward crown, and dizziness sets in again. How can I feel both lonely and accepted at the same time? I feel a million miles away from what I know, yet everything here is the kind of familiar found only in a place where people knew you before the world set in.

A family of four waves at me as I pass Déjà Vu, the indoor movie theater that people only go to in the winter when it's too cold to go to True View, the drive-in on the outskirts of town. The three movies listed on the marquees in black block letters create an unfortunate sentence when strung together—*Fantastic*

Four Knocked Up Nancy Drew—but what makes me really smile is that the movies' release dates were five years ago. New releases are a big-town luxury, like McDonald's or higher education.

In between the movie theater and the police station is a new brick building, still under construction. A temporary vinyl banner hangs from the roof, boasts *Home of the True City Thespians*. Since when did True City have real, live theater? And then another surprise that hits me like the first, deep-bellied note of a big brass band. *Coming soon… The Music Man.*

My pulse speeds up, flutters at the very thought of it. Mother's very own Harold Hill right here in True City. But then a hole forms somewhere in my heart, and toxic *could've been*s spill out everywhere, pump through my veins. I sink into my seat, Dad's meticulous upholstery job holding tight, and I think of all the things they're going to miss out on.

When I pass Strickner's Mercantile, a sharp pain announces itself in my core. I feel my small hand in Dad's. *Pick one out, kid; the butterscotch ones are good.*

When I finally get out of the car and enter Happy Days Funeral Home, it does not smell like death. It smells like casseroles. This is the midwestern way to console; flowers are just not practical. I imagine dozens and dozens of them—tater tot, hamburger pie, tuna noodle, and other mothers' versions of Mom's died-and-gone-to-heaven scalloped corn casserole—lined up in Happy Days' main room, in the form of neighborly, rectangular mourners bathed in butter.

Happy greets me at the door, and despite his name and the funeral home's name, looks neither like the Fonz nor one of the seven dwarfs. He is a very tall Vietnamese man wearing a very outdated suit in the middle of rural America. Yet another surprise in this land that I thought had no surprises.

"Willow," I say and shake his hand. "Jane Willow."

Happy lets out a subdued, "Janie," like it's an apology. There is something off about him. He cups his other hand around both of ours. These are the same hands that touched my parents as he prepared their bodies for this day. An achy cold shoots through me, which is when I realize I'm still wearing all four of Mom's cardigans. I should take them off, but if I do, that means there will be no more lilacs, no more Mom.

Happy turns out to be the antithesis of his name. His pouty countenance makes way for his childlike, melancholy voice. "Such a sad, sad day."

Isn't he supposed to keep things positive? Isn't there a class in mortuary school devoted to distracting the mourners so they forget how damn sad they are? I force a half smile. "Trying to keep it together. For my parents."

His eyes widen. He places his hand on his chest in the "oh dear" position and begins to shake his head. Then he takes my hand. "Janie," he says quietly, pathetically, like I am mentally challenged, like he knows something I don't. "Your parents are...*dead*."

Hearing this and seeing the confused look on my face, a woman wearing an apron over her church dress flutters over to us. "Now, Happy, we talked about this. Don't upset the mourner, remember?" The woman whispers to me, "He's got the mind of a seven-year-old but the heart of an old soul."

It turns out Happy is the one who's mentally challenged. "Why... What..."

The woman puts her hand on my shoulder. "Happy's part of

True City's Special Jobs for Special People program. Happy's dad, Happy Sr., ran Happy Days for years, but he recently passed away, God rest his soul, so Happy Jr. here is helping out. Happy gets lonely. He's an adopted only child."

I want to ask why they don't just make him a greeter at the Walmart, but then I remember there is no Walmart here, no Starbucks, no cynicism. Midwesterners historically see the best in people. They always find a place for everyone.

I grimace and softly say, "Should he be touching dead bodies?"

The woman adjusts her apron and raises her strong, ung-roomed brow. "I hardly think they mind, darlin'. Plus, Hank over there"—she points with her head, and Hank raises his hand to say hello—"has been taking care of the embalming since Happy Sr. passed. Happy Jr. just talks to the deceased. I think it makes him feel better, ya know?"

I am officially in the Twilight Zone—not the Rod Serling, quirky television version, but the John Landis do-you-want-to-see-something-really-scary film version—and here's how I know I'm in another dimension: My parents are dead. A six-foot-four man-child of a funeral director named Happy, who possibly has a G.I. Joe action figure in his pocket, probably had a better con-versation with my parents today than I have had in years. Farmers and little girls, strangers, know me better than I know myself. All the while, the Music Man prepares to sing and dance his way in and out of True City's hearts and minds and into my dreams. So as it turns out, there is another dimension, but it doesn't lie in either fear or intellect; it lies in the middle, the heartland, between a willow tree guarding my shame and two giant grain silos that I swear are watching over me. This is the dimension of reinvention, my home, redefined, revised. It is an area which we call...Iowa.

Happy lowers his head but keeps eye contact with me and speaks like he's rehearsed it. "I'm sorry for your loss." He looks to the woman for assurance of a job well done.

I hand him a CD I've burned just for today, and he tells me there's no sound system, that's for the fancy funeral homes, but he's brought his very own stereo system today just for me.

"Thank you," I say, for Sid. "I've got everything else lined up. This is the last thing." I clear the regret from my throat. "I'm not letting them down. Not this time."

My parents, I want to explain, but somehow Happy, who shouldn't know, now knows. He pats my shoulder, one parentless child consoling another.

Just when I think it is Tim Burton who has been following me around with a camera, transforming the plain, predictable home I used to know into some fantastical, macabre landscape as only true auteur could, the master shot changes into a slow pan of the room, a Wes Anderson-inspired collection of misfits—my parents' funeral attendees posing as Royal Tenenbaums stand-ins—a father and son in matching track suits, a woman in her house coat and work boots, a man in an Elks' Club sweater and cowboy hat, and yet another in his letterman jacket from 1959 over top of freshly soiled overalls.

I glance down at Mother's sky-blue cardigan, one of the four that I've layered over my black Betsey Johnson dress, and realize I have more in common with the characters in this scene than not. This ensemble, no doubt a disgrace to my three-hundred-dollar shoes, would have gotten me laughed off an LA street, but the ever-present smell of lilacs makes me forget that. I reach into the pocket and pull out a neatly folded handkerchief—one I knew would be there—and dab at my messy mascara to avoid looking like the predictable, grief-stricken only child.

By now, the entire town has arrived. Happy has opened up the two extra rooms, and since it is late summer, not yet harvest-cold, they've opened up the double doors and placed metal folding chairs they'd borrowed from the Lutheran church on the outside patio. There was a small service on Friday, but my parents would not have wanted two big events devoted to them. *That is to say, never be a damn nuisance, kid.*

"Janie." A woman touches my shoulder and gently takes my hand as I move through the whispering throng. When I see her face, I feel like a child back from summer camp.

"Mrs. Davis." Without thinking, I hug the woman, my other mother growing up, and for a few seconds, forget to let go. "Is Charlotte here?"

"She'll be 'round later. She's got her hands full on the farm with Steve gone and all." And because I've been gone so long, Mrs. Davis had to explain. "Pheasant season."

"Of course." I try not to think about how many times my childhood best friend Charlotte has sent me Christmas cards over the years, none of which I reciprocated. "I heard the house has become some sort of tourist attraction—tell me she's charging admission."

Mrs. Davis shook her head. "My home…a circus sideshow." Her home, the house Charlotte now raised her family in, was the birthplace of Grant Wood and the backdrop for the iconic *American Gothic* painting.

I search the room for words to break the tension. "Lots of casseroles."

"Hot dishes." Mrs. Davis squints a bit as if she felt sorry for my forgetting the proper term.

Used to being the corrector, not the corrected, I give Mrs. Davis a polite but awkward half hug and make my way toward the main room. I feel the crowd watch me, taking in what they can see of my dress, much shorter than everyone else's, and my leg line, much thinner.

"Guess they don't eat much out in that Los Angeles," I hear a woman whisper as I walk by.

I glance down at a body that is ten pounds heavier than it ought to be and remember these people consider butter a food group.

"At least she has the good sense to have a cardigan on, what with this weather comin' and all," I hear another woman say back, "but Good Lord, she must be cold, she's wearing enough of them to clothe half the Ladies Auxiliary Club."

As I pass, I see a woman in her own black cardigan look toward the reception room and say, "I don't think I used enough butter in the hot dish I brought." Shaking her head, she adds, "I hope they don't run out of the fancy paper plates."

Happy appears from a back room. "It's time to celebrate," he says and rings a cowbell—an actual cowbell—and the entire population of True City, whether they were in the main room, the patio, or adding butter to hot dishes, hush. Happy turns up the volume on a small amp, and then taps on a corded microphone until it thumps. "Friends," he says, closing his eyes for a moment to remember the next memorized part, "it's time to celebrate the lives of Jack and Mary Willow."

With no hesitation, an endless line forms behind Happy and his microphone. Dozens of almost-familiar people take polite turns talking about my parents. The six-o-clock supper siren had blared at the beginning of the "celebration" and now I see the sun setting as the mini eulogies play out like a well-edited montage.

The whole room nods while Stew Jenkins boasts about Mother's food drives and the hundreds of young people she'd helped put through college with her philanthropy. By the time he begins to rattle off just what Dad meant to True City, I start to wobble in my heels, not from exhaustion, but from a combination of pent-up pride and shame.

"Jack Willow was the only guy I know who could convince you it was totally appropriate to swear in church." Stew laughs. "He wasn't a religious man—only went to church to see his friends." Stew looks out the window. "There they are." He points to the silos, standing tall and firm, together forever. "Jack and Mary held us up." He pauses. "True City has a crack. We're wide open today."

Stew hands the microphone to the last person in line, Larry Peterson. He speaks in slow succession, sure of every word as he defines Dad—his best friend. "Jack Willow: Justice-bringer. Peacemaker. Confidant. Mayor. Weekend farmer. Parade director. Elks' Club president. Benefactor. Story-time host. Prankster." He smiles. "Friend. Jack liked having the last word, but since he can't this time, I'll speak for him, which he truly would've hated." The crowd grows quiet. "He'd say, 'Mary and I are just fine; don't worry about us. We're happy. That is to say'"—and with that, the crowd erupts in smiles—"'we're flying high.'"

Larry lowers the microphone for a moment, and then brings it back up as if he's going off the script. "You know what I loved about Jack and Mary the most? They both had the daggum, hair-brained notion that they could will anything to happen. They believed anything was possible. They did things that mattered." Larry lets the silence grow thick. "That is to say"—his voice now sounds like he's lost his best friend—"the sky's the limit. *Believe so.*"

I turn my head away from the crowd to blink away potential tears as Larry hands Happy the microphone. The heaviness of the day pounds in my head. This is almost over. I will do what I came to do as people begin to exit, then sneak out the back.

But instead of the crowd getting louder and dispersing, it suddenly gets funeral-home quiet. When I turn, I'm startled to find Happy an inch from my face, breathing his mid-funeral tuna casserole snack on me.

"Fuck, Happy!" I say under my breath. But the words aren't under my breath. Without my knowing, Happy has plopped the microphone right in front of my foul mouth so that all of God-fearing True City can hear my always-inappropriate-under-pressure self say the f-word on Happy's highest volume.

"Bad word!" Happy scolds, covering his ears, and drops the microphone on the floor with an amplified clunk.

CHAPTER ELEVEN

$\mathcal{A}$ WOMAN WEARING A CARHARTT jacket over her dress blurts, "Gads-zukes!" a favorite curse word in this part of Iowa. "Is she drunk?"

Oh, how I wish I was drunk.

I hear a man explain, "She's from Los Angeles," and the crowd around him lets out a collective understanding with nods and aahs.

Fuck Happy. And Peaceful. And Content. And Hopeful, while we're at it.

"I guess she used to be funny and clever when she was young," another woman tells her husband, loud enough for me to hear. "Now she's just mean, rumor has it. Writes things about movies. Is that even a job?"

I'm right here! Do you think I can't hear your mean little critiques?

I usually observe others' mistakes, but right now a naughty little halo hovers above me, and I look out at the crowd like an uninvited child who's crashed a birthday party.

Happy is not happy. He looks at me like the ungrateful child I am, picks up the microphone, and then dangles it until I take it.

Dad fathers me from afar. *Fix it, kid. That is to say, make it right.*

"Um, thank you," I force out, "for coming." Uncomfortable silence and disapproving stares compete for attention until the microphone screams out a mean feedback screech that I know I deserve. "My parents were a lot of things to a lot of people." I look out and now recognize Henrietta, the town librarian; Dr. Nance; and Mrs. Jones, my high school history teacher who has a kind, pitiful smile on her face. I let out an honest laugh, try to softly say, "Who knew that you could be so many things here," but it comes out loud and clear, so much so that a few skeptics have begun to show traces of affirmation.

I need to say goodbye and get the hell out of here.

But my grip on the microphone only tightens, and to my own surprise, I begin to talk with intention. "Did you know"—I smile, looking up at the people who had spent their entire lives with my parents—"that Dad never complained when Mom turned off James Bond so she could watch *The Music Man*? All he wanted to do was fantasize about shooting people in the kneecaps while wearing a sharp suit, but instead, he sang along with Harold, made her believe in the impossible."

I cling to the microphone cord like a lifeline. I conjure up Dad's gruff delivery and say, "'*Believe so*, kid,'" and my voice breaks. With this, Mrs. Douglas begins to cry, and Larry's upper lip trembles as he proudly tries to sniff away the moment.

I want to run, but I hear Mother's voice: *Work hard. Be nice.*

Mrs. Davis is on the verge of rescuing me when I muster up the strength to continue. "My mom told me that a girl knows she's in love when she'll ride on a tractor with a boy and not want to say a word. And with my dad, well, he liked to talk, so that worked well."

I concentrate on keeping the tears from unleashing. "They sure loved it here." I hear the wind pick up outside and imagine the August breeze traveling in waves across the county, one cornfield, one family at a time. "And they loved each other. After all this time." I try to disguise my quivering voice. "It's a good thing they went together."

Then, with the closing credits of this tragedy looming, I realize what I need to say—what I've come here for. "I make a living from words. My dad always liked that. But sometimes words aren't enough." I decide to say exactly what each of my parents would've wanted to hear, what they deserved to hear. Here it goes. I look to the sky and say, "Mom, I'm home," then straighten up tall. "And, Dad, here's the song you requested many, many years ago," I say, seeing him tap his foot in time, drumming his fingers on the roof of the Aston Martin. "That is to say, you're right. *Believe so*, Dad."

I motion Happy to bring me what I've asked him for, and he delivers what he promised. It is ridiculous and perfect. Happy hoists up a giant boom box like he's John Cusack on a mission. It is loaded with the CD that's traveled five states to get here, and the song that transcends space and time.

I blow out the two candles that are flickering by Mom and Dad's pictures on the display table. Two tiny puffs of smoke billow into clouds much bigger than I expect them to be.

It is time. I look over at the door and give a farmer nod as a signal. A boy lugging a standing bass leads in the rest—four trumpet players, a drummer, a French horn player, one flutist, one baritone saxophonist, one alto saxophonist, and twenty-three of True City's finest singers.

Just yesterday, I'd called the members of the True City high school band and choir to personally ask them if I could pay them for a favor. They all declined payment because Dad had raised money each year to send them to the Iowa State Fair, and they said he'd always given them more than they'd needed.

But given what they are about to do for me—my father, really—I feel gratified to give them all the envelopes I have tucked in my purse. Inside each is a generous check, courtesy of the *Los Angeles Times* scholarship fund, to put toward their futures. I had thought about hiring professionals at first but heard Dad's voice: *Hell, kid, there's nothing you can't find in True City if you look close enough.*

I give Happy a wink, and he pushes Play. The room first fills with the sound of a schmaltzy snare drum, then deep notes plucked on a bass, and finally Frank Sinatra's smooth, cool voice. "Fly Me to the Moon" rings out as clear and crisp as a full harvest moon. Frank sings of playing in the sky, life and love on faraway planets. That is to say, being in love.

In a seamless, uniform maneuver, evidence of a late night's practice, horns erupt in little sections all over the room—first trumpets, then the French horn, then the saxes, and like a little bird who wants to contribute to the song, the flute sings in airy little chirps—together, their small group plays like a big band. When Larry Peterson bobs his head and begins to snap his fingers, the citizens of True City follow suit, and soon Happy's funeral parlor lives up to its name.

The choir, planted strategically among the crowd, flash-mob style, explodes into perfect harmony and joins Frank on the second verse. This time around, Frank's heart, Dad's heart, is full, wanting to sing until the end of time, wanting his love to never die. That is to say, a love that lasts an eternity.

I walk over to the two coffins, side by side, the way it should be. Trying not to sound like a broken little girl, I whisper my final words. "Goodbye, ambassadors. Outta this world."

CHAPTER TWELVE

I AM LOST.

I don't know where I'm going, but I've torn off into the dark night on the blacktop road that leads out of town, and I intend to drive until I've composed myself enough to confirm my reservation and pay for one night's stay at the Sandman Motel. I can't sleep at home for my first night back in True City. The idea of finally sleeping in my mother's home without her being there seems wrong. I'll pay a moving company to pack everything up and send it to storage, and when I can, I'll put the house on the market. Everyone will live not-so-happily ever after. The end.

Goddamn it, I hate it here.

I drive past farmhouse after farmhouse, aglow like fiery magnets for happiness. The more I drive the worse I feel, and finally, after bouncing past every corncrib, flying around every road surrounding True City, I cannot outrun the lie: I am not from here. Someone from here would not have avoided coming home for any reason, no matter how shameful. Someone from here would have come home to visit her parents, no matter what.

I am used to city lights, so I am humbled by the absolute blackness that I see before me. My headlights illuminate my way through the darkness—the same darkness I normally relish in brings me no comfort tonight, yet without darkness, there would be no stars.

And how can I describe the stars here? I used to think we all saw the same stars, but these are not regular stars. I've seen those. These stars are archetypal, like somehow they are the originals and all other stars are mere imposters. No, these luminescent balls of fire are the ones from which copies have been made, to be scattered all over the universe, like borrowed wishes.

Right now, Los Angeles stargazers watch the sky—at Eagle Rock, at the Griffith Observatory, splayed out on their backs like little disciples next to the Hollywood sign—and they think they've cornered the market on stars, that their stars are brighter, more real, that the rest of us poor saps in the world are looking at inferior stars.

But in this exact moment, I know something they don't.

Here, in the black Iowa night—a place for beginning and ending, birthing and dying, loving and losing—this is where the stars are.

Every culture has looked for pictures in the stars. We want so badly to make sense of it all, find meaning from nothing more than chance groupings, and tonight, so do I. The Navajos believe the Milky Way is a bridge linking heaven and earth. So I gaze at it, take in its vastness, frantically search for them, my ambassadors to the moon.

I extinguish my doubt of all things ethereal and instead embrace divine possibilities, create my own celestial story where my parents, temporarily in the dark, awaken as stars. Born of a gravitational collapse, now held together by their own gravity, they burn brighter than the rest, and I worry—because the more massive the star, the shorter its lifespan. But I know them. They're optimists. Workers. Philanthropists. They will evolve, recycle part of their matter into the interstellar community, and create a new generation of stars. In my star lore, they inspire billions. In my star lore, my parents own the sky.

So I drive. The stars surround me, but I need them to guide me. Like a sailor who needs help navigating in the dark of night, I look to the sky. Give me something. Some sign as to where to direct my lost soul. An extra twinkle somewhere, maybe in some constellation. I'll figure it out. Come on. Give me something. A flicker in Orion's belt to tell me I'm a boastful jackass. A glint in Cassiopeia to verify my vanity. A shimmer in Canis Minor to remind me I'm the lesser dog.

I glance out the driver-side window for my sign.

Nothing.

Why the hell am I even here? I don't know. I admit it.

Here are the bravest, weakest words I've ever uttered: I surrender.

Together, the Aston Martin and I travel down the blacktop. One barn. Two barns. Three. I scour the sky for a sign.

Nothing.

Screw you, Universe. Thanks for mocking my vulnerability.

I pass the Stephens' farm. Exhausted, I glance down for a split second to check the clock. 9:15 p.m. When I look back up, a flash of a white, shadowy shape enters my peripheral vision from the right side of the road, and in a blur, it streaks toward my car.

Before I can slam on the brakes, there's a loud thud, and a

louder thump, as whatever it is flies up and bounces off the front grill and then the right side of the hood.

With my foot still on the gas pedal, I scream, then scream again just to make sure I'm alive.

Oh God.

Oh God.

I hold my breath as the iridescent, yellow dashes on the blacktop flash by in quick succession.

That did not just happen.

My hands grip the steering wheel, and my foot lets up on the gas for a moment, but something in me won't allow me to slow down completely. To turn around to see what I've hit.

It's too dark to stop. It was probably a raccoon. This damn state is teeming with nocturnal wildlife, and with the Raccoon River nearby, it makes sense that animals would be out hunting food.

Yes. That makes sense.

I drive.

There's no law against hitting a raccoon, right?

No. There isn't.

I drive.

I drive until I recognize the Smiths' farm. Then the Holts'. Then I drive back into town, settle into the Sandman Motel, and vow to sleep away the day.

Morning comes. Doesn't anyone honk or yell here? I force myself out of the lumpy motel bed, decide I will not make the instant coffee sitting in a packet on the nightstand.

Then, like an alarm clock, my conscience rings. *Thump*. The night before floods back in short, mean flashes.

Thud.

And then again. *Thump*.

Fine. I will retrace my evening drive, find the poor animal I've hit, stiff legs pointing to the morning sky, say sorry, and clear my mind.

This whole trip will fade into a hazy, neutral blur.

I sit at the foot of the bed, put on the only other outfit I've brought: jeans, my Ramones T-shirt, and leather jacket I scored from the UCLA Thrift Shop. While dressing, I watch one of the few stations that come in on the small television. When I hear the words, when I see the picture in the top right hand of the screen and my eyes meet the eyes of a beautiful young girl, I freeze.

The words won't stop. They keep coming.

Breaking news. Gruesome hit and run. Small town of True City. Victim: eighteen-year-old girl. Left in the ditch.

And I stop breathing.

Chapter Thirteen

*I*N IOWA, GUILT IS a religion. The people bow down to it, make sure it's always with them, a talisman-like conscience to keep small sins from becoming big ones.

I buried my guilt years ago.

But now, just like that, just like riding a shiny red bicycle down a long country lane, I ignite my former relationship with my old friend: Guilt, sister to Shame, brother to Blame.

I slide off the lumpy motel mattress, fall to my knees, and let the guilt flow through me; I let it punish me for a sin bigger than words—a sin so big it makes the horror of burying both of my parents merely seem like a bad day.

In my mind, I hold up a dewy-wet daisy—the He-Loves-Me-He-Loves-Me-Not kind—the kind with which one makes deals with God. But this time I'm not looking for a boy's affection. I'm looking for salvation.

I will be a better person.

I pluck an imaginary petal.

I will do things that matter.

I pluck another dewy, white petal.

I will be nice to shitty movie producers.

Just make this a bad dream. A nightmare. A wake-up call.

Another petal. I close my eyes.

When I open my eyes, please let the television show me any-thing—a weather report, the current price of corn and soybeans—anything but her face.

I pluck.

Then open my eyes.

He loves me.

Not.

I look at the television screen, and the young girl stares back; her bright eyes sparkle with youth and possibility. *Left near a blacktop road. Intensive care. Critical condition. Coma. Crocker County Regional Care Center.*

I grab my knees, rock on the dirty shag carpet. A flood of emo-tion settles in my throat where words should be. What I've done, this insidious thing, blocks my airway, chokes me with guilt.

Words finally break through. "No, no, no, no, no, no!" I am Superman yelling to no one. I close my eyes, fly around the Earth, turn back time. My life flashes in reverse. I move in high speed, backward, out the motel door, back into last night, jet-black except for a few billion of the brightest stars I've ever seen. The Aston Martin drives backward down the blacktop, but this time, I don't keep driving. No thud. No thump. Instead, I go to my house, watch the stars from our front porch, in Mom's red rocker, while nestled tight in four layers of lilac-infused warmth. I find my parents, shining bright. I bow down, tell them I'm sorry.

But I can't stop. I need to go back farther, so I keep flying, keep reversing time. I spin, spin, spin back three days, ten o'clock Central time. Mom and Dad are getting ready to take up Hawkeye, fly away the afternoon. I pick up the phone, tell them, "Don't go flying today. I'm coming home."

But it's still not enough. I fly harder. Faster. Back to where it all began and ended. One year, two, ten, eighteen. I am surrounded by corn, a labyrinth full of tall rows, switching this way and that, confusing me, forcing me to succumb to fear. But this time, I don't leave her.

Sunlight pours through the motel window, reflects off the face of my watch. Time has not stopped. It has not reversed. This isn't Hollywood. And it sure isn't heaven. It's just Iowa. You have to do your time here. Do the hard work. I recite a midwestern commandment: "Nothing worth doing is ever easy."

No redo. No revising this time.

I put on my shoes, grab my keys to keep my hands from shaking, and walk to the door. I need to make it right. I have a confession to make to the True City Police Department.

Chapter Fourteen

I DRIVE DOWN MAIN STREET, the road to all destinations in True City, until I reach the police station. I turn the car off, listen to the *tick-tick-ticking* of the resting engine, unable to touch the car door handle. Instead, I look out the window. Farmers and mothers alike move down the street in a small-town cadence, and farther away, Jack and Mary still stand tall, still reach for the sky. From across town, they watch me. I hear my father. *If you're wrong, kid, make it right.*

I make myself open the car door. And step out. One foot. Then the other. My heavy feet heel-toe their way in autopilot fashion until I reach the front door of the station. Everything slows. Bullet time, as they say in the movie business, made famous in *The Matrix*. One millisecond, one frame at a time.

On the drive over, I'd practiced a confession in my head, and now, I practice it again. I must pay penance for this, I'll say. I must pay penance for everything. In between steps, I imagine my life's mistakes playing out on the film screen in my mind. It's clearly an Alan Smithee film. What real director would claim such a pile of shit?

I see the mise-en-scène staging on Main Street as a brief diversion on my way to incarceration. In my panoramic mind, a passerby wearing a ruby-red cardigan swirls with the blue storefront awnings and stark trim around storefront doors.

The police station door comes into sharp focus, and right on cue, the musical score in my head juxtaposes a melodic female vocal with harsh minor chords that say *transgressions, retribution, impasse*, all pointing to some existential struggle. I know what Paul Thomas Anderson would add here. Symbols of biblical proportion, no doubt. Frogs falling from the sky. Reminders that the future is unknown in this midwestern *Magnolia*.

An urgent gust of wind shocks me back to reality. I grab the police station door handle, but when I do, the wind sweeps down the sidewalk, makes hats fly, tree branches dance, and storefront signs on hinges swing themselves into a frenzy.

I look toward the wind, try to understand it. My world darkens when something blows in front of me, blocks the light. I put my hands to my face and find the culprit: a piece of blue paper stuck to me.

The sky-blue flyer with black print speaks to me. Wants me.

To come see…*The Music Man*?

The Music Man?

I am in so much trouble. True City, River City—it's all the same. I. Am. A. Criminal. The surrealism of it all swirls in my mind, and yesterday's dizziness returns. How can this be happening? How can any of this be happening? I think of what this movie meant to Mom and Dad, and my heart aches.

The flyer flies out of my hand. It whirls in a small eddy formation, suspends for one exaggerated moment, then lands flat against
the glass station door in front of me. It reads *Coming This Christmas*.

"Hey, give me a hand?" A boy has somehow gotten the slide
of his trombone hooked on the door handle of the building next
door, True City's newly renovated community theater. He stands
half-in, half-out of the arched theater door tangled in humiliation
and brass. A Sweethearts candy falls from a small box in his back
pocket, falls onto the sidewalk and shatters.

The old brick building, now new with possibility, features a
dark-blue awning with the tragedy and comedy masks donned in
John Deere hats. Above the front door, a sign lit with marquee
lights reads *True City Community Theater*. On the left side of the
building is a thirty-foot-tall mural of True City, complete with my
parents' grain silos watching over endless cornfields.

"Sure, just a sec…" I take one last look at the police station
door, turn away from it, and run toward the boy to help him
dislodge his trombone.

His kind voice and Opie Taylor freckles make me think he
might say, "Gee, thanks, lady," but like so many other things that
have surprised me since I've returned to this place I call home, his
reaction is not what I expect.

"I hate this trombone," he mutters. When he looks at me, I see
something familiar in his eyes, something I've seen before, something that reminds me of a long-lost friend. "My mom's making
me be in this dumb musical. It's so friggin' stupid!" His eyes pale,
letting sadness in. "Especially now."

I continue to hold the door while I look at him, listen to him.
His impolite tone is unusual for a God-fearing Iowan boy, but it's

hard for a woman on the verge of being arrested to be critical. He looks at me, waits for me to react, but when I don't defend his mother or the fine art of musical theater, he says, "Thanks," and squirms his free hand out to half shake mine. "I'm Connor," he says, and scoots inside, now holding the door open for me.

He starts to walk toward a deep and shiny stage at the front of the large room, an amphitheater that still smells new. Actors, townsfolk really, bustle about. Some hand out props. Others clutch their scripts.

I almost say *you're welcome* when he thanks me. I almost tell this stranger-turned-Connor how I'm in the middle of something and have to go. But when I try to speak, time slows; a relentless zoom shot pulls me in with it, up toward the stage. Something beyond my control takes hold, and I can only listen. A middle-aged man in the middle of the stage begins to address the actors, plead, really, and I feel compelled to walk toward him.

"Now I know you're upset about Bliss, but bloody hell…" His voice trails off, unable to find the right tone. I now recognize him—it's Mr. Linart, my foul-mouthed high school English teacher, who is apparently the closest thing to a drama coach True City can find. Because he always thought British profanity was less likely to get him in trouble with the school board, Mr. Linart would replace American curse words with British ones when he felt passionate about something, and he often felt passionate— "Hey, you bollocks had a crap ton of verb-tense errors in your last essays" and "Holden Caulfield is such a bloody wanker"—but he was so fun and taught us more than any other teacher so that none of us ever ratted him out. It appears the habit has stuck with him in retirement.

"Look. I know you're all upset. I'm upset. But stop arsin' about. The show must go on." He gives a sad, nervous tug on his argyle sweater vest. "Bliss would want it to."

With this, the teenage boy who is playing Harold Hill begins a series of slow nods. My legs weaken, and with my gaze still fixed on the stage, I slump into one of the new, plush theater chairs, two rows back from center stage.

"Okay, Josh, good job, lad! Your lovely Marian, the librarian, can't be here right now, but we have work to do." Mr. Linart rubs Josh's head with a new vigor. "You are Harold bloomin' Hill! Not some lousy git." Mr. Linart is a whirling dervish. He darts to left stage center, slams his coffee-to-go cup down on a prop table, and addresses the cast. "Harold Hill is so bloody brilliant that he can will things to happen, or pretends to anyway." Mr. Linart is now waving his hands in the air like a half-bloke, half-dude crazy man with patriotic identity issues. "And it doesn't matter anyway, does it, as long as somebody, even one person believes it?"

"*Believe so*," Josh says—declares, really—from across the stage. Then louder. "*Believe so.*"

"Abso-bloody-lutely!" Mr. Linart yells. "It's not the unofficial mantra of True City for nothin', lad! *Believe so* allows a total duffer to play Beethoven when he doesn't know how to play a barmy note! Harold Hill isn't a con man, kids; he's a bloody shaman!"

I can't take my eyes off the faces on the stage before me. There is a reverence here, a palpable gravitas I would mock under normal circumstances, but I am in my last hour of desperation, so I take it in, lean into it. The six brass players now look ready to play. Connor's scowl has disappeared, his trombone back in his hands. Josh now holds his head a little higher, with the promise of an against-all-odds glimmer in his eyes, looking like a young Harold Hill on the verge of a miracle.

For a predictable moment, I am Jane Willow—the After Jane who is ruled by doubt and cynicism, who knows all of this malarkey is nonsense.

And.

Yet.

Small stirrings of Before Jane awaken from somewhere I can't quite place, and she says, *Believe so. Just think it so, and Bliss will be all right.*

"I know what you're thinking," Mr. Linart says. "Why does it matter? Why does this stupid little musical even matter right now?" He plops down onto the makeshift park bench courtesy of the fictional River City set. "You know why it matters? When you want something so badly, and you just know it's sure to be a total cock-up, and you do it anyway. That's why. And when you're gutted, absolutely gutted over how cruel and unfair this life can be, but you keep going, you believe in the miracle of an impossible transformation. That's why."

Mr. Linart takes a deep breath, for everyone.

"Across those hills, Bliss sleeps. Dreams, maybe. But we need her to come back to us."

Then like a testament to doubt itself, Connor breaks in with a declaration that seems to represent the collective fear in the room. "She's going to die."

It spreads like a cancer. Two other trombonists lower their heads, a little girl starts to cry, and Harold Hill, who has returned to being just teenager Josh, looks to Mr. Linart as the deflated room awaits his response.

Mr. Linart nods, waits for several seconds, suspends the heaviness in the room while he buys some time. "Okay. You're right. She might die. But none of us are getting out of here alive, ya know." He points to himself. "I'm going to die." He points to the little girl, the cutest member of River City's townsfolk, who is already crying. "Even little Carrie's going to die." Carrie, now acutely aware of her mortality at the ripe age of five, turns her cry into a full-blown sob, and I start to question Mr. Linart's motivational strategy.

"But quitting is for tossers. Quitting is rubbish. We owe it to her to not bugger this up. We owe it to Bliss to have a little faith. So either we do this thing full monty, or we don't do it at all." For the first time in this diatribe, Mr. Linart tears up. "We want—we need—a shaman; we need a…" He then whispers *miracle* as if it's too embarrassing to say out loud. "But I'll settle for a first-rate, bloody con man." He winds up now, unapologetic, totally off his trolley, his Union Jack flying high. "We are not a bunch of dodgy quitters. We are River City champions." And then softer: "True City's finest. We work hard, mates."

Work hard. Be nice. Mom is everywhere.

"'Believe so' will save the bloody day." Mr. Linart now stands, directing his people, guiding those who need to find their way. "Now, make it happen, lads and lassies!"

And just like that, with the predictability of a midwestern thunderstorm on a humid, August afternoon, everyone gets to work.

"Hey, help us out," Mr. Linart hollers out at me as the crew take their spots on the stage. "We're short one Marian Paroo. Please. Just a few lines."

I sit up, heart racing, unable to move as everyone now stares at me, their only audience.

When I remain seated, he adds, "Just a few lines. Please. Come on. I could really use a bloody hand here."

I think hard, hoping it will save the day, but knowing it won't. I get up anyway and walk to the stage. Mr. Linart takes my hand as I climb five steps to center stage. "Just so you know, I'm not an actor." And I start to laugh, thinking about the lousy reviews I would get from myself. "I'm actually a—"

"I know what you are, Janie." Mr. Linart squeezes my hand, smiles, and winks at me. "Welcome home."

Someone whispers Corn Queen, but right now I am Marian Paroo, for Bliss, and Mr. Linart is feeding me my line.

I read my line as Marian. Teenage Josh stands up a little straighter as Harold Hill, takes my hand, and stares into my eyes. It's all about today.

Josh needs no prompting, no script, and I realize at that very moment, neither do I. The giant room shrinks. The world outside disappears. Harold Hill and I, the two of us, exist in some other plane where people know things.

It's all about today. He stares so deep inside me, I lose myself in the smooth strength of it. *Believe so*. Just say it, and it shall be.

Just like that.

Just like that, truth emerges, revised, redefined. *If you're wrong, kid, make it right*. But this time, right is not next door, sitting in a jail cell, following the letter of the law. The real right lies asleep in a hospital bed, waiting for someone to say the right words that will call her back. The real right will be much more difficult, calling upon a thing as heavy as a miracle, unmovable as one's will.

The real right involves a girl, temporarily lost, being found.

"Thank you, Mr. Linart," I say, but I am already down the stage steps heading toward the door. "And thank you, kids. You make River City…True City…proud!"

"Wait, Janie! Your big scene is coming up!"

It is. And I have to go. Out the door and past the police station door, toward the hills where she dreams.

Cheerio.

CHAPTER FIFTEEN

RUN OPENING TITLES OVER:

INT. SOMEWHERE—TODAY

BLISS (V.O.)
(dreamy)
I don't know where I am, but I
know who I am. I am Bliss.

FADE IN:

Establishing Shot: Eighteen-year-old BLISS ANDERSON,
in an ethereal state, floats in space, tries to
figure out where she is. The borders of her world
are fuzzy, cloud-like. She watches herself below,
some in-between place.

CUT TO:

The earthly BLISS sits, waiting for her name to be called for something. She beams in a sunshine-yellow organza gown, a warm spot in a cold, colorless auditorium.

> **BLISS**
> (surprised)
> God, I look good. Really good. Not to sound totally into myself, but I look pretty. Like this is the biggest night of my life, maybe. That dress is epic! I definitely did not get *that* in True City.

BLISS now settles into her body below…

TIGHT ON:

BLISS's hand first touches her body, then her gown, and finally her hair pulled painfully tight in a fancy updo. BLISS proceeds to ask several rhetorical questions like it's a well-practiced habit.

> **BLISS**
> (growing tired)
> Is this why my head hurts? Why am

I so tired? Can't I just take a
little nap?

WOMAN (O.S.)
(urgently)
Bliss, don't fall asleep. Whatever
you do, don't fall asleep.

BLISS wants to obey the voice. She lets the famil-
iarity of it wrap around her. She sniffs the
air to take in a sudden, overwhelming scent of
hollyhocks, then as if it were not strange at
all, BLISS watches a live monarch butterfly land
on her dress.

A fluttering spot of orange and black hovers in
a sea of yellow. She looks around for the origin
of the voice, but when she can't find it, she
observes the people sitting in the auditorium
seats near her. They are beautiful strangers.

STRANGER
Where are you from?

BLISS
Somewhere…with golden cornfields,
red barns, and lots of twinkling
stars in a sky as black as the
soil.

STRANGER

Sounds lovely.

BLISS

Not really.

Suddenly, like a dream interrupted, details about
BLISS's life come in flashes. As they float in, BLISS
relays them to the STRANGER, who nods politely.

BLISS
(drifting)
I'm eighteen. I'm going to be an
actress. I have a boyfriend named
Mitch. And I'm tired. So tired. My
head feels like a bowling ball.

STRANGER

Why are you here?

BLISS
(confused)
Not…sure, but I think I'm on
the verge of something amazing. Something. That will change
everything.

A SUITED MAN steps up to a podium. Award-show
music plays and beams of light crisscross around

the giant auditorium. He reads a list of names.
Nominees. Finally, after several other names…

> **MAN**
> (excitedly)
> Bliss Anderson.

The audience erupts into applause.

> **STRANGER**
> That's you! Maybe you're going to
> win!

> **BLISS**
> But I haven't been chosen yet. Time
> will tell. Whatever "time" is.

> **STRANGER**
> (giggling)
> There is no time here.

> **BLISS**
> Yeah, I'm getting that.

> **STRANGER**
> Is this your final destination?

> **BLISS**
> I don't think so. I think it's

something in between…in the middle.
The Middle. That's what I'll call
it. The Middle—like a red carpet,
a gateway to somewhere else when
you're not sure which way to go.
Right now…

BLISS nods off.

WOMAN (O.S.)

Bliss! Open your eyes, Bliss.
It's. Not. Your. Time.

BLISS looks up toward the voice, notices the
auditorium has no ceiling. It is made up of
wispy, cartoon clouds—the kind in a Maxfield
Parrish painting, adorning the bluest sky she's
ever seen.

BLISS

Right now, I want to rest my eyes.
I'm a lifetime of tired. Maybe
I'll sleep.

Or maybe I'll wake up. For now,
waking up sounds like the hardest
part.

CHAPTER SIXTEEN

*L*OTS OF THINGS THAT people do in life are irrational. Screaming at the sight of a tiny field mouse as it scurries by. Hiding behind one's hands during a scary movie. Avoiding secrets from one's past when they surface.

To an outside observer, my plan to save this girl would be considered irrational. Beyond irrational. Even to me, it reeks of bizarre. In fact, I could easily offer an even harsher revision of the word irrational.

Illogical.

Illegal.

That is to say, fucked-up crazy.

But for me, there is no going back. Righting my wrong means bringing this girl back from wherever she's gone, and I can trust nobody else with this task. Some things in life you have to do yourself. The gaffer can't do it. The grip definitely can't do it. This is a job for the director, the storyteller. Serious cinematic skills are required here; the lighting, the angles, but especially the words, need to be perfect. I alone can will it to be so.

I go back to my motel room to check out. I've decided to give Mother what she always wanted, eighteen years too late. The remainder of my stay will be at my parents' home. Maybe it will ground me.

I pack the few things I have and force myself to speed-dial Sid.

"Hey."

"Hey!" Sid's voice, warm and concerned, pours over me. "How are you? *Where* are you?"

"I'm so sorry, Sid."

"You're practicing your manners. Good for you." He pauses. "But sorry for what?

"Something happened."

"Jane, I can't imagine how hard it must've been—"

"No, Sid. Something else. Something I have to fix." The weight of my own voice makes me stop for a moment and take a deep breath. "I can't come back. Not yet."

"Okay…"

I know sheer panic hides behind his patient response. This plot twist is not making the story better. In three days, he will need something to print. He'll need words about films that are three-thousand miles away from me.

"I can't…. I just can't come back yet." I pause again, try out another idea. "There are other film critics in Los Angeles, you know. Kate or John could fill in until I'm back."

His silence cuts through me.

He sighs. "They're not you, Jane. People read your column because of you. You are Cinegirl."

Silence.

"You have an uncanny way of seeing through the bullshit and

politics of film. Even the most jaded in Hollywood know that." His voice softens. "You make pretentious people love unpretentious films, and you make the common man love the avant-garde."

Silence.

"How you write…your common sense…is what made your parents the proudest, you know."

I do. But Sid is wrong. They're all wrong. I'm a fraud.

"Sid?" I try not to sound as vulnerable as I feel. "It's this place. It's got me totally confused." I want to ask how a person is supposed to know where she belongs.

"Jane? I'm getting worried now. You don't sound like yourself."

"That's the thing! Who the hell am I, Sid?" I throw a pair of shoes into my bag and slump onto the bed. "I don't think…" I shake my head for no one to see. "I don't think I'm a very good person."

I try to think of something—anything—that I've done since I've left home that mattered. Nothing. Nothing that *really* mattered. I wasn't a good daughter. I wasn't a good *anything*. And now I don't have anyone in my life to care about, anybody who needs me.

I went straight from film school into writing about film, and I can't think of one thing I have to show for the past eighteen years besides words on paper. I can't think of a thing I've done that can't easily be erased. The idea bleeds into me like ink on paper. I could be erased without consequence.

I don't want Sid to have the chance to comment on my lack of humanity. "Look, I have to go, Sid. I'll figure something out. I'll send you something."

"Jane…"

I hang up, drive down Main Street, out of town past Jack and Mary, and finally make my way home.

After unpacking, settling into my childhood room, and eating another square of Mom's corn casserole, I park the Aston Martin in the garage, its birthplace, and cover it with a tarp. I don't have the courage to look too closely. When the dented front bumper disappears under the canvas disguise, my stomach contracts at the sight of it. I hear the thump, feel it, and want to vomit. I feel a respite from the guilt when I imagine myself in an orange jumpsuit, jailed for my crime, after this is all over. After I save her.

But for now, I will need to drive my parents' old Ford pickup truck and make a plan. How am I going to get into this girl's hospital room? How am I going to keep from getting recognized in a place that seems to know me better than I know myself?

As if it's 1990, I sit down on the little stool in front of my vanity and talk to the shrine before me. She's still here—between my stand-up swivel mirror, my worn Rubik's cube, and my purple, BeDazzled jewelry box—the late, great, one and only Pauline Kael.

I sigh. "Where do I begin, Ms. Kael? All I've ever wanted was to become you, which I could never do, but I've come as close as I can. I've recently pissed off the hottest director in Hollywood by denouncing his manifesto on film about world hunger. And… nobody likes me. And…yesterday I buried both of my parents. And that's not even the worst of it."

She looks up at me from her black-and-white glossy photo, speaks confidently in her signature second-person voice. *If you can't make fun of bad movies on serious subjects, what's the point?*

"I know, right?" I say back, like I'm talking to an old friend.

And being liked is overrated. Lots of people hated me. I was fine with it.

When she says this, the tone of her voice betrays her, and I wonder if she's being totally honest. But of course she is, she's Pauline Kael.

About your parents…people die. That's it. End of story.

I lower my head. "It is what it is. No encore."

Nope. So live your life. Every day. I think I see her blink her steely eyes, full of wisdom. *So what's the worst of it?*

"I did something…" I can't even find an adjective horrible enough. "I need to fix it, but I don't know how."

She lets out an impatient sigh. *Well, where there is a will, there is a way,* Ms. Kael assures me and lifts her chin up ever so slightly like it's an invitation to sack up. *If there is a chance in a million that you can do something, anything, just do it. Pry the door open, or, if need be, wedge your foot in that door and keep it open.*

"But what if being me won't work?"

Then be someone else. She adjusts her writerly scarf. *Look to what you know. For you, for us, the answers are all on film. You know this.*

"But how do I—"

You'll figure it out. Look to the giant movie reel in the sky. I can tell she's finished with me, and the animated Pauline Kael now starts to flatten back into her less glossy, lifeless head shot, but not before she gives me one more urgent plea. *Now, go.*

I plop down on my little-girl bed and look out the window. What movie reel in the sky? I am seriously losing it. Leaving the scene of an accident. Talking to dead idols. Making plans to bring a coma patient back to life.

Then I see it. A puffy cumulus cloud in the shape of a circle. I imagine another circle, followed by a number seven. 007. Right there in the clouds. My gaze moves from the sky to my bookshelf filled with twelve Ian Fleming novels, and I laugh, thinking of my dad doing Ernst Stavro Blofeld's German accent, telling Mr. Bond that he only lives twice.

What would Dad tell me to do? *If you're wrong, kid, make it right.*

He'd tell me to do what James Bond does. Improvise.

That's it.

Flashes of James Bond in various disguises—a Zorin Industries blouson in *A View to a Kill*, a keffiyeh and tunic in *The Spy Who Loved Me*, and sadly, the most pathetic Bond disguise ever, a clown in *Octopussy*—remind me what I need to do to get the job done.

CHAPTER SEVENTEEN

*T*O MY SURPRISE, IT only takes me fifteen minutes to become someone else. Perhaps I'm so disgusted with myself that shedding the old me comes with great ease. Or maybe transformation isn't as difficult as I thought. Either way, after going to the attic and digging through costumes from my high school drama club productions—Rizzo from *Grease*, Liesl from *Sound of Music*, Nellie from *South Pacific*—I settle on Cleopatra's wig.

With my Ramones T-shirt, Mom's pink cardigan, Dad's horn-rimmed reading glasses, and my jet-black and trendy blunt-cut bangs, I look like a hipster Zooey Deschanel on the way to the Brentwood Whole Foods. I make sure my blond hair is tucked into the wig, no trace of Jane anywhere, and get into character. Today I'm not Elizabeth Taylor's Cleopatra from Joseph Mankiewicz's 1963 big-screen version in all its Ptolemaic splendor. There's no Richard Burton to woo, to slow me down.

Today, I am an ordinary woman with an extraordinary task.

Today, I am Bliss's savior.

So Cleopatra walks into a hospital.

With the getup I'm in, the insane situation I'm in, I realize I'm the punch line of this sick joke. But when I walk through the front entrance of Crocker County Regional Hospital—a self-contained city—nobody seems to think anything out of the ordinary, except perhaps that my fashion choices are not homegrown, and this is exactly what I want.

Unlike True City itself, the hospital seems to be disconnected from the land, and the people here bustle past one another like strangers rather than neighbors. Thank God. In the heart of True City, everyone seems to know me, but here I will be among strangers, and after this morning's quick Google search, I know the first lie in a series of necessary lies—I know exactly who I need to be.

"Hi, I'm Kate Snelling," I say to the nurse behind the desk. "I'm a representative for the National Institute for In-Transition Coma Patients."

"ID?" the nurse says, nonplussed.

"Oh, shoot," I mumble, rummaging in my laptop bag. "Left it on my… I'll bring it next time." When the nurse meets my stare, I speak in a calm voice. "I can give you a number to call… to verify…if you want… I won't be here long, but as you know, the first two weeks are crucial in terms of long-term prognosis."

The cranky nurse scans her finger down a clipboard, then shoos me in the direction I need to go. "Bliss Anderson. Room 212— they just moved her from ICU."

Bliss. What a beautiful goal.

I look back at the nurse's name tag, which reads "Marsha," but that must be a mistake. Clearly she is Nurse Ratched. Milos Forman himself has conjured up some high-key lighting to accentuate the grayed-out, lifeless hallway. The extreme contrasts and muted camera movement make this cuckoo's nest seem movie-fake.

But it's not fake, and I'm not a cinematic character, a live-free-or-die Randle McMurphy who inspired his twelve disciples to find their voices. I am Jane Willow. Barely hanging on. Where are you, Milos Forman? Where are you, Randle McMurphy? Where are you, Hollywood? Nobody is going to save me, because I'm not the one who deserves to be saved. I tuck this feeling away where nobody will see it, then walk away, faking the confidence of a real health professional.

When I reach the room, I enter after a soft knock. I see her, and my heart grows heavy, each beat held hostage with guilt, accelerated with remorse. This girl in the bed looks nothing like the girl on the television. This girl—swollen, bruised, still—shows no signs of life.

I step back out into the hallway to catch my breath. My heart hurts. A sharp pain shoots through my chest. I face the hallway wall, pretend to read a sign, but then bury my face in my hands.

I did this.

This is my fault.

I want to run, and almost do, but I have to face what I've done. I have to help her. I force myself to walk back into the room and see her. They've wrapped the top part of her head in gauze. Shiny blond hair spills out from underneath, and bandages cover both arms, resting frozen on top of the blanket.

Hello, Bliss.

I watch her chest move up and down, and, in solidarity, synchronize my breathing with hers.

Mid-breath, a voice startles me. "Are you family?" A nurse enters the room and begins to check the monitor hooked up to Bliss.

"No," I blurt. "Therapist."

"Already? That's great. Her dad will be happy. He's just grabbing some coffee—hasn't slept a wink."

Dad? Of course she has a dad. My heart free-falls.

The nurse, an Altman-inspired character from some dark comedy, a less-sexy Major Margaret "Hot Lips" Houlihan—tucks a blanket under Bliss's side. "Physical?"

"Physical?" I repeat.

"*Physical* therapist?" The nurse turns around, takes a break from checking vitals.

"No, not *physical* therapy." I don't want to hurt the poor girl any more than I already have.

Believe so.

Will it to be.

That is to say, a leap of faith.

I stick my hand in my bag and pull out the only book I have with me—my parents' copy of my own award-winning book, *Real Movies for Real People: Living in the Dark*, and try not to choke on the fact that, at the moment, I am a completely fake person.

"Story therapy." I turn the book over so the nurse won't see my black-and-white author photo on the back cover.

"Story therapy?"

"Yeah, it's like music therapy…but with words." I nod in hopes of believing it myself. "Research shows"—I scour my memory for my five-minute research—"that sometimes it isn't anything physical that wakes a coma patient. Sometimes it's a word or phrase that stirs something in the cerebral cortex, prompting the emotional and physical to work in sync once again."

The nurse walks over to me, speaks with sincerity. "That's wonderful. Just wonderful."

"Two years ago," I say while looking at Bliss, "the family of an Iowan farmer who was in a coma after falling off his machine shed decided it was time—after eight weeks only one percent of coma patients recover—so they prepared to say goodbye, turn off the life support. But then"—I touch Bliss's blanket, wanting to caress her face—"his wife, as part of her goodbye, whispered to him the exciting news that their daughter had given birth that very morning to their first grandchild. To this, the man who had not spoken, let alone moved on his own accord for two months, simply sat up and said, 'Is it a boy?'"

"No!" the nurse says, hands on hips, her pink scrubs clinging to her curves. With an excited nod, she said, "I've cared for many coma patients over the years… People give me grief for talking to them. But I don't like the idea of giving up on them, you know?"

"I know." I glance up at Bliss and once again match her breathing cadence.

"Loves Audrey Hepburn. Guess she can quote every line from *Breakfast at Tiffany's*." She sighs. "Wanted to be a movie star." The nurse stops fiddling with the IV bag and stares at Bliss.

"*Wants* to be a movie star," I correct her.

The nurse smiles, nods, embarrassed by her pessimism. "Right." She moves toward the door, then turns around, extends her hand. "Stella." She stares just long enough for me to panic. "Have we met before?"

I tuck my book back into my bag and readjust Dad's reading glasses. "No, I don't think so."

"Something about you seems familiar. Like our paths have crossed before."

"Nope. Don't think so." I choked out the next words, pulling Mother's cardigan tight around me. "I'm not from here."

"Funny...you seem right at home." Stella stands at the door's threshold. "Well. We cross paths when we need to in this life." Years of experience show in the lines on her face.

After she leaves, I walk to Bliss's bedside.

Believe so.

Wake up.

I look for movement in her eyelids.

Please wake up.

I shut my eyes and try to remember what the great thinkers—Einstein, Gandhi, Buddha, Harold Hill—said about the law of attraction and the power of thought. Everything is energy, and that's all there is to it. Match the frequency of the reality you want and you cannot help but get that reality. It can be no other way. This is not philosophy. This is physics.

But I can smell the faint hint of manure as this New Age philosophy tries to ring true. I think of Harold Hill and realize a truth. He is actually not in this camp of believe-in-yourself-and-you-can-do-anything; his true transformation came about from recognizing his negative effects on others and understanding that he could give rather than take.

I imagine what I will give this girl if—when—she wakes up. Together, we'll watch some of the greatest moments on film, starting with Truffaut's *Jules et Jim*. I'll watch her face light up when she sees the famous bicycle scene where three carefree people, lost in joy, ride their bikes in the sun in France before they are ruined by war. I won't even lecture her about the film's genius—the newsreel footage, the panning shots, the photographic stills, Jeanne Moreau's on-screen definition of *smart equals sexy*. I will just help Bliss see the beauty in sadness.

And then, with no time to catch our breath, we'll watch Spielberg at his bold-faced-storyteller-of-humanity best—when Stern tells Oskar Schindler that he who saves a life saves the entire world.

Please be right, Dad. Please let life be one big work in progress, every situation changeable, revisable. Please let one person be able to change the course of history.

Yes. There will be so much to do after I've saved her.

After I've saved her, I'll tell her how they thought she was as good as dead. *Fin.* Lights out. Final curtain call. Fade to black. I'll tell her how she now has her whole life ahead of her.

Until then, I will keep reading about times when mere words prompt a coma patient to awaken. What will make Bliss want to come back to life?

She's eighteen. Wants to be an actress. Acting class! That's what I'll tell her. I'll get her into Lou's coveted acting workshop. He owes me a favor.

I stand close to her, feeling her warmth through the bedsheet, and breathe with her, the only thing we can do together. I try to imagine what Bliss imagines, wherever she is. I try to imagine which one of us is more lost. I tell her I'm going to help her dreams come true.

Believe so.

Will it to be.

That is to say, open your eyes.

Open your eyes.

I wait for some sign—any sign—that my words have reso-
nated, but she is still. Not the right words, I guess. I search her
will for hope.

But there are so many words.

I pull out *Living in the Dark*, turn to page one, and begin to read.

Preface

Film unites us. Like a sunrise peeking out from behind
whatever landscape we call home, movies bring us
together.

Most people need to look backward, dig deep, to
envision that scene, which plays every day, every hour in
some home, some theater somewhere in America.

Movies have always been the thing that connects us to
other people, the thing that reminds us of our shocking
sameness. No matter where we come from, they remind
us who we are, who we've loved, where we've been,
where we want to go.

I fell in love with movies on a Tuesday morning.

CHAPTER EIGHTEEN

INT. THE MIDDLE—TODAY

> **BLISS (V.O.)**
> You know that feeling when you know you're dreaming, but you can't wake up? Well, that's not how I feel. Not even close.

FADE IN: Auditorium ladies' powder room

BLISS stands in an enormous bathroom complete with a sitting area for two plush, purple settees. She looks into a rectangular mirror surrounded by vintage, theater globe lights.

> **BLISS**
> (to her reflection)

This place, The Middle, is real.
And I'm glad, because my hair
looks *amazing*. Really. The mirror
doesn't lie, especially in this
kick-ass bathroom I'm in.

BLISS stares into the mirror, lets the golden,
ethereal light from the mini globes bathe her in
a warm glow. BLISS remembers she's from a place
called True City; that's what people call it,
but it doesn't seem true at all, more like a lie
to use words that have no meaning, to talk of a
place she doesn't really recall. She decides to
call it The Other Place until she remembers what
it means to her.

BLISS
(looking at her reflection)
The Other Place did *not* have one
of these. Not even close. This
bathroom is bigger than my bedroom. Hmm. There's another detail.
I had a bedroom. Back there. It
was yellow, my bedroom. Not a dumb
baby-pastel yellow, but a canary-
yellow. Happy yellow. Like liquid
sunshine.

WIDE-SHOT

Over the whole bathroom, which is flooded with the sound of elevator Muzak. One by one, as if choreographed, several mirrors in a long row as far as the eye can see, come into view. Four female FIGURES—in different-colored dresses, fantastical gowns all magically swaying and flowing without as much as a breeze in this still, windless bathroom—stand in front of their respective mirrors, and lean forward over sparkly, gem-adorned sinks. The FIGURES examine their reflections. BLISS follows their lead. They turn their heads to the left, letting the light hit all facets of their perfect faces. BLISS turns to the left, then when they do, to the right. They take lipsticks out of tiny red purses and color their lips in unison.

The first GIRL, in a tea-length, red organza dress, turns to BLISS. She's older. She knows things.

RED-DRESS GIRL
(with a pouty face)

No purse?

BLISS shakes her head, then touches the top of it, piled high with shimmering blond hair, and winces in pain.

RED-DRESS GIRL
(snobbish)
You're gonna be here awhile. You
should have a purse.

RED-DRESS GIRL's tea-length dress suddenly grows
longer, the color deepening to a bloodred.
Suddenly it forms an exaggerated pool around her
on the shiny marble floor, making BLISS's head
throb.

BLISS
(whispering)
I *definitely* don't have a purse.

(a smile creeps onto her face)
My dad says I have an unhealthy
affinity for adverbs.

(Pauses.)
Hey! I have a dad! I just remembered. I totally have a dad!

RED-DRESS GIRL
(Rolls her eyes)
Congratulations.

BLISS looks at RED-DRESS GIRL like this place is

indeed real—right at home with the reality that mean girls are everywhere.

Camera drifts left to the next GIRL, wearing a full-length, green mermaid gown. There is a peacock pattern on the front, and when BLISS looks at it, the bird comes to life, blinks its small black eyes, displays its vibrant plumage.

BLISS
(baffled)
Your dress is alive.

GREEN-DRESS GIRL
(smiling)
This kind of thing happens here.

GREEN-DRESS GIRL hands BLISS her crimson lipstick, and BLISS puts it on. She looks just like the other GIRLS now. When BLISS thinks of her dad telling her to wipe the lipstick off, she realizes that he is back in The Other Place. Some cobwebby corner of her mind tells her this might be bad. She knows it's bad, for sure, when she remembers his sad eyes.

BLISS
(to herself)
I wonder if my dad would be happy
here.

GREEN-DRESS GIRL

Probably not. Sad people are sad
wherever they go.

BLISS

Totally.

(pauses, stares at GREEN-DRESS GIRL)
Do I know you? There's something
familiar…

GREEN-DRESS GIRL smiles at BLISS.

Just then, a memory from The Other Place arrives
like a gift, a tiny silver box wrapped in yellow
silk ribbon. BLISS closes her eyes and opens it.

BLISS
(eyes closed, recalling)
Yeah, he's all up in words, my
dad.

(smiles)
He likes to mock me. "'Never' is
a very strong word, Bliss," he'd
say.

She floats around the memory, breathes it in. His
words come to her in flashes.

To GREEN-DRESS GIRL

> **BLISS**
> (opens eyes, saddens)
> *"'Always' is worse, Bliss. Adverbs never live up to their bold promises."* God, his delivery is so… like, award-winningly depressing. Totally. What happened to this guy? What happened to my dad?

BLISS remembers a hint of her dad's smile, but it drifts away, like something is making it impossible for him to smile. She opens one last gift.

> **BLISS**
> (concentrating)
> *"Adverbs are a writer's worst enemy,"* he'd say, even though he's not a writer. He does something else…
>
> (closes eyes again—
> tries to remember)
> It's bossy… He wears a uniform.

To GREEN-DRESS GIRL

BLISS

(teenage-confident)

Anyway, thanks but no thanks,
because I'm not going be a writer.
I'm going to be an actress. And not
one of those after-school-special
actresses who tell you to love
yourself and all sorts of other
cheesy crap—and no offense, Miley,
but I don't want to be one of those
Disney sitcom actors either, with
a built-in laugh track. There's
nothing funny about the kind of
actress I'm going to be. I want
to be totally serious, you know.
Like Audrey Hepburn serious. Like

(forces a sweet lisp, Hepburn style)
"Which accent do you want me to
do, Mr. Huston, because I can do
them all." Seriously. Really.

But before an answer comes, the elevator Muzak
stops and an invisible guitar strums the notes
to *My Fair Lady*'s "Wouldn't It Be Loverly." The
third mirror lights up, and AUDREY HEPBURN in her
prime appears wearing her signature *Breakfast at
Tiffany's* black dress, sixties updo with tiara,
black gloves, and pearls.

                    BLISS
                (wide-eyed)
    It's you!

                AUDREY HEPBURN
            (smiles, removes her
            oversized sunglasses)
    It's me.

                    BLISS
    What are you doing here?

                AUDREY HEPBURN
    I should ask *you*. You're writing
    this screenplay.

                    BLISS
    I am?

                AUDREY HEPBURN
                (nods)
    All of this…

AUDREY admires the endless layers of yellow chiffon cascading down BLISS's skirt, then looks at
the other girls.

    …is your design, your dreamy little
    story. You alone know what it all means.

(pauses)

But it's time to get back, Bliss.

BLISS

Back to what?

AUDREY HEPBURN

What we're here for.

(whispers)

The Show.

BLISS

(confused)

The Show?

RED-DRESS GIRL flares up; small flames erupt from
the hem of her dress.

RED-DRESS GIRL

(rolls her eyes)

Get up to speed, newbie.

BLISS

(to AUDREY HEPBURN, pointing
her eyes at RED-DRESS GIRL)

Red makes me nervous. So different than the blues.

BLISS raises her eyebrows, wonders if AUDREY HEPBURN gets the *Breakfast at Tiffany's* allusion.

AUDREY HEPBURN smiles knowingly, impressed that someone BLISS's age even knows the classic film.

> **AUDREY HEPBURN**
> (sighs)
> Everything I learned I learned from the movies.

> **BLISS**
> Me too.

BLISS turns to finish this conversation, but in a flash, AUDREY HEPBURN is gone. RED-DRESS GIRL and GREEN-DRESS GIRL leave, and just when BLISS starts to follow them, she notices the fourth mirror light up. Her voice sounds familiar. A woman in a dewy, flower-petal-pink gown stands in front of the mirror but doesn't turn around. She has no reflection. The scent of hollyhocks floods the room, and a monarch butterfly flutters around her.

> **PINK-DRESS WOMAN**
> (softly, sweetly)
> Bliss? Stay awake, Bliss.

BLISS listens, but her head starts to throb again, her eyelids grow heavy, her consciousness drifts.

> **BLISS**
> (drifting in and out)
> I have to pee. This bathroom is beautiful, but I can pee in a cornfield if I have to.

> **PINK-DRESS WOMAN**
> There are no cornfields here.

> **BLISS**
> Thank God, right?
>
> (suddenly remembers)
> Cornfields are *everywhere*, where I come from. Cornfields as far as the eye can see.

> **PINK-DRESS WOMAN**
> Sounds like a fairy tale.

> **BLISS**
> Not really. Actually, I like it here. Really. It's different. Different is good. Who wants to live in the same old, boring place for their whole life?

PINK-DRESS WOMAN doesn't say anything. BLISS feels like she's in trouble now. BLISS doesn't tell her how a super-small part of her does wonder where the sun is. When the sun decided to come out in The Other Place, it was big and golden. And the stars there? So clear and bright. BLISS definitely doesn't tell the WOMAN that she misses them.

PINK-DRESS WOMAN heads for the powder room exit. Words trail behind her as the butterfly darts to and fro.

> **PINK-DRESS WOMAN**
> Bliss? Don't fall asleep.
>
> (fainter)
> Enjoy *The Show*, Bliss. Enjoy *The Show*.

> **BLISS**
> (drifting)
> Totally. Absolutely.

The door shuts.

CHAPTER NINETEEN

$\mathcal{F}$OR ME, THE ROAD to salvation now stretches so far into the horizon, through acre after acre of today's and yesterday's cornfields, a landscape riddled with my sins, that I wonder if the road even has an end. Every time I turn around, every time my heart feels a pang of regret, it becomes clearer that asking for forgiveness might be my only way out. But who the hell is going to forgive me for my transgressions, and who the hell should? There is Bliss, yes, and there will be Bliss, every day, until I will her back to life with my words. But there is someone else I've wronged. Yet another person I've abandoned.

Today, since my visit to the hospital is over, I will drive straight to her. I know the way. I've traveled this road thousands of times. For years on a bicycle—then later in my 1975 Monte Carlo that backfired out of a rusty exhaust pipe when it reached fifty miles per hour—and now, in my parents' Ford.

When I drive up the lane, I breathe in Charlotte's farm—fresh-cut hay, unearthed soil, smells from my other childhood home. Memories arrive like a montage fit for a queen. A Corn Queen. First scene—the memory of the lemonade stand from when Charlotte and I thought we could earn enough money to go to Dick Clark's American Bandstand. Second scene—cleaning chicken coops as punishment for being at Joey's house when we said we were at the library. Third scene—Charlotte and I in shiny, purple and blue prom dresses, posing on the front porch. Fourth scene—our last summer together, walking beans for Charlotte's father, learning exactly how to cut down velvetleaf and buttonweed so it didn't ruin the yield. Fifth scene—and this should be bittersweet, but instead it's just bitter—Charlotte and I sitting in her car on my last day in True City twenty years ago, wanting the courage to tell her the biggest secret of my life.

But if I had told Charlotte, that would've made it real, and that would have been unbearable. I could never tell her, that much I knew, but being around her, keeping the secret from her, had posed a problem of best-friend proportion. Charlotte would've sensed it. She would have eventually seen it in my eyes, so I had said a silent goodbye I thought would be forever.

Until today.

I drive toward the little white farmhouse and think of so many weekends spent watching *E.T.*, *The Goonies*, and with my insisting, James Bond marathons, into the wee hours of the morning. So many sleepovers devoted to Charlotte listening to my endless pining over Joey Darnell, and role-playing what on earth I would say if Joey and I ever had a conversation that lasted more than three sentences. So many summer afternoons wasted away listening to the Go-Go's, singing into hairbrushes. Halfway up the lane, past the apple tree, past the big red barn, I notice a series of square signs nailed to solid, white posts jutting out of the ground. More signs. So many signs here.

I read the signs as the truck inches forward. The first sign, a tidy collection of red lettering, bears an affected, colloquial greeting. *Welcome to the backdrop seen 'round the world.* The second one, swirling with shiny blue paint, invites strangers to *Pose in your very own American Gothic painting.* The third and last sign states the obvious. *No appointment necessary.*

At my parents' funeral, Mrs. Davis said that hard times had prompted Charlotte and her husband, Steve, to open up their home—the front yard at least—to tourists and passersby who were searching for an up-close look at the history of *American Gothic.* In 1930, when Charlotte's mother was just a baby. Grant Wood, the young aspiring artist and native Iowan, had driven by the house and fallen in love with its Carpenter Gothic Style. He had his sister, Nan, get out to pose in front of it, and later painted in the man based on the likeness of his Cedar Rapids dentist.

I stop the car and take in the panoramic view of the farm, a sight that should've been familiar. But everything looks somehow different now. This can't possibly be the same sky I'd seen as a girl. This sky, a vibrant azure blue, is nothing I remember witnessing before; and what is going on with this late-afternoon sunlight? Whatever it shines upon—the oak treetops encircling the farm, blankets of cornfields swaying in unison—gives everything a heavenly glow. At first glance, I'd say the enchanting radiance is but a mere scientific shine explained by light refraction, but something deep inside me says there is no need for revision, I have the right word: shimmer. Everything shimmers here. An otherworldly shimmer, like an offering from the sky above, like a gift for those who choose to live on such hallowed land.

More surprises. First, the rich air that made me dizzy yesterday, and now a heavenly shimmer cast upon things as mundane as a muddy combine threatens to make me doubt my own eyesight and sanity. At least the people are predictable here. This I can count on. Midwesterners are polite, yes, but don't forget that the first musical number from *The Music Man* is "Iowa Stubborn" for a reason. If you are disloyal to a midwesterner, expect an affable termination of your friendship, a well-mannered cutting of the proverbial cord—a cord that Charlotte will, no doubt, sever today.

A breeze, urgent and purposeful, sweeps past me as Charlotte Davis rushes out her front door. I imagine myself cleansed by the sudden gust, baptized by its purity, and in my dreams, forgiven. But when Charlotte emerges from below the famous arched window, I feel as dirty as the brown, stained dish towel she has flung over her right shoulder.

"Sorry, I was upstairs…" she says, a little breathless, not yet looking at me. When our eyes meet, she pauses, stares.

Charlotte looks a little like my best friend, and a little like a woman who is in the middle of something. Lots of somethings.

"Hey, Char."

At the sight of me, Charlotte stops for a moment, lets the midafternoon sun, now on fire in the August sky, kiss her creamy, porcelain skin dulled by years. Her once-shiny red hair has lost its sheen and is pulled back into a sort-of ponytail, she looks like an exhausted Julianne Moore, not camera ready. She takes a long look at me, her old friend, hair a bit matted down from the wig I'd worn this morning, and surveys me from heels to cardigan.

I stand motionless. How could I blame Charlotte for not wanting to see me? There was so much I'd missed. Her wedding. The birth of her two children. Her sickness—God, when I think of how devastated I was to hear the news, but how I didn't know how to reach out to her—my stomach cramps up with shame.

Moments turn to seconds while I await Charlotte's verdict. Just when it looks like she is on the verge of blasting me with the truth, I see her blink away a lifetime of resentment. "Nice outfit," she says. She peruses my schizophrenic fashion ensemble. "I'm no fashion plate, but I think the layered look died in the late eighties."

I let out a decade-long sigh. "This look, you should know, is big in LA." I smile. "Very cutting-edge."

Charlotte walks toward me, hugs me with the kind of authority earned by truly knowing someone. "I'm so sorry, Janie." She places her warm hand on my cheek. "I was at the funeral. In the back. Didn't know if you'd want to see me, so... God... I just saw your mom last week. I can't believe"—she releases her hand, swipes tears from her face like they are a nuisance, and whispers—"they're gone."

"I know." I nod away my own tears. "You look great, Char."

Charlotte tries to tame her disheveled, gray-streaked bangs that have escaped her afterthought of a ponytail. "Your eyebrows do funny things when you lie, Janie. I happen to know this." She wipes her hands on her jeans and gives me a you're-full-of-crap look that no one in Los Angeles would've dared give me.

I take her in. In the montage of my life, Charlotte Davis is in every scene. She's the supporting cast member who never got top billing—my Marissa Tomei, my Geena Davis, my Shelley Winters.

"It's good to see you, Char," I say, standing now as a stranger on the porch of a house that was once my second home. I feel the porch boards sag beneath me and remember two young girls in first-day-of-school outfits standing in this very spot, posing for mothers who wanted to freeze time.

The horizon fills with new shades of orange and pink, colors that, for farmers, promise a generous harvest. The smoldering sun inches its way behind twenty acres of Davis cornfields, and I know time is not frozen, but passing right before me.

To my surprise, Charlotte holds the front door open for me. The heavenly smell of a hot dish, slow-baked with intent, wafts out, and she lets me in.

Maybe the farmer was right. Maybe our true home can forgive anything, even when we're at our darkest.

After all, this is home, and I'm at my darkest. Charlotte seems to know this, so she opens the door.

That is to say, she has to.

"Welcome home, Janie."

CHAPTER TWENTY

*C*HARLOTTE LOOKS UNSETTLED, AND not just because of me—it's like somehow her life has developed an unsolvable complication during my too-long absence.

After checking what I can assume is some sort of meat concoction in the oven, she glances up at the clock, only to be interrupted by Lady Gaga and her "Poker Face" blaring from her cell phone. I can't help but wonder about her choice of ringtone. The Charlotte I remember—sweet and hopeful, now the choir director at her church—would've chosen something uplifting, more inspired by her faith, like "Ain't No Mountain High Enough" or "Don't Stop Believin'." What hand has she been dealt that makes her need to hide something?

I can just imagine Charlotte at church sporting the perfect poker face—a pleasant, almost-smile, a deadpan gaze out toward a congregation who looked to her to keep their hearts singing—when she was supposed to be listening to Pastor Larson's sermon about commitment. Come on, God, cut Charlotte some slack. She looks exhausted. After all this time, all these years of doing the right thing, deciphering right from wrong has probably started to become muddled gibberish, like goo-goo Gaga.

As I watch Charlotte fumble with her phone, a heavy truth settles into me. We are all faking it, bluffing our way through life, pretending to have all the answers while really having none. Here is my childhood friend, trying to disguise her sigh when a number flashes on her phone screen, but still she answers the call—probably a friend in need or some other selfless quest for a woman twice as thoughtful and dignified as me.

"Charlotte's Meatloaf Hotline," she says, mustering a perky tone from a place of necessity. "What's your meatloaf emergency?"

Oh. My God. I stand corrected. Nothing dignified here.

After she says the words—and I can't believe she's said them—I try to disguise my shock and horror by squirming in my vinyl-covered kitchen chair. I bet she knows what I'm thinking—*Oh, sweet Jesus, thank God this is not my life*—and something tells me she wishes the same thing.

"Uh-huh. Oh, sure. You bet," Charlotte says. "And so it's all crumbly, right?" She bends her head to the left, wedging the phone between her neck and shoulder and takes her own dinner out of the oven. "No, no, no, I'm not in the middle of anything at all," Charlotte says. "It's okay… No, no, ma'am. Oh, please don't cry, ma'am. It'll be fine… Ma'am, don't cry. You're just hungry. And tired. I get it." It sounds like Charlotte might be describing herself. She stops moving for a moment, slumps into the kitchen counter with an ease that looks practiced, and speaks as honestly as someone wearing a Sponge Bob oven mitt can.

"Believe me, I totally get it."

She lifts her unmitted hand and raises an apologetic finger toward me, letting me know it won't be much longer. Then, with the get-it-done flair of a good midwesterner, she regroups.

"Okay, ma'am, when will your guests be there?"

She pauses to listen.

"All right. I think I know what you did wrong."

I relax into the kitchen chair, finding comfort in the familiar territory of critique.

"You used too much oatmeal, no biggie," Charlotte offers. "Just reglaze it with barbecue sauce and ketchup and turn the oven up another fifty degrees. It'll be fine."

Then she turns her head to steal a private moment with this meatloaf-making stranger. "Ma'am?" I hear her say in a softer voice. "Listen. Tried and true's overrated." She gazes outside. Charlotte breathes in. "Sometimes we gotta cut our losses, try a new recipe"—she softens her voice—"and not look back."

I bet Charlotte hopes I didn't hear that. I bet she thinks it will sound like justification for my own reckless abandonment, especially since she knows how I love being right. I wish I could tell her that I know how wrong I've been.

"It is never, ever about the meatloaf," she says, the phone still resting on her soft cheek as she leaves her meatloaf stranger with this loaded advice.

Memories flood my brain, and I start to feel the weight of Charlotte's life. Meatloaf is serious business, because supper in the Midwest is serious business. A good family eats supper together. A good mother, a good wife, makes sure of that, and she doesn't do it out of obligation; she does it because it fulfills her, completes her like the last ingredient in a perfect recipe. Tried and true.

Oh, Charlotte.

"Sorry about that," she says and hangs up the phone. "Here." She hands me a plate stacked high with slices of fresh-baked sourdough. "And have some homemade jam," she says before she scurries back to the counter.

"Char," I say to Charlotte's back.

She knows what I'm going to say, what sort of drama we're on the brink of, so she ignores me and begins to fill a tray with vegetables from her garden. "Um, let me give you some of our fresh peaches with our own cream. I remember how much you love that."

"Char. Stop."

She finishes piling up the tray and then begins to rearrange things on the counter. "The corn this season is out of this world," she says. "Just wait until you—"

"Char, stop!" I erupt, then soften my voice. "Look at me. Please?"

She stops moving but doesn't turn around. I have dreamed of this moment so many times—how confident, how strong, how right she'd be when she tells me how selfish I've been. Like life has caught up with her and I'm not sure she can take this on top of everything else. She ends up saying the opposite of what I think she means in the form of a passive-aggressive stall tactic.

"Whatever," she mumbles and wipes the already-clean counter.

At this, I throw my hands up. "I'm sorry, Char. I'm so sorry." I pause, stand up, tug at my one, two, three cardigans, doing nothing to ease this cold ache. "There's so much I'm sorry for," I tell her. A heavy sigh escapes me in one guilty breath. "Say something, Char," I say, then I pull my shoulders back, stand up straighter, demanding a verdict.

Charlotte finally turns around, her face full of tears, and musters nothing but silence.

"Don't you dare tell me it's okay, Char. What I did was shitty." My voice now screams the truth as I reach my crescendo of guilt. "It was so super fantastically shitty!"

She leans into the counter, trying to settle her trembling legs.

I walk over to her, forcing eye contact. "What? Want specifics? Okay. I abandoned my best friend, the only friend I ever had. Without as much as a phone call. Or a goddamned Christmas card. Not even when you were sick. Who does that?" My eyes well, and I try to will my tears to obey, but when I say, "I don't even know your kids' names," my tears unleash.

"Connor," she tells me as she looks past me toward the kitchen doorway at her second-born child. "This is Connor, my little sweetheart."

When I turn around, I see her Connor—all freckles and strawberry-blond hair—standing in the kitchen doorway. He waves and then places his trombone case on the linoleum floor. Connor and I look at each other with the knowingness of recent acquaintances.

"And this," she says when her sullen-faced teenage daughter sulks up and stands next to Connor, "is Janie."

CHAPTER TWENTY-ONE

AUGHTY, CRUDE DAGGERS SHOOT from the girl's eyes. "Janelle," she says in a biting tone that rivals mine when I'm dressing down a pompous producer. I tilt my head back to avoid the blow. "I like to be called...Janelle." Unlike Charlotte's muted red hair, Janelle's is fiery, the waves angrily straightened out, and her flat, teenage midriff is on display without apology. Her nostrils flare, teenage-girl style, and OMG, she is not LOL. I'm not sure if I should cry over my best friend naming her daughter after me or apologize for it.

"It's okay. I don't like Janie either." I give her an awkward smile, looking as out of place in this kitchen as a foreign film playing at the Déjà Vu Theater.

"I don't hate the name," Janelle-Not-Janie says, enunciating each word like it's a sucker punch. "Only where it comes from."

"Janelle Elizabeth Davis!" Charlotte's eyes scold her daughter like only a mother's could.

If Charlotte is an exhausted Julianne Moore, and Connor is

an irreverent Opie Taylor, Janelle is a really, really mean Molly Ringwald. But I can't help but side with her. Who can blame her? Janelle Davis is only protecting her mother from a best friend who abandoned her. She represents what everyone in True City thinks of me—just without the polite filter. Underneath her pissed-off exterior, I see a glimmer of softness, something that looks like she might have the capacity to forgive. When this shines through for a fleeting moment, the thought of having a child to love—to love me back—makes me sink even further into my chair.

Connor Davis now seems to be the yin to his sister's yang, as he stands sweetly, at attention in the doorframe, prepared to tend to his mother, his sister, whomever might need it. He emits something that begs to be gobbled up, the kind of something a young girl might not yet know she wanted. Something simple but comforting.

Charlotte herds Connor and Janelle to the red Formica kitchen table, the same one her own mother had called her to each night growing up. The three of them sit down next to me, one on each side, and they stare, sober-faced, at the centerpiece: a giant pan of meatloaf. Perfect, tried and true.

I break the silence. "Smells amazing, Char." A pregnant pause fills the room. "Is Steve back yet?"

Both kids now look even more uncomfortable hearing this question, and Charlotte doesn't answer. Her gaze belongs to a woman who is somewhere else. "It's the *Mona Lisa*, you know."

My confused look prompts her to elaborate.

"The number one most recognizable painting in the world. Not *American Gothic*." She comes back from wherever she was, slices up four pieces of meatloaf, and plops them on four Corelle plates. "The power of just one woman." She speaks in a murmur. "Imagine that."

"So we're in second place." I nod and look out the window at the photo-op cutout in the front yard, and two college kids who are putting money in the donation box and taking their picture in front of Charlotte's *American Gothic*. "Second place isn't so bad." And then I notice Charlotte bristle. Was it second place that troubled her or my assumption that I'm part of it?

"Sorry for our mood, Janie." Charlotte hangs her head, scrapes her fork in no particular direction across the meatloaf. "It's... I don't know if you've heard." Connor and Janelle break all eye contact, a popular teenage coping mechanism. "Janelle's best friend, Bliss... There was an accident."

Janelle bursts into tears and scoots out her chair with teenage urgency. Mid-cry, her manners flare up, a sign of good rearing. "May I please be excused, Mom?" She sniffles.

Charlotte says yes by saying nothing at all and continues to poke at the perfect square of meatloaf.

I am amazed, horrified by the levels of sorry one human being can feel, and collapse further into my chair. *Three more reasons to make it right, kid.*

"Don't eat this," Charlotte says after she takes a bite of the meatloaf, the cornerstone of a happy family. "It's cold."

"It's okay, Mom," Connor says, rescuing his mother from what any good midwestern boy knew was a failure. "I'm not hungry anyway."

"Go ahead, honey," Charlotte tells him, pointing her head toward the nearest exit before he even asks.

"Come again tomorrow," he says to me on his way out. "You

were good." He stops, gives me a sad smile. "Linart's right. She'd want us to keep going."

"I met Connor earlier…happened to be walking by the new theater," I tell Charlotte after Connor is gone.

So now it is just Charlotte and me, once again, like old times. Almost. "At least I didn't ruin the corn," Charlotte says with a resolve that makes me want to cry.

"Char, it's okay, you went to the trouble." I plunge my fork into the biggest portion of red meat I'd seen since the eighties. "Let's just eat."

Charlotte reaches over, puts her hand on mine. "Don't. We waited too long. It's not good cold." She hangs her head. "And some things just shouldn't be reheated. Maybe you should go."

So this is what giving up looks like.

Charlotte gets up from the table, walks into a small room off the kitchen, and comes back with some sort of big scrapbook. "Here. Take it, Janie. It's yours, really." She manages a *Mona Lisa* smile.

I look at my friend, think about the time we've lost and that if I would've known, I would've called the meatloaf hotline just to hear Charlotte's voice.

It's not about the meatloaf, after all.

It's never, ever about the meatloaf.

CHAPTER TWENTY-TWO

1993

I WAS SIXTEEN YEARS OLD, consumed with sixteen-year-old things, but all people were talking about were the crops.

Could they save us?

Our farmer neighbors focused on my birthmark one afternoon to take their minds off the impending farm crisis. With determined squints, then raised eyebrows, they all chimed in with their observations. *I'll be damned—that's an ear of corn, Janie Willow.* Farmers debate things only farmers would consider. *Look at the hull. It's not field corn—no dent in the center. It's definitely sweet corn.*

But like my birthmark, the bad news was here to stay. The news told me things I didn't really understand. Interest rates skyrocketed. Land values plummeted. Reaganomics had done whatever it had done. John Cougar Mellencamp and Willie Nelson sang songs about the farming crisis, and Farm Aid showed up on MTV's *Friday Night Videos*. The Hawkeye football team wore ANF on their jerseys to show that America Needs Farmers. To make matters worse, it hadn't rained in six weeks, and after the dry winter, the drought threatened the harvest crop, the only hope our farmers had. Charlotte worried her family would lose their farm, and families all around Crocker County braced for the financial devastation that was on the horizon if rain didn't come soon.

All across Iowa, especially in True City, congregations prayed for rain. Methodists and Presbyterians filled their church marquees with God-inspired puns. *Even God's lawn is brown* and *Dear God, I'm thirsty. Love, Corn.* Even the Lutherans attempted humor. *May the rain be with you…and also with you.* Right on cue, Catholics joined in with jokes about holy water. But no one laughed when two more weeks went by with no rain. Children started performing rain dances at recess. Teachers talked about worst-case scenarios. Parched cornstalks drooped alongside our dwindling hope.

With all of my friends going to church more than usual, I got curious. "Dad, how come we don't go to church?" I asked one night at dinner. I had gone to Mass with Charlotte several times— Catholics didn't mind if you wore jeans to church, which was cool—and the repetitive and aggressive stand–sit–kneel combos felt a little like Jane Fonda aerobics for sinners.

"It's just a building, kid."

It seemed ironic that our town's only judge wasn't a fan of judgment, but I kept my mouth shut. I figured my parents had figured out something everyone else hadn't yet—that what really mattered was how we treated people, regardless of where one spent his Sunday or what was on their altar of choice. So even if my parents didn't prescribe to organized religion, they were quite organized about helping others and were the first to volunteer for all of our local churches.

When True City's Annual Corn Festival rolled around right before my sophomore year, Mom organized a craft booth for the Methodists, a food table for the Presbyterians, and a mock confession booth for the Catholics. Dad was grand marshal of the parade and helped make the Lutheran's "Aw, Shucks" corntastic float.

When I told my parents I'd been nominated for that year's Corn Queen and mentioned it was all a bit stupid, my practical mother surprised me with a dressed-down scolding. "Don't be ungrateful, Jane Marie Willow. It is an honor, and you will treat it as such."

"Okay, then," I said, preparing to lose.

Mother dyed my *Moonraker*-inspired, white halter gown a maize yellow, and with the fresh greenery in my golden hair, I was a not-so-subtle tribute to corn itself. The other nominees, Lisa Heart, Cheryl Smith, Lori Richmond, and Charlotte, planned on playing piano and singing for their talent portions, so I thought I'd do something different. Really, really different.

It was heartfelt. It was risky.

But to me, it was exactly what True City was lacking, what they truly needed: a trip down memory lane and a healthy dose of hope. With the help of Charlotte's church and my relentless door-to-door skills, I acquired all the necessary props. Then, for days, I practiced my routine in front of my mirror, sorting out the subtle nuances between making arm movements that said *anguish* versus *despair* and how to make a shaky pirouette act as a worthy transition of emotion.

On the day of the festival, Dad walked me to the garage, pulled off the tarp, and unveiled the long-awaited reveal of the fully restored Aston Martin. It had taken eight years, but the labor of love that I saw that day was worth every lost Saturday afternoon, every missed matinee.

"Dad," I said, staring in awe. "She's beautiful."

"She is," he said, looking back at me, taking in the sight of me in my festival gown, nervously adjusting the crown of Mom's ivy resting on my head.

When Mom walked in wearing a blue chiffon dress that matched the blue Iowa sky—a total departure from her usual housecoat—Dad stood speechless for a beat, until he was able to speak again.

"My corn queens, your chariot awaits." When he opened up the passenger door, we settled into the newly upholstered seats, rolled down the windows, and in the spirit of the moment, we let the fresh breeze tousle our hair as we headed toward True City.

Main Street was transformed into the nerve center of the festival, and every single person in Crocker County showed up. The residents of True City temporarily suspended their drought fears and celebrated. The smell of sugary funnel cakes wafted down Main Street. Corn was everywhere—corn dogs, corn pudding, grilled corn, roasted corn. Halfway down Main Street was a long table set up for the corn-on-the-cob eating contest. As we passed, True City's hungriest devoured ear after ear, butter oozed, and mouths of all ages became motorized chomping machines. I imagined a *Stand by Me* puke fest if they didn't slow down.

When the noon whistle blew, Charlotte and I made our way to the stage, a borrowed set of risers from our high school choir. We sat down in the first two folding chairs, and both of us laughed at how serious the other girls looked. Lisa sang her way through a creepy rendition of "Every Breath You Take," Cheryl did a so-so version of Bonnie Tyler's "Total Eclipse of the Heart," Lori attempted Michael Jackson's "Billy Jean," and then Charlotte brought the house down with an angelic tribute to Night Ranger's "Sister Christian." The ladies' auxiliary tapped their toes, clearly unaware that the lyrics warned a slutty not-so-Christian sister to tone down her sexual escapades.

After each contestant's talent portion, Mr. Simon, the host, conducted the question-and-answer segment. The highlight being Cheryl Smith's one word answer to his question: "What do you think the world needs more of?"

"Me!" Cheryl said, followed by the crowd's uncomfortable laugh, a testament to midwesterners' aversion to boastfulness.

When it was my turn, I put on tap shoes I'd borrowed from Charlotte's cousin and took the microphone. "My dad wanted me to do Bond's monologue from *Diamonds Are Forever*, but I thought our current, unfortunate situation calls for something… more personal."

I cleared my throat and raised my arms. "We are people who value tradition. Am I right, True City?" I yelled, trying to rally the crowd, but they just stared blankly, looking exhausted and parched in the unforgiving sun.

"Um, well, here's to…um…us?" I said, quieter, holding up an invisible glass full of invisible rainwater. "My performance today will be True City's agricultural journey as told through…um"— my throat started to dry up along with all of True City—"the medium of dance."

Mom and Dad, with front-row seats to this train wreck, were now wide-eyed with concern. Their looks said *Dear God, I hope she has a plan B.*

This was plan B. Plan A was a monologue from *Stripes*.

Long, uncomfortable silence. Blank faces staring back at me from the endless rows of folding chairs should've stopped me right there, but knowing when to stop has never been my strength. I cued my first background sign, one of many I'd painted last week with a set of watercolors I'd found in the garage. When I nodded to Cheryl, she held up her sign, which read *1920s* and featured a happy ear of corn.

I started with whistling. Not my best, but clearly "Singin' in the Rain."

Then a hint of a notes—"Doo do do doot, do duh doo do doot do dah"—and then I did my best tap dance as recollected from abandoned dance classes.

With two clicks of my metal heels, I cued Mrs. Peterson at the piano, and she began to plunk away as I wielded my still-closed umbrella and attempted the Charleston, hands spastically waving like a flapper on crack. When the happy notes turned sad, I cued Charlotte. She walked my hand-painted tractor sign across the stage, depicting the passage of time, and Cheryl followed with *1929* and a sad ear of corn squished under the failing stock market.

Somewhere between my tossing of "Dust Bowl" dirt at the audience—Mrs. Smith was not a fan of this—and Cheryl's upside down *1950s* sign, I really lost the crowd. The watercolor ears of corn on my signs may have been getting happier as time rolled on, but the audience was not. Some were fanning themselves with the pageant programs, and most were just scowling, looking at their watches, bitter reminders of how long it'd been since their fields had seen rain. Mrs. Thomas whispered "Shh, it's almost over" to her son Leo as she bounced him on her lap.

Was my jitterbug not up to par? I really thought my hand jive and my twist were quite good. Maybe I'd left out key parts of history. I should've paid more attention in Miss Fordham's history class. Thank goodness there was still a lot of show left.

Just how much show was left seemed to show on my parents' faces.

But they hadn't even seen my *Saturday Night Fever* yet. Everyone loved disco, right?

By the time the real farm crisis of the eighties moved across the stage and the minor piano chords slowed to a painful cadence, I was sure I could save the show with a isn't-it-comforting-to-know-things-have-been-worse? finale. Cheryl showed us a picture of a family being evicted from their foreclosed farm as I did a breathless running man trying to escape a bank note, then I cabbage-patched my way over to the edge of the stage to get the audience involved. With Mrs. Peterson and her piano really hitting all the right notes now, singing the hope of rain, I wondered why the crowd still looked so glum.

I moonwalked the length of the stage, which was hard to do in a tight evening gown and tap shoes, and when I surveyed the faces of True City, they did not appear to be fans of the eighties, but I knew what would save the moment: the dance move of the decade.

The robot.

Before my stilted, mannequin-like moves even made it to the other side of my body, I heard "Oh my God" come from somewhere in the front row.

It was Dad.

Things went downhill from there. In retrospect, maybe doing the sprinkler move during a drought might have been in poor taste. When I ripped my evening gown attempting the worm, I decided to call it quits.

By now, the imagined Gene Kelly was no longer singing or dancing. He had gone fetal, left to die in my desert of shame. Mrs. Peterson gave me a sad, sorry look as she put away her sheet music, and an off-put Mr. Simon attempted host humor. "Well, there you have it, ladies and gentlemen. That was 'Singin' in the Rain' with, ironically, uh, no singin'." He then added a sad and quiet "Just the robot."

And no rain, I thought.

That's when I knew what I had to do. I'd come here to give True City hope, but instead, I'd reminded them just how awful things were. I stood up, straightened my dress, and grabbed the microphone, but Mr. Simon did not entirely let it go.

"Tough crowd," I mumbled. "I get it." I paused to muster up the strength it was going to take to do what came next. "Everyone is hot and tired and scared they won't be able to take care of their families." The only sound coming from the audience was Mr. Dearborn's ever-present farmer's lung cough, along with the collective din of disappointment.

"Janie. For the final question of the day," Mr. Simon said, saving me, "what…do you wish for?"

World peace? A lifetime pass to the movies? Joey Darnell to notice me?

Then, without any warning, without any sense at all, a smile crept onto my stupid, young, hopeful face. In the crowd, I saw Mrs. Lindsay, my fifth-grade teacher who'd given me a B on my Iowa history project—an Iowa-shaped plaque covered in hot-glued corn kernels—because I'd put Des Moines in the wrong spot. I saw Dr. James, who refused to remove my ear-of-corn birthmark when I brought him my whole piggy bank to do so. I saw Mr.

Stephens—I'd detasseled his corn, walked his beans, cleaned his corncrib for way too much pay. And then there was Mom and Dad, along with everyone else, who measured distance with acres, hope with bushels.

"I wish it would rain!"

The words hung in the air for a moment, then swirled sadly through the crowd. Nobody moved. The damage had been done, too late to revise. My parents smiled in solidarity. Mrs. Davis blew me a *Good try, darlin'* kiss. Mrs. Peterson readjusted herself on the piano bench to interrupt the awkward silence.

When I looked at Charlotte, she knew what to do. She began passing out all of the umbrellas I'd been collecting for weeks. Everyone had parted with them easily, eager to get rid of things that reminded them of rain. Some umbrellas were borrowed; others were new, donated from Twila at Strickner's Mercantile. Charlotte's Catholics helped me get the rest. Originally, they were going to be distributed to the crowd for the finale, simple as a gesture of hope, but now I needed it to be so much more.

"Go ahead," I urged all of True City. "Open them up!"

Seconds went by as I looked, row after row, at angry, umbrella-holding doubters refusing to budge.

I unfurled mine, trembling, and raised it toward the sky. Then with a wink, Dad opened his first, followed by Mom, and there we were, the three of us, a trifecta of hope.

Charlotte followed suit, along with a few others, but most refused to be duped by the con man, con woman, who stood before them.

Mr. Simon cleared his throat into the microphone. "Well, yes…a little rain would be nice, wouldn't it?"

"*Believe so*," I said into the microphone. I leaned into the moment and winked at my dad.

The audience began to leave, heads down; others squirmed in their seats, losing patience.

"*Believe so!*"

I thought about what was at stake: livelihoods, lives, hope itself, and wondered if I'd committed the sin any rational midwesterner would never commit—promising the impossible.

For the moment, the audience allowed themselves to enjoy a cloud that had temporarily obscured the oppressive sun, and I prepared for failure.

"*Believe so*," I said under my breath one last time.

I waited.

When too much time had gone by, I gave the audience an apologetic smile, closed my umbrella, and turned to sit down.

Halfway to my chair, I felt it. First on my right cheek. Then on my shoulder. Then two more dropped on my dress, turning the maize yellow to mustard brown as it soaked into the fabric, bled through to my skin.

One by one, the citizens of True City stood up, arms outstretched, palms reaching toward the sky like little pairs of offerings, catching drops of rain. One by one, they unfurled their umbrellas. The lone cloud from earlier had company now. The sky turned dark gray, a thunderclap rumbled, then let out a sweet boom, prompting grown men and women to beam in disbelief.

"Ladies and gentlemen," Mr. Simon began, laughing, "I believe it's raining." Today, though, nobody ran for cover. Instead, we let it ruin our hair, our stoic midwestern attitudes.

When I looked out at the crowd, I spotted Joey Darnell, all

button-down, jeans, and boy muscles. People were in full, rain-induced commotion, bustling about with their multicolored umbrellas, but he was coming toward me. With a purpose. Why was he coming toward me? I looked behind me, waited for him to call out for Cheryl, Lori, Lisa—anyone but me—but then he spoke.

"Hey, Janie." His smile melted all the ligaments in my knees.

I stared, but no words came out.

"That was great." He took a breath. "What you did."

My "thanks" came out more like a question than a statement.

His smile morphed into a smirk. "You're a horrible dancer, but you're gutsy as hell. And the whole rain thing was pretty amazing… Maybe you could create some miracles with my allowance—"

"Let's do this quickly, before we're all soaked," Mr. Simon interrupted, calling Joey over to center stage. "Mr. Darnell here is going to reveal this year's new Corn Queen." All of us girls had sat down again, mascara starting to run, dresses damp with rainwater. Joey opened a sealed envelope and pulled out a card. Maybe the rain obscured my vision, but it seemed like he didn't even look at the name on the card. He spoke into the microphone with confidence.

"And True City's Corn Queen for 1993 is…Janie Willow!"

The crowd cheered, and all of the other girls except for Charlotte sported pursed, congratulatory smiles. I slowly stood as Joey placed a diagonal sash over my gown and a crown of metal corn husks on my head.

When he leaned in to readjust my crown, he whispered, "Meet me at the corn maze tonight. Nine o'clock. Don't bring the rain this time."

CHAPTER TWENTY-THREE

*O*N MY THIRD DAY back in True City, I am getting what I
deserve, but I need to get on with the business of unlikely
miracles. I am alone on the road I travel, except for the white,
porched farmhouses predictably placed every ten acres. It is
midmorning, which means each house smells of bacon, pancakes,
probably over-easy eggs—the second breakfast of the day for folks
whose chores begin when the sky is still black as night.

But these are not the farmhouses I remember from my childhood. Not exactly. Back then, they seemed old, outdated, without
individuality. Now, with eighteen years in between, they suddenly seem not old, but quaint. Not faceless, but teeming with
life. Sleepy-eyed children in footy pajamas. Fathers with calloused
hands, drinking from coffee cups stained with years of early morn-
ings. Mothers wearing cardigans over their nightgowns.

An ache forms somewhere deep inside me, in the place where
one misses those who have gone away and memories that will
never repeat. I imagine myself in each little farmhouse, walking

around in each kitchen, taking care of people. I imagine having a purpose.

Midway to the hospital, I open the car windows until the air rushes over me with a gust strong enough to remind me that I'm alive, but someone else is barely hanging on. I take the rich Iowa air deep into my lungs—air I'd recently discovered is capable of strange things, powerful things—and imagine breathing it into Bliss as a life force.

"Make it right," I say out loud to nobody and everybody. Dad. Charlotte. Connor. Janelle.

Bliss.

When I arrive at the hospital as Kate Snelling, the nurses wave me past the front desk this time like I'm an old friend. Guilt and shame quietly twist and wrench in my gut as I walk toward Bliss's room and try to play the part of a decent human being.

When I enter the room, I put down my bag, pull up a chair next to the bed, and get to work.

"Good morning, Bliss."

I watch her breathe, and then after a few seconds, we synchronize. Inhale. Exhale. Inhale. Exhale. This conversation goes on for five minutes, until I get up the courage to change the subject.

"So how was your night?" I take my book out of my bag. "Quiet, huh?" I say, and lower my voice. "Well, that's gonna change. One day soon I'll say the right thing, that one perfect word, and out of nowhere you'll answer and then…"

I let the words trail off, wishing them safe travels to wherever Bliss is. I remember my own words. *Sometimes it's a word or phrase that stirs something in the cerebral cortex.* I ponder possible phrases that could inspire a person to awaken from a coma. *It's Monday.* Nope.

We need to talk. Definitely not. *It's time for dinner.* She's probably not hungry.

I stare at her beautiful face, wonder what her eyes look like. When I imagine what hope looks like there—how she looks at Harold Hill on stage, how she squints when the afternoon Iowa sun is too bright with promise, how she looks at her mother—the tears come. I swipe them away like they were never there. My crying will not inspire her. I need to think of something else for a minute. Get my crap together. Okay. What will Charlotte make for dinner tonight? Will Connor be going to *The Music Man* rehearsal afterward? How does Harold Hill make his willpower *work*, and how do I get Bliss to listen? What does it feel like when the impossible becomes possible?

Answerless, I pull the blanket up around Bliss, but it is folded over in a perfect crease, unmoved from yesterday. Of course it is.

"Well," I say, shoving my guilt out of reach, and take *Living in the Dark* out of my bag. "Where were we?" I flip pages. "Oh, yeah. I'd just fallen in love," I say, "with film."

Most people catalog their most treasured life events, commit them to memory based on their significance. In the scrapbook of their minds, they can thumb through some of their best moments—reaching that summit at sunrise, watching their newborn baby sleep. And I get it. This is what people do. It's just not what I do. My brain's Rolodex is filled with Gene Kelly dancing in the rain, birds assembling on monkey bars, and Rocky Balboa training for his life in the cold, early morning before a Philadelphia sunrise.

This love affair with film began on a Tuesday morning in 1985 when my father had me watch *Heaven Can Wait* on VHS. I had no idea what happened to us after we died, so when Warren Beatty as Joe Pendleton showed me, I was relieved. It looked nice. A white, fluffy dream. But when he discovered that he wasn't supposed to be there, that it was an angel's mistake, I realized that our fate is sometimes out of our control. Life is merely possibility and fallout. From that day on, I kept my head about me. I looked to movies to remind me of the important things, like how we could all go at any time. I started memorizing my parents' faces—Dad's freckles on his right cheek and Mom's impossible cheekbones—in case there wasn't a tomorrow.

I place the book, facedown, in my lap, and stare at Bliss's swollen face. I don't want to remember her like this. I want to remember the vibrant girl I saw on the news, the one that had so much to look forward to. I am the hypocrite in the room, the one who as a child memorized her parents' faces, yet never went home to see them when it mattered.

I am not supposed to be here.

"She can't hear you, you know."

I don't hear the big hospital door open or shut, but I feel the faithless words of a faithless man hang heavy in the air.

I look up to see a man with pale, sad eyes look back at me. His shirt has been buttoned wrong, so it puckers in the middle; that, along with a series of long, slow blinks, announces the presence of a man who is in a state of complete exhaustion.

I extend my hand, prepared to be someone else, but he walks past me, keeping his tired eyes fixed on Bliss. He runs his hands first through his unruly hair, then over his stubbly cheeks, and finally shoves them into his front jean pockets like they are good for nothing else. But then, as if he's had a change of heart, he collapses in a chair and takes Bliss's hand in his.

His overall essence seems buried, sealed for self-preservation. My throat seizes up.

He rescues me.

"Rob Anderson," he says when he finally turns to me. "This is my daughter. This is my Bliss."

CHAPTER TWENTY-FOUR

1993

CHARLOTTE WAS MY ALIBI. I had never lied to my parents before, but the chance to be alone with Joey Darnell in a moonlit corn maze trumped my midwestern guilt. I wasn't doing anything wrong, but parents of a teenage girl couldn't possibly get behind something so right.

"Can I take the car? It's the Browns' annual hayride. Remember, they did it last year after the Corn Festival? Charlotte's going too."

I held my breath, faked confidence. Somehow, my parents deemed bouncing around precariously in a hay-filled flatbed with flimsy railings—driven by the teenage need-for-speed Martin Brown—perfectly fine. I grabbed my Iowa Hawkeyes hoodie, got in the Aston Martin, turned left like I was headed to the Browns' farm, then took the back way to the outskirts of town where the corn and Joey waited.

My heart fluttered when I pulled up and saw his white, muddy

Chevy pickup truck. I glanced in the rearview mirror, checked to see if my cherry lip gloss was on my teeth, then imagined how my face would look smiling at him as we talked, and if things went really well, as we laughed.

The entrance to the corn maze was marked by two hay bales, makeshift benches for those who mastered the maze and had to wait for those who had gotten lost. A large sign made of two-by-fours announced the corn maze rules in bright-red paint.

After yearly childhood trips to the corn maze, I'd committed the rules to memory.

Rule #1: No smoking.

Duh.

Rule #2: No alcohol.

I was already drunk thinking of Joey's smile.

When I crossed the threshold into the maze, I heard him. "Janie!" His voice rang out confident from somewhere in the center of the maze.

Rule #3: Do not run in the maze.

I ran, with abandon, toward his voice, still hanging in the autumn air.

Rule #4: Please stay on the path.

The straight and predictable man-made path knew nothing of young love, so I left it behind, veered right, bolted into the pure, unadulterated stalks that slapped me in the face as I ran.

Rule #5: Dare to get lost.

Too late. I was lost ever since last year in English class when Joey convinced Mrs. Johnston that *Raising Arizona* should be mandatory viewing in our curriculum. "Mrs. J., it's one giant fable of Shakespearean proportions, an allegory, if you will, about a childless couple in love seeking the impossible," he'd said, looking like a young and muscular Paul Newman in a tight, gray T-shirt. "Think pathos, think symbolism, the perfect companion to your Faulkner and O'Connor." Mrs. Johnston's eyes came to life, likely from the shock of a teenage boy using not only one but four literary terms she'd taught us, and then Joey sealed the deal with his killer smile. "It would be irresponsible, Mrs. J., not to expose us to cutting-edge popular culture rooted in classic storytelling… We've grown up in a cornfield, for God's sake."

When he'd turned and winked at me, I tried not to react, but my body collapsed into a predictable rom-com state of weakness, so I gripped the seat of my sturdy desk chair to look more in control than I was. But I wasn't. Not at all. I didn't know if the wink proved that he knew I existed or if it was a simple, everyday thing that confident, beautiful people did, but I prayed the wink was for me. He was perfection in the midst of mediocrity. All the other boys in my class were nice enough, corn-fed cute, solid and simple, but Joey watched movies, real films, not just Déjà Vu's Friday night showing of whatever. Sometimes he wore a bow tie to a potluck. He read old books. He smelled like a cool rainstorm in a parched summer. He was a bewitching alien dropped from another world into my own personal cornfield. Joey Darnell was a Superman among mere mortals.

"Hey," I said breathlessly when I finally reached him, swiping bits of corn tassels from my hair. I willed myself to look casual, placing my hands in my front sweatshirt pocket, like I'd just happened to run into him here, in the corn maze, under a giant harvest moon larger than life. But when I thought about what it really was, our designated rendezvous point, like Marian Paroo meeting

Harold Hill at the footbridge, their crossroads of love, I felt like I might float away—up up and away, above the corn, into the never-ending moonlit sky.

His words tethered me. "You came."

I would've showed up if the planet was on the verge of destruction. "Nothing better to do." I smiled.

He walked toward me, and my body froze, but then he stretched out his hand, holding a bouquet of the saddest, most beautiful flowers I'd ever seen—three yellow mums, one beheaded, the other two wilted, on their last stem. He'd stuck three corn leaves in to try to revive the ensemble, but it's hard to improve upon perfection.

His hand grazed mine when he gave them to me, and a shiver shot straight to my toes. "I stole these from Mrs. Jackson's garden on the way here."

I already knew that. She was his neighbor, and everyone in Crocker County knew Mrs. Jackson's award-winning mums. A smile took over my face as some gravitational pull drew me closer to him. "Best in the county."

"Yes," he said, now close enough to caress my cheek, "best in the county." Moonlight glimmered off his blue eyes while we stood in our own spotlight, surrounded by our private walls of twelve-foot-high field corn. He reached inside his coat and handed me a VHS tape. "Terry at the video place said he's sick of you renting it, so…I bought it for you."

I couldn't stop smiling as I stared at True City's only copy of *Stripes*. "You didn't. Shut. Up."

"Well, I had more to say, but…"

I looked up, fell deep into the moment. "Thank you," I

managed, but then unstoppable words came. "So…you've been in my dreams for, like—"

"You made me want to go to kindergarten," he blurted, confident, unapologetic.

This was it. I was going to explode into tiny pieces, fertilize the corn maze, never to be seen again. "Kinder—"

"You sat next to me." He took my hand in his, like he knew what he was doing, like it was as natural as breathing, and followed my gaze even when I looked away in embarrassment. "You refused to take Miss McIntyre's coloring book pages and drew your own. You shared your peanut butter sandwich with me every day, and you were the only girl who played baseball at recess. You smelled like lilacs and sometimes like motor oil. I wanted to listen to you read aloud all day." His gentle hand touched my face when I turned away, blushing, telling me he wasn't finished. "Kindergarten was lame. Except for you. You were the most beautiful thing I'd ever seen. Still are."

After that, I couldn't feel my body. The smell of burning leaves wafted through the night air, and my inhibitions floated away with it.

"Remember that time in fifth grade when—"

"Shh." I put my finger over his mouth, leaned in, and faked my way through knowing how to kiss a boy. My numb body came back to life, working on its own. First, I got on my tiptoes to reach him, then my head turned to the side and my hands cradled his head. My front teeth clinked into his, and when I flinched, he reassured me by pulling me into him. I don't know what my mouth was doing, but I know I wanted all of his boy taste, all of his boy smell. The only other boy I'd kissed was Jacob Stevens in seventh grade, but it was for a dare, and I enjoyed it about as much as I enjoyed helping Charlotte clean out the chicken coop.

I finally pulled away, even though I didn't want to.

He smiled and touched my hair. "That…was a proper kiss."

"Was it?" I asked, not sure.

He answered by giving me the kind of kiss I'd seen in movies, the kind people described feeling in their knees, their toes, their dreams.

Within seconds, my childhood drifted away, and I suddenly felt the weight of a changed girl-woman. If this feeling existed, how did adults ever go to work or make dinner or do other boring things? Why wouldn't people just do this all the time?

There was something gentlemanly about the way he stopped kissing me, took my hand, and invited me to sit with him. He took off his coat, spread it out over the cold, hard ground, and we lay down together, watching the stars.

He looked to the sky like some long-lost lover. "Ever wonder what the stars look like in other places?"

I wanted to look into his eyes, but I remained fixed on the big dipper, fixed on the illusion that I was cool and collected. "Same galaxy, same stars, Joey Darnell."

"But how do we know, really? We've never left here, right? Maybe they look different somewhere else."

I turned toward him. "You joking?"

"I would never, ever, ever joke in a corn maze," he said, straight-faced. "It's against the rules."

"Nope. Not a rule." I linked my little pinkie finger with his.

"Should be." He verged on laughing.

"You know what else should be?" I added, matching his ability to stay in character, "Mini movie theater inside the maze."

"Huh, interesting."

"Yep." I readjusted my head so it fit into his coat hood.

He abandoned my pinkie for my whole hand and shook his head. "Girl loves movies."

"Yep."

"Okay. Movie night at the corn maze... What's playin', Janie Willow?"

"*The Thing.*"

"What?" His laugh made his chest move up and down. "No hesitation? *The Thing*? True City's youngsters will never sleep again."

"And then a *Stand by Me* and *Raging Bull* double feature."

"Not much of a romantic, huh?"

"Fine," I said. "End-of-summer finale... *Casablanca.*"

"Ooh, very nice. Unrequited love, cut short by...life."

"And Nazis," I added.

He turned to me, his whole face smiling. "When I get outta here, I'll send you a picture of the stars from wherever I go."

My heart sank. I didn't know where Joey Darnell was going, but wherever it was, I was going with him.

"Well, just so you know, restless spirit, wherever you're going will never be as glamorous as this." I grabbed a handful of black Iowa soil, lifted my arms, looked around, grinning, and presented our perfect little house of corn.

He whispered, "We'll always have the corn maze." And with the stars, our stars, as witnesses, he kissed me like we owned the night.

CHAPTER TWENTY-FIVE

*R*OB ANDERSON IS A broken man. This is obvious to any astute observer, and I can't stop observing.

"Don't you have somewhere else…someone else…you could pretend to help?" He keeps his eyes on Bliss, leans forward in his chair, the only thing holding him up.

I try for a moment to be offended by his comment, mean and biting and warranted, but his devastated voice and sad eyes make me want to fix this miserable disaster even more.

"Faith is just pretending that…" I say, abandoning my sentence and resisting the urge to walk toward him.

Still fixed on Bliss, he lets out one long, faithless sigh. "Well, I'm a bad pretender."

Go for it. Be Harold Hill. Make him believe we can wake her up. "Sometimes, you know, coma patients can sense—"

"Sense?" He shakes his head, then with an angry twist, turns to me. "Hasn't moved in forty-eight hours, but she can sense…" He stops, stands up. "I hope she can't sense this utter nonsense." He hangs his head, and we breathe in silence, the three of us. I wait for him to send me away, kick me out like I deserve, but he just stands with me, like he wants someone to yell at. This, in some perverse way, makes me feel useful.

"Yesterday"—I tread lightly—"when I said her name, I swear there was a little flutter in her eyelids." He stares me down with irritated disbelief, so I walk to her bedside and speak in a gentle voice. "Bliss?" When nothing happens, I try again. "Bliss?"

"Just stop—"

"Bliss?" I say one last time, pretending not to pretend.

At first it looks like it might be nothing, but no, it's something.

Rob Anderson moves with a purpose toward Bliss and stands next to me. "How many times has she done that?"

"Just these two," I admit.

A nurse comes in to check the feeding tube and gives us an apologetic look when she overhears us. "They do that sometimes. Their eyes may flutter. Just brainstem reflexes." She touches Rob's shoulder. "Sorry, Chief."

Chief? His ivory skin and blue eyes rule out any Native American heritage. I look around for context clues. Then I see it sitting on a small side table along with a worn, black wallet—a police officer's badge, shiny, and for the moment, useless. So this is who I would've met if I'd turned myself in two days ago. All of the air left my lungs, and my mouth, a criminal's mouth, is dry with guilt.

When the nurse leaves, Rob slumps into the chair again, looking like he's been broken before; the nightmare before him—Bliss, his only child, not yet dead, not really alive—has broken him in a new way. Like a fracture on an already broken bone, except this time, the fracture hasn't made him stronger, it's made him want to give up.

"I can't lose them both," he says, barely audible.

Before I can ask, he answers my question. "My wife, her mother... Cancer... Two years ago."

"I'm so—"

"I actually thought staying here, the smallest of small towns, would keep them both safe." He takes a big, disappointed breath and turns to the window. "I used to watch them, Bliss and her mother, out in the garden—she loved her hollyhocks—and I'll be goddamned if every time she told Bliss she'd find her a monarch butterfly, one would fly over, like she'd conjured it up. Magic Mommy, she'd call her, the bringer of butterflies. Every time I see one..."

His emptiness, our emptiness now, settles into me.

"All she ever wanted to be was a mother. I'm so grateful she can't see this."

When he turns his attention back to Bliss, he bows his head, unable to look at her swollen face and closed eyes.

"I'm sorry. I'm so, so sorry," I say.

"Don't be sorry. Just don't tell me she can hear you...because she can't."

"She will," I say, the unwanted, resident charlatan.

"You're the '*expert*,'" he fires, his hands erupting into angry air quotes. "I haven't slept for two days, mind you, so I'm a little off my game, but tell me something." His eyes widen and a desperate sigh escapes. "How many people have you saved with your little stories? That's what they said you do, right? Tell stories to people who can't hear a damn word you're saying?"

"I think you're full of shit." He watches me, curious. "Yeah. I think you're full of shit," I repeat, like I am even surer the second time. "Chief."

With this, he stands up. "Excuse me?"

"Excuses are for pussies." I sigh. "And I'll have none of them in this room." I shove my book in my bag and then stop to look into his eyes with a truth he is not prepared to hear. "I know why you don't want me to tell you she can hear me...hear us." I tell my eyes not to well up. "If I tell you she can hear us, I might be right." I nod myself on. "And that's a lot to hope for."

He lets the chair catch him, and he slumps into the cushion; his brokenness upgrades to full-blown shattered. "She is slipping away, and I can't help her. I can't bring her back. Three weeks, they said. Three weeks, and then the odds..."

Together, we listen while Bliss breathes life into the silence. I walk to him, extend my hand. "Kate," I say. "Altered state special-ist. Storyteller." I crack a smile. "Ballbreaker."

He doesn't smile back—that's asking for a lot—but he does something better.

"What were you saying...about how she can sense things?"

"It's called salient stimulus," I say, grateful for the question. "When something emotionally significant to the patient—a song, a voice, but usually words—prompt them to wake up."

His almost-nod indicates a hint of hope, but he suddenly looks like he needs rescuing. Words. Words will save the day.

"Mr. Anderson, I'm going to come back here every day until you have your daughter back." I let that rain down on us, three broken people, and wait to see if the chief is going to charge me with wrongful hope-giving.

He looks back at me one last time. "How are we supposed to know which words will wake her up?"

"We don't," I say and open the door to leave. "That's where faith and pretending come in."

CHAPTER TWENTY-SIX

1994

I'M PREGNANT," I SAID, and then I puked into my mother's country-blue kitchen garbage can.

For once, Joey Darnell had no words. He came to me, touched my back as I retched into the Hefty extra-strong trash bag. "Do you... I mean, are you..."

With my head still in the can, I threw up again, then turned back to Joey, pale and still, slumped onto a kitchen chair. "Yes," I gasped. "I'm sure." I pulled two positive pregnancy tests from my back pocket.

"Shit, Janie. God... When...?" he stammered. "How...?"

I wiped my mouth with my sleeve. "Valentine's Day. Your truck. The Simpsons' cornfield." In an attempt to address the "how," I added, "Reckless hormones. Prince on the radio. Bad judgment."

My head pounded, and I leaned into the punishment. I couldn't get enough air. "My God, what....what are we gonna do?"

He let out a defeated exhale, shut his eyes for a moment, like he was thinking it over, and then he sat down with me on the linoleum. What he did next made me want to cry. "Nothing." He kissed my forehead. "We're gonna do nothing. We are gonna do this. Together." He cupped my tear-soaked face in his hands. "I love you, Janie Willow."

"Oh, Jesus." I hid behind my hands. "Nightmare. Total nightmare."

"Not exactly what a guy wants to hear after bearing his soul, but okay, all right. Uh, let me regroup. On second thought, I don't love you. Because you're kind of gross." He smiled. "And there's a chunk of your lunch stuck to your lip."

With this, a conundrum of the human condition—a moment that's simultaneously devastating and beautiful—I fell apart. After a year and a half of dating, a year and a half after our corn maze rendez-vous, Joey and Janie had evolved into Joe and Jane, and Joe and I had become the happy couple that outwitted and outlasted other typical, fleeting high school romances. We weren't your typical high school lovebirds only concerned with prom themes and Friday-night foot-ball games. Joe and I watched films together, studied together, cooked together. We even garnered the attention of True City's grown-ups, who gave us the *my God, Marge, they just might make it past high school* look. But we weren't looking for approval; we were looking toward the future. And now we were looking toward it together.

"Where are your parents?" he asked, breaking eye contact.

"Out flying." My stomach knotted, realizing why he'd asked. I attempted to stand. "No. No, Joe, I can't do it. I can't tell them—"

"You have to tell them. We have to tell them—"

"It will kill them, Joe. You don't understand. I'm all they have. All they've ever wanted is for me to…"

He tried to hug me, but the idea of admitting to my parents that I was not who they thought I was made my body clinch into one giant, guilty knot, and I backed away.

"Look, it will be weird and awful and probably be the hardest thing you'll ever say, but we can tell them we have a plan."

"Plan?" I almost laughed, but I still felt like puking.

"Yeah. Look, we're graduating in a year. We'll have the baby, I'll help you with everything I can, and we'll still go to school, maybe just part-time for a while, and it won't be like we had always planned, but—"

"Like we planned? This is nothing like we planned! This is not engineering! This is not film school! This is not making our parents proud…and don't say that word."

He looked angry. "What word?"

"Baby," I whisper-cried.

He exhaled from somewhere deep. "Janie, we screwed up, okay? And we're gonna have to suck it up, try to make this right. As right as we can." He offered me the other kitchen chair. "I'm gonna go home. Get my parents. When I come back, we'll tell both of our parents together."

My silence screamed compliance.

"Okay?"

I nodded.

An hour later, the phone rang. "Joey, what's taking you so—"

"Janie?" Joey's mother managed, but there was something wrong.

"Did you talk to Joey?" My shame was palpable. "Are you guys on your—"

"No… Joseph…never made it…home." I heard a loud thump, the phone dropping to the floor, followed by crying.

"Hello?" My voice grew more desperate.

"Janie?" Joey's dad said. "There was"—he cleared his voice, trying to push the emotion away—"an accident."

I held my breath. Began making deals with God. *Anybody but him. I will tell my parents everything. Anybody but him. I will make everything right. Anybody but him.*

Mr. Darnell let out a raw sound, an audible open wound, then changed my life forever. "He's gone, Janie."

CHAPTER TWENTY-SEVEN

OR THE FIRST TIME in eighteen years, I am going to act like a friend. Something tells me Charlotte needs one right now. Showing up, late or not, is the least I can do. I owe her.

Besides the wonderful childhood we shared, I owe her for leaving her. I always had the aching feeling I'd left a void in her life, but it wasn't until last night, after leaving Charlotte's house with the scrapbook she'd given me, that I realized how big the hole was that I'd left in her world.

When I'd settled into my father's rocking reading chair with the worn armrests and opened the cover on the scrapbook, I expected to find pictures of her last eighteen years—her wedding, her children, everything I had missed that she wanted me to know about. But when I flipped to the first page, the already big hole I'd left gaped wide open.

Staring back at me on page one was a picture of me from the *True City Gazette*, a picture my mother had sent in of me after getting my PhD in film studies from UCLA. On page two was a clipping from the *LA Times* of the first film review I ever wrote for *My Own Private Idaho*. The next several pages were dedicated to my climb to fame as Cinegirl. When I saw my cartoon likeness staring back at me, the alter ego I'd taken on, I began to rock faster, as if I could somehow rock away the guilt. Page by page, my life unfolded before me, cataloged and highlighted by Charlotte Davis, the best friend I hadn't bothered to send one birthday card to in eighteen years. The newspaper articles and pictures overlapped, just like the years.

After I'd looked at the last page, and after I'd rocked alone in silence, the flashes of my life still fresh in my mind, I decided to do what my gut, what this place called home, told me to do.

If ya screw up, kid, make it right.

Work hard. Be nice.

Tonight, on this very special night, I arrive at Charlotte's front porch, holding something that will make it hard for her to turn me away. I take in one deep breath and let the humility pour over me. The traveling passersby, there to take pictures in front of the genuine *American Gothic* backdrop, have long since gone, and all that's left is the moonlight hitting the tips of cornfields and bouncing off the famous arched window. With my feet planted firmly on Charlotte's porch, I wriggle my toes inside Mother's worn slippers and let the weight of what I'm carrying push into the belt I've cinched to keep up Dad's pair of work pants.

Charlotte answers the door, gives me a once-over. "Only brought one outfit, huh?" She gives her attention to the very large, lopsided, three-tiered chocolate cake I'm holding. When she sees there are lit candles, one for each of her birthdays I've missed, her mouth contorts into a shape that I've seen three times before.

In second grade when Charlotte broke her arm after falling off the monkey bars and didn't want anyone to see her cry. At her grandmother's funeral when she went to the casket for her final goodbye, but didn't want tears to ruin the makeup Happy Sr. had applied to make Charlotte's grandmother look like her Nanna again. And finally, in tenth grade, when Joe Henning asked Jenny Whitman to the prom instead of her.

"You remembered." Charlotte fights back eighteen years of tears.

"Happy Birthday, Char. Made it myself. Make a wish."

For the second time in two days, Charlotte lets me in. I cup my hand around the candles, protecting each mini flame as we walk in the house and I place the cake on the kitchen table. Charlotte glances out the kitchen window, out into the darkness, then back at the candles, each a silent apology for sins too big for words. She inhales, then exhales with purpose, extinguishing what appeared to be yesterday's flames. Eighteen mini blazes of red and orange disappear, just like that, but then in one seamless evolution, they become little apparitions of smoke, each one swaying to its silent tune.

"Well, that's that," Charlotte says.

I stare at Charlotte, who seems lighter, like she's undergone her own evolution of sorts and is prepared to float away.

"We'll save some for Connor and Janie-Janelle," I say while grabbing some napkins and plating two pieces, "and Steve?"

"We'll put it in the freezer." Charlotte nods, automatic and resigned, and I begin to think midwestern deep freezers are the keepers of all untidy sins.

Charlotte glances out the kitchen window like something beyond it calls her. Then she gives me a mischievous look, one I recognize from a lifetime ago when we could finish each other's sentences. "Wine?" she says, followed by a smile.

I nod, but before she can get the wine, I give her a hug and have a hard time letting go. Neither of us says anything for a while.

"Here's to thirty-six," we finally say, and we clink glasses. "God, Janie, after Joey…I didn't know what to do. You were just…gone."

My lip quivers, and I almost tell her. I almost tell her the thing nobody knows, the thing that put Janie Willow to rest forever. But some secrets, if you keep them long enough, become so buried, like ancient lore, that unearthing them requires the strength to chisel through layers and layers of shame and regret that has solidified into impenetrable sadness.

I slip my index finger under my bracelet, let it slide over the inscription, and then nod an apology that looks more like a simple acknowledgment. "I want you to know that what happened…my drifting away…leaving…was my fault…all of it. I know that's not an explanation, but—"

"No." She grabbed my hands. "Don't say any more."

"You still the choir director at church?" I say, before I say too much.

She nods. "Been doing more repenting than directing lately." The faraway look returns. "People always want to tell me their sins, can you believe it, like I'm Father Larson or some kind of bartender—"

"I did something horrible" escapes me and ends my silence.

"See?" She smiles. "Come on, Janie, I forgive you for abandoning me. Let's cut our losses, huh?"

The word *abandon* cuts deep, but I need to stay on my game, keep from doing any more damage than I've already done. "No, something else," I say, not sure if I'll end up in Rob Anderson's station cell tonight. I imagine Bliss's wrecked body, breathing in sync with her father in a hopeless, dark hospital room.

"Wanna talk about it?"

I shake my head.

"Well, all right then. I'll pray for you." She paused. "I've been doing that for years, anyway." Charlotte poured us a second glass of wine and sighed. "You know why I go to church, Janie?" She laughs and takes a gulp. "It's not what you think. Mostly, it's because I like to stare at the stained-glass windows. They're so beautiful; they make me forget so many things." She takes another aggressive gulp. "I'm not even sure if God exists anymore."

Whoa. What's in this wine? Charlotte just went from God-fearing choir director to atheist in two gulps.

After a sigh, she says, "But there's gotta be something bigger than us, right?"

Charlotte and I have somehow switched roles, and she looks at me like she's the one who needs forgiving and I'm the absolver. "Lately, I go to church to try to forgive myself, to try to remember that when life presents us with an irreconcilable dilemma, that we can transcend, we can embrace the wreckage, we can somehow find the courage to throw up our arms, open our mouths, and say 'hallelujah' despite the impossibility of it all."

Right. Love is not always a triumph. True desperation calls for Leonard Cohen, so I throw up my hands. "Hallelujah!" I yell and raise my glass. "Here's to impossible tasks—"

"Steve wants his kidney back," she blurts, then guzzles her whole glass of wine like the farmhouse has turned into a frat house.

A few seconds go by before I can process what she's said. "Wait. What?"

Despite the alcohol, her face takes on a sober countenance. "We were so young. And then we had Janie when I was just twenty. And all of a sudden, it's two decades later... He was the only boyfriend I ever had. I hurt him. He is hurting so much. He doesn't know what to do with his anger so... He's not hunting, Janie; he wants the kidney he gave me back."

"He's not serious, Char... That's, like, totally crazy."

She walks to a kitchen drawer and pulls out a large stack of papers. "Divorce document. Page thirteen..." She follows her finger and, voice shaking, reads, "Client asking for one left kidney donated by said client in 2004 as part of compensation for—"

"Char, he can't be serious. He must be asking for the value of the kidney—"

"No! He wants my kidney! His kidney. Our kidney."

The whole thing sounds like some horrific semantic joke, some sort of tragic possessive pronoun conjugation or a Robin Cook novel under piles of failed meatloaf. Wow. Hollywood is not so far away after all. Zoom in for the close-up on the face of devastation and a montage of the just plain bizarre.

When Charlotte, a very light drinker, pours a third glass of wine, I imagine her body trying to filter out the alcohol, and I begin to get concerned about the kidney in question. "My lawyer says a donated organ can't be a marital asset, that it's just a stalling tactic, but it's not. I know him. That's how betrayed he feels. His own lawyer has advised him it's insane...it won't stand up in court...but he won't let it go."

"So let me get this straight: He'd rather see you dead than just let this go?"

Charlotte, looking like a child who'd just been shamed, traces her finger around the wineglass rim. "He's just hurt. Love makes you do crazy things."

Suddenly, just how well I actually know Charlotte Davis comes into focus. It all falls into place. The way her eyes tonight seem empty on first glance yet hold an unexplained gleam. She is in love with someone else. This is why she'd been somewhere else all night, looking out the window somewhere into the darkness. Guess we both have big secrets.

A drop of red wine falls from Charlotte's lower lip and splashes onto her white napkin lying on the table. We watch it bleed into the napkin's corrugated designs. I take a piece of leftover dinner bread, break it into two halves, one for me, one for my Catholic best friend. Together, we take a bite, giggling, no doubt thinking of how many times we'd done this together years ago, and we wash it down with the wine, letting our sins swish, swish, swish out of sight. Here we are, body and blood, laughing our way through an impromptu communion.

Lady Gaga and her poker face interrupt our redemption, and lacking her usual good judgment, Charlotte picks up in an altered state. "Charlotte's Meatloaf Hotline," she says, slightly slurring her own name. "What's your meatloaf…meatloaf…"

"Emergency," I whisper to Charlotte, who is snapping her fingers, trying to remember a line she's spoken thousands of times.

Charlotte listens for a millisecond and then something in her— years of good, sensible, church-going behavior—breaks loose. "Just forget it, ma'am; you're totally fucked," she says, somewhere between desperate drunk and midwestern polite. "That meatloaf is fu-ucked up… Time to call Pizza Hut, darlin'.""

The darlin' on the other line must be expressing dissatisfaction, because Charlotte says "I'm sorry. I'm really sorry," then begins to drunk-whisper, which isn't a whisper at all, and speak in an exaggerated annunciation: "My. Husband. Gave. Me. His. Kidney. And. Now. He. Wants. It. Back."

Charlotte listens for a second, then switches to speakerphone and makes the universal sign for crazy while the woman with the fucked-up meatloaf says, "What, honey? Your husband's name is Sidney?"

"Jesus, Mary, and Joseph," Charlotte yells. "'Kidney'! I said 'kidney'!" And then after one deep, regretful breath, she begins to cry. "One in 700,000. He was a one in 700,000 match. He saved my life. He gave me his kidney…and I broke his heart."

I turn off speakerphone and grab the handset. Someone needs to end this meatloaf hotline train wreck.

"You're gonna get me fired, Janie!" a pouting Charlotte says about the most humiliating job on the planet and wrestles to get the phone back.

"You're welcome," I tell Charlotte. "Ma'am?" I say into the phone, unearthing long-ago midwestern manners I'd forgotten about. "Look, my friend is too nice to tell you this, but I'm gonna be straight with you. Nobody likes meatloaf."

"Nobody?" she says, deflated.

"Nobody. It's like the Christmas fruit cake of weeknight dinner." I pretend Cinegirl is a food critic and wind up. "A gelatinous hunk of dry bread crumbs and low-quality beef glued together with ketchup, which we Californians call ghetto salsa."

"California!" she says like it's a curse word. "But my daughter says—"

"She's lying," I tell her. "People lie, ma'am. For lots of reasons. Sometimes for the noblest of reasons." This liar needs support, so I sit down.

"Thank you," the meatloaf-maker says, "for telling me the hard truth."

"It's what I do," I say, trying to remember the last time I told the truth. "Now go give your beautiful daughter a big hug and order out. And, ma'am?" I pause, unsure why I care about this woman and wonder if I'm coming down with something. "Enjoy your family. It's not about the meatloaf. It's never, ever about the meatloaf."

Right when I end the call, Janie-Janelle bursts through the front door with Connor trailing behind. "Mom!" she yells, not waiting for a response. "Mom! You're not gonna believe this. Mitch Blackman is such a jerk!" When she sees Charlotte and me and the empty bottles of wine, she stops. "So Bliss's boyfriend has totally been cheating on her with that skank Scarlet. What kind of poser only wears red just to match her name anyway? Whoa, are you drunk, Mom? And what's she doing here?"

I am now used to Janie-Janelle scowling at me, but a little surprised when Janie-Janelle explodes into a hormone-induced, teenage meltdown. "So Bliss is dying, and you're here getting drunk with someone who hasn't bothered to talk to you for, like, forty years!"

I correct her lack of accuracy. "Um, we're not that old—"

"No wonder Daddy left. You don't care about anybody."

Connor runs out of the kitchen and upstairs. I am single, lonely, recently orphaned, and probably going to jail in the near future, but looking at Charlotte—drunk, kidney-stealing, meatloaf-peddling Charlotte—slumped over the kitchen table right now, I suddenly don't feel so bad.

When Charlotte says "I'm sorry, honey; I'm so sorry" and goes to give her daughter a hug, Janie-Janelle softens for a moment. Her fiery-red hair seems to get demoted to a mere smolder.

"I'm sorry too, Mom," she whispers, midhug.

I feel like I'm interrupting some teen-edition Lifetime episode, so I start to make Charlotte some coffee—it's still exactly where Mrs. Davis used to keep it. "How's Bliss?" I ask, afraid of the answer.

Janie-Janelle whips around. "Why do you care?"

I can't answer that question, not here, not now, so I say it's tragic and sad and unfair and lots of other true things. "I've been reading, Janelle," I say, taking the risk of getting something thrown at me, "and even though it may seem hopeless, it's not. It's really not."

Wait for it. Wait for it. But instead of contempt, I get a warm "Thanks," and when she says this, she looks just like Charlotte. "Mr. Anderson told me that's what this lady—some sort of therapist or something—said too, that she thinks Bliss will wake up." Tears fill her eyes. "He says he wants to believe her."

My mouth goes dry and my lips stick together. Worlds…colliding… How am I gonna pull this off? But when I think of Rob Anderson wanting to believe me, a warmth comes over me.

I am reminded how young Janelle is by her T-shirt featuring a BeDazzled green-and-blue peacock with satin feathers. Just sixteen. Bliss is probably the older sister she never had.

I hand Charlotte a cup of coffee, and when Janelle leaves to go upstairs, Charlotte hollers after her, "I'll be up in a minute,

Peacock, to tuck you in…and no, I don't care if you think you're too old. Tell your brother he's not too old either."

Peacock? I ask with my eyes.

"Steve's nickname for her. Once, when they were stargazing, she asked if the stars were eyes, watching over everybody at night to keep them safe." She sighs. "Well, peacocks' feathers are called the eyes of the stars…so…" She drifts away for a moment and then says, "Speaking of stars, when I come back downstairs, can I show you something?"

After giving Charlotte another cup of coffee, we put on Carhartt jackets from the breezeway hall tree and walk together, guided by starlight, past the faceless and now spotlit *American Gothic* cutout, then past the barn. My slippered feet step alongside Charlotte, who is walking with a curious purpose. We make our way halfway down the lane, turn left, and take the path that leads toward the Simpsons' farm. "Char, where are we…"

"Shh." Charlotte touches my shoulder, and her eyes widen when she sees light glowing through the cracks of the four-story barn. "Wasn't sure she'd be flying tonight."

"Flying?" Now I'm really confused.

"Shh."

"Yeah. You already said that," I whisper. "Tell me we're not going to visit Heather Simpson. That bitch has hated me since first grade."

Charlotte's voice is quiet but sure. "Not the Simpsons' farm anymore. They moved three years ago."

The sky seems clearer than usual. The absence of clouds gives Charlotte and I, two clandestine women on a mission, the special privilege of watching the stars awaken for the evening. Thousands of flickers announce their presence as if they are preparing for something grand.

When the light from a tall lamppost shines on Charlotte's face, her breath accelerates in anticipation of something. She turns away from me and toward the barn. Light seeps from all corners like some sort of celestial homing beacon amid the monotonous cornfields.

I let Charlotte take my hand and lead the way. What could possibly be in a barn in the middle of the heartland that has Charlotte so out of her mind? Charlotte's grip intensifies with each step, and by the time we reach the barn's side door, I feel Charlotte's pulse quicken.

I scour my brain for something, anything that could generate this kind of excitement from Charlotte, but I have no idea. I probably have walked a quarter of a mile, in my slippers, to see a prized heifer, maybe a mare, or worse yet, someone's new tractor.

But Charlotte had mentioned *flying*.

Oh God. It's probably an owl. Charlotte loves owls. My desperate friend has made a pet out of a wild animal that is probably a carrier of the Avian flu, and I'll die before I can save Bliss.

I crane my neck to look up at the largest, oldest barn in Crocker County—it really is majestic—and when I glance up at the topmost window, I notice intermittent shadows appearing in a rhythmic pattern. One one-thousand. Two one-thousand. Three one-thousand. The shadows dance with the unexpected grace of a nighttime ballet four stories above the most fertile soil on Earth.

"Char, are you sure we should…"

Charlotte doesn't answer. After a deep breath, she nudges the small side door and leads me inside. We stay huddled next to the barn's interior wall, hidden in the dark. Six giant beams of light land on what we've come to see.

A woman who flies without wings.

Tendrils of shimmering, ebony hair trail behind her, undulating in slow motion as she glides through the air. A silky, white bodysuit showcases the woman's olive-skinned body, a perfect marriage of delicate curves and strong muscles. She sits perched atop a silver trapeze bar and holds on to hefty nylon ropes. I look upward, follow the lines to their origin—enormous rafter beams, the backbone of the barn—and then my gaze falls back upon the raven-haired flyer.

"A trapeze in a barn?" I say, too loud. "So is this a thing now?" I had been gone so long. So many surprises in this place I thought I knew. Maybe the farmers had turned to circus acts due to hard times and hard labor.

Charlotte places a finger on her lips to quiet me. "When the Simpsons moved, Roland and Celeste Love moved in. Used to run Love's Circus in Fort Dodge. Their daughter, Julia, does trapeze lessons here, and the occasional circus-themed birthday party." Charlotte stops, smiles, as if she's somehow proud of what comes next. "Only for the brave," she adds. "For those who can learn to let go."

I whisper, "Don't you need two people to...*fly*?"

Charlotte keeps her gaze fixed on the angelic flyer and nods. "Two is better," she whispers back, but when she follows with an even softer "Two is infinitely better," I suddenly understood. The woman flying through the air glances down at Charlotte, smiles at her in a knowing way, and yes, it is now as crystal clear as a crisp, starry night sky.

Love's Circus.

Love *is* a circus. A scary, exhilarating, death-defying act. A leap of faith we all hope we'll have the chance to dive into.

Well, I'll be damned. I did not see this coming. Memories of Charlotte and I hanging up posters of heartthrob boys from *Teen Beat*, and crying over how Peter Stevens didn't ask her to the Homecoming Dance, and now this? A new Charlotte. Or is this the real Charlotte we didn't know existed? Reversals, opposites, mysteries everywhere. Is this Iowa? No, it's just lesbian heaven. Charlotte's favorite movie, *The Way We Were*, swirls in my head, in all its past-tense glory, and I realize that after all these years it isn't Robert Redford in Charlotte's dreams. Her Hubbell Gardiner isn't wearing a beige trench coat and writerly turtleneck. Her Hubbell Gardiner has a vagina and is flying through the air in the Iowa night.

The woman releases her hands from the ropes and sits balanced on the bar.

My nerves resonate in my voice. "Should she be…"

Charlotte silences me with her hand. "Lista," Charlotte whispers up toward the woman.

"Lista?"

"Ready. It means 'ready'…in trapeze-speak."

Suddenly, the woman flung her arms up and behind her.

"Oh God!" I grab Charlotte, calm and lost in the moment.

"It's okay, Janie." Charlotte's body now mimics the woman's as she watches her next move, a backward swan dive. Charlotte slightly arches her back and tilts her head back in sync with the woman, and just when I expect to see a stranger free-fall to her death, she catches the bar where her knees bend and swings upside down.

Charlotte floats on an invisible cloud. "Timing is everything," she says, eyes still fixed on the woman who saw the world from the other side.

I let a few seconds pass, knowing that despite years of botched timing and faulty geography, at that moment, I am in the right place at the right time.

I turn to Charlotte. "Char?" I whisper. "So how long have you been in love with a trapeze artist?"

"About a year," she says. "Forever," she whispers. "Something like that."

"The two of us are a mess, huh?" For some reason, despite how illogical it is for the circumstance, I feel compelled to be optimistic. For Charlotte. "Maybe there's hope for us after all, Char."

She nods, staring at me now with a newfound understanding, like maybe we can get through our messes together.

"Char, do you believe in second chances?" I whisper, wondering if Dad can hear me, if Dad is revising at this very moment.

A soft truth escapes, as sure as a birthday wish. "I'm banking on it. So should you."

"Hallelujah," I say, as all stars, all eyes, watch the unlikely angel soar through the night.

CHAPTER TWENTY-EIGHT

1994

ANIE WILLOW, THE BEFORE Jane, died on April 16, 1994, at
6:14 p.m. when Joey Darnell left this earth. While I was
preparing to tell my parents they were going to have a grandchild, a semitruck carrying 1,100 bushels of corn crashed into
the driver's side of Joey's Chevy on Highway 71, killing him
on impact.

All that was left was Jane, a hopeless shell of Janie. The After
version of my better, Before self. While Janie knew love was pre-
cious, Jane only knew its pain.

I went to Joey's funeral with part of him growing inside me,
and told no one. Maybe tomorrow, I thought, maybe tomorrow
I would tell. But as the Methodists cried and sang "You've Got a
Friend in Jesus," I protected my secret and my belly while all of
True City hugged me and attempted condolences for a life taken
too soon.

Such a shame. Hug. *Everything happens for a reason.* Hug. *Such a shame.* Hug. *Such a shame. He's in a better place.*

"No, he's not," I said to Mrs. Nelson after she'd tried to convince me that Joey Darnell from Crocker County, a land where a boy could be a girl's King of the Stars, was in a better place. Janie would've walked away, but Jane bulldozed through the tension. "That's what people say," I snarled. "Better place... That's what they say when they know the universe has totally screwed someone over."

My mother scolded me, whisking me toward the front entrance of the house of God, but I continued my tirade by hollering, "And 'everything happens for a reason' is the biggest line of bullshit I've ever heard!"

Maybe it was the pregnancy hormones, or maybe it was the grief-induced posttraumatic stress disorder I'd heard people whispering about, but the Corn Queen was officially dead. Janie had been replaced by some bitch named Jane, and everyone was nonplussed. Look, if a pregnant girl at her baby's father's funeral can't show a little frustration, where the hell can she? So just like that, Jane Willow was born. Born again in the house of God. Alongside Joey rested Janie Willow, the Corn Queen, the girl who believed in rain and love and the beauty of a place called home.

You'll be okay, they said. *You have your whole life ahead of you,* they said.

That's exactly what I was afraid of; this pain would have no expiration date.

I had planned on telling, but one day turned into five. Five days turned into twenty. Twenty days became a month. Every time I thought about Joey's eyes, whether this baby would have the same blue, dreamy eyes that always seemed to know things, I pushed the truth—how much it would hurt to love this child without Joey—into a faraway place. Every time I thought about how many nights I'd have to see the stars without Joey, I realized this baby *was* Joey. If I attached emotion to this baby, it would mean saying goodbye to Joey all day, every day, forever.

"You feelin' okay?" Mom asked one day, but I could tell she was concerned about my emotional health, not my physical health, suspecting nothing more than depression. My teenage boyfriend had died tragically and I was sad, Mom and Dad thought. So sad that every afternoon I ate half a pan of Mom's corn casserole and then helping after helping of her chocolate chip bars. My parents, even Charlotte, viewed my personality change, my added weight, as a reflection of death, not life.

One afternoon, midbite, I finally spoke some truth. "I'm so sorry for everything, Mommy." A hint of a childlike whimper snuck out, and Mother hugged me like a mother does.

She pooh-poohed my guilt as a what-could-you possibly-have-done-wrong kind of ridiculousness, but she didn't know a thing. Only I knew the truth: this was all my fault. It was my body that got me in this mess in the first place, and it was my lack of courage that sent Joey out the door that night to his death. If only I'd told my parents myself, and then told Joey, or maybe had him wait with me to confront my parents straightaway. He was distracted, in a hurry, thinking about me, when he pulled out onto that highway. This was all on me, and it always would be.

And this baby? She was pure happiness. Happiness I didn't deserve. As I thought about how my mother used to sing to me each night, I mourned for a love I would never know. I said goodbye to the life inside of me. I would secretly love her for the rest of my life, but she would never be mine.

For my parents, I found the strength to pretend to be Janie again, to be what my parents wanted me to be. "So, I think I need a change of scenery, Mom."

I talked my parents into letting me spend the summer in California, taking a UCLA course offered to high school students interested in film history. By the time I got back, I hid my swollen belly under one of my dad's old Carhartt jackets.

"You'll die of heatstroke, kid," Dad would say, but I told him I was cold—I'd gotten used to the California sun—which was partly true. Every day in Los Angeles had made me feel farther away from the only home I'd ever known. By the time I'd gotten back, it felt like Janie's home, not mine, full of memories too painful to be near.

Charlotte reached out like a good friend should, but unlike her, I was not a good friend. I pushed her away, unable to tell her the truth. Charlotte was Janie's friend, and being around her only made me miss what I'd already lost.

I was on my own. Telling my parents at this point would rob them of everything they'd ever wanted: for me to be a good, happy, midwestern girl with a future. If I told them, not only would Janie be dead for me, but for them too, and the Willow home couldn't take any more disappointment. How could I not tell, you ask? How could I create the biggest lie imaginable? Shame. Contrary to popular belief, shame, not love, is the master emotion when you're seventeen.

My eighth and nine months of pregnancy involved lying on a whole new level. Sorry, Mom, I'm just not ready to hug yet. Yes, I'm feeling fine, just tired, Dad. Charlotte and I just grew apart,

Mom. Well, I need to read all these film books up in my room so I can be prepared for college. Um, dressing like an overweight truck driver is more comfortable.

Mom and Dad's blind optimism was finally a benefit for me—we see what we want to see, I guess. A disaster of this magnitude didn't even register as a possibility for them, so how could they see it? Dad had even mentioned, during one of his juvenile pregnancy cases, how irresponsible the parents of the teen must have been to not know their own daughter was pregnant. Thank God for his rose-colored glasses now.

I didn't know the details of how I was going to pull this off, but I did have an idea what to expect, thanks to *What to Expect When You're Expecting*, which I'd bought in California and threw away in a bathroom garbage can in the Denver airport on the way home. I tried not to think about episiotomies, mucous plugs, or the fact that poop coming out of a woman during labor was totally normal. Nothing about this was normal, and at night I lay awake, terrified of what could go wrong. But I had one job. Get this baby out safely. I owed that to her. To Joey.

By the time the Braxton Hicks contractions I'd read about had turned into full-blown contractions, I was sure I was going to have the baby right in the middle of some family meal. After a day and a half, I felt a warm rush of fluid, kind of like I'd peed my pants, and knew it was really happening. I told my parents I had bad cramps and needed to lie down, which wasn't entirely untrue.

They always went flying in the afternoon, which meant my window was a few hours, and I prayed it would be enough. When the front door slammed and I heard Dad's truck drive away toward the airport, though, I panicked.

"Come back!" I cried to nobody, in between wails of pain and sheer fear. "Please come back; I'm so scared," I whispered, a child about to have a child.

This went on for forty-five minutes, the pain escalating with each minute, until the only way I could find relief was to crouch down on my hardwood floor and groan. Each contraction made the last seem like a mere spasm, a twinge. The dull aches turned into intense twisting and wrenching in my lower back, then subsided. But not for long. When it returned, it was the worst agony I'd ever experienced, like someone tugging at my organs from the inside, followed by a stabbing sensation. I was sure my organs were going to fall out, that they'd find us both here in a pile of guts and intestines.

That fear didn't last long, because I suddenly felt immense pressure and a burning sensation, like someone had taken a blowtorch to my vagina. I'd read about this. The baby was crowning. I crawled into my bathroom, flopped into my claw-foot tub while pulling down the jogging pants that had been acting as my maternity pants, and fulfilled my urge to push. This felt surprisingly good. For a minute. Then my body ripped apart, hip to hip, bone to bone.

When I felt like pushing, I did, acting as my own uninformed and deranged birthing coach, but it seemed to never end. In the movies, it's over in a couple of pushes, so I feared something was wrong. Thoughts of women in covered wagons dying while giving birth flashed through my mind, followed by nightmarish images of me dying in a bathtub wearing bad sweatpants with a baby sticking out of me.

"Come on!" I yelled. "You have to come out!" I wanted to cry, but I was so exhausted I could barely talk. I managed one last, breathless directive. "No one can help us. It's just us."

I drew on strength I didn't know I had and mustered up one more push along with a guttural, universal, primal scream, the kind that puts you in the women-mother club, and I felt her come out, first her head, then, with one last push, her body. I reached down between my legs and pulled her slippery body up to me. She was a girl, but I'd known that all along.

Shaking, I tried to remember what I was supposed to do. Clean nostrils and airway, keep her warm, but all I could do was look at her blue eyes. When she first cried, I should've been worried someone would hear, but all I felt was an unexpected pride.

"You are beautiful. And strong." A new emotion I'd never felt before showed up; perhaps it was extreme fatigue. "And perfect."

I cleaned her off with a bath towel and quickly let her suckle on my breast—something about inducing a hormone that helps push the placenta out. Plus, I'd read that the buttery stuff that came out right after birth was full of nutrients. She'd already had a rough start; she needed all she could get.

Everything that seemed super gross from my reading now seemed natural, rooted in necessity. I knew I had to clean up the bathroom and try as best I could to get moving, but for one long moment, we just sat there, the two of us, breathing, living. For the first time in months, shame evaporated, replaced by the absolute miracle of what had happened. After cutting the umbilical cord with Mother's Fiskars sewing shears, the first act of our inevitable separation, I prepared for the impossible. I retrieved the blanket I'd made thanks to my 4-H skills, a blanket I'd embroidered with hundreds of stars because I wanted her to be near Joey and my stars, her stars, always there to wish upon.

The rest is a blur. My weak, oozing body trudged through

the motions, each step producing throbbing pain in my tender, swollen self. I washed all traces of what had happened down the bathtub drain and hid the bloody towel in a garbage bag. Then I wrapped her in a blanket, placed her in my canvas Gap tote bag I had prepacked in my closet, and made my way to the Aston Martin. We drove together first down the long lane, then down two gravel roads, before I could admit that I had no idea where I was going.

Where does one hide and protect something delicate and valuable in the middle of Iowa? I had no Nile River, no tall reeds of grass to hide her in…and just like that, I knew. Iowa had its own brand of tall grass. I turned around, headed back toward the outskirts of town toward the only place worthy of her. A perfect place for a child—equal parts rules, fun, and love.

Just one year ago I had been on this same road. No, Janie had been on this road. Now, a lifetime later, I arrived in the same place, but this time in the far back, a secret entrance that not many people knew existed. A small car path led to it, through the Stevens' adjoining cornfield, so if something went wrong, Mr. Nelson could get to the center quickly without going through the crowd of customers in the height of harvest.

That's what I was looking for, a way to get to the center without being seen. I grabbed a baseball cap from the glove box and tucked my hair up in it. I lifted up the tote bag, got out of the car, and let her suck on my pinkie so she was quiet. Together, we walked into the back entrance of the corn maze, uninvited guests on hallowed ground.

I pulled the wall of corn back like a curtain, and we made our way through two lesser-traveled parts of the maze, until we reached the center, the heart, the goal of True City maze-goers, as if heartland heritage instinctively lured them to the centers of things.

Formerly muffled voices grew louder and clearer, which meant I was running out of time. I placed the bag down gently in an open part of the path where I knew she would be found. It was time to go, yet my feet remained still, heavy and frozen with the weight of leaving her.

The voices drew nearer.

My mind had already walked away, but there I stood, looking at her, unable to move. With the last of my strength, I ripped off a frayed corner piece of the blanket with multicolored stars I'd wrapped her in and clinched it in my sweaty palm.

I heard a child and her parents talking like families do, getting closer.

The *Titanic* was sinking, and I was leaving her behind. I prayed I'd drown and never be found.

"This way, baby." A mother guided her child like a mother does. "We made it!"

They'd made it.

They'd made it.

I blinked tears away and squeezed the scrap of blanket in my fist, the only part of her that would make it out of here.

"I think there's someone up there!"

All of the air left my lungs, and the weight of the world pressed down, stealing my breath. I gasped for air, forced my heavy legs to move, now just swollen, lumbering, guilty stumps, one foot after another until I'd exited the corn maze. All that stood between us was one temporary wall of corn.

"Mama, there's a big bag, there's a big bag!" the little girl called to her parents. "It's a prize for making it to the center, I bet!" As I approached my car, I heard the little girl's voice change. "There's a baby in the bag, Mama. Mama? Mama, there's a baby."

I slumped into the driver's seat, grabbed the steering wheel to calm my shaking hands. I let the world open up, swallow me whole, so I could drown, sink down, down, down, watching pieces of me float away.

When I stumbled through my front door, barely able to stand, Dad was reading the paper and Mom was making dinner.

"Janie!" she said with her signature smile. "I was starting to get worried." She walked over to me, placed her warm hands on my face like only a mother does, and then brought out the semi-pout, the one that says *I'm so worried about you but I don't want you to know.* "How's my girl, huh?"

Of all the things I could've cried over in the last eleven months—fear, death, birth—it was this, these four words, a mother asking her daughter how she was, that destroyed me. A lump throbbed in my throat and sent a surge of pain and pressure to my already aching head. Tears formed so fast that they began dropping onto the hardwood floor, falling and crashing like abandoned dreams.

"Think it might rain," she said, stirring the Crock-Pot of meatballs.

"Yep," I force out, trying to disguise my gasp-sob. I couldn't let her see me cry, so I wiped the evidence away with my sweatshirt sleeve and tried to control my breathing. I squeezed the small piece of afghan blanket with one bright, colorful star, the only part of her I had left.

"Have a good afternoon?"

I let out a silent gasp-cry, disguising it as a little cough, and used the last bit of energy I had trying not to audibly sob. I had become a mother at 2:42 p.m., and by 6:48 p.m., I'd become a mother who'd lost a child.

As Mother peeled potatoes, something she could do in her sleep, I took off my coat, set the table, my back to her so she wouldn't see my tears or wrecked face. When I placed Mother's plate down, the place where the matriarch watches over the table, something happened, and my weakened body gave way, and I sat down so I wouldn't collapse.

"Did you go to Charlotte's today?" she said, peeling in a fury. When a few seconds of silence went by, she added, "That's so great, honey. I knew you girls would work it out. It's so important to have someone to talk to. Loneliness can destroy your soul."

My back still to her, I let her see me nod my head, while my secret tears continued to flow.

She stopped peeling. "Janie?" Her sense of urgency made me nervous. "Stand up. Come over here."

I froze.

"Stand up, honey. Let me see you; you sound funny." She stood in the middle of the kitchen, holding a paring knife and serious concern.

Slowly, I helped myself up using the back of the chair for support. When she saw my face, she gasped. "Janie! You look awful. You must have caught an autumn cold. Why didn't you tell me? Now, let's fix you right up with some corn casserole."

Then her face turned serious as she looked my body up and down. I tugged at my sweatshirt and pulled it down, hoping blood hadn't soaked through my pants.

"Darlin', you've lost some weight!" She smiled. "Yeah, you've lost a lot."

She had no idea what I'd lost.

"See? Things are looking up, sweetheart," she said and then gave me the kind of hug that makes you believe anything, just like a mother does.

CHAPTER TWENTY-NINE

*H*ELLO, SID."

"'Hello'? Is that all you have to say, Jane? Where the hell are you?" Sidney wastes no time expressing his frustration.

I switch to speakerphone and distance myself from an angry Sidney Poitier Parker.

"I'm a criminal in disguise, Sid, on my way to perform a covert operation to bring someone back to life."

Silence.

"You think this is funny?"

"Not. At. All."

"I've called you, like, thirty times. What could be so important that you can't even pick up the phone?"

His tone is slightly reckless, three shades past his usual lilt of concern, and I know right now he is nervously running his fingers through his dark-and-in-charge hair in the hopes of gaining control.

"Well, Sid, I've been simultaneously hiding from and spending time with the chief of police, trying to figure out how to save an innocent victim. All this plus consoling my best friend whose husband wants his kidney back because she's in love with a trapeze-flying woman."

"Wait," he says. "You have a friend?"

Even in the most dismal of times, Sid can make me laugh.

"Either you've lost your mind, Jane, or you've been watching too many Charlie Kaufman films…or Iowa is a lot more interesting than I thought."

"I know, right? Who knew?"

Silence.

"Sid? You there?" Something tells me he's ready to go all father-figure on me.

"Seriously, Jane. What's going on?" When I don't say anything, he defines his version of a nightmare. "So Frank says—you remember Frank, right, Janie? That's my boss. A very important man who signs our paychecks in case you've forgotten… Well, Frank says that he doesn't care if you're half-dead or in jail; he wants something to print for Cinegirl's column by tomorrow. Oh, and Nick Wrightman really, really, really wants to know where you are, like a stalker wants to know where someone is, Jane."

"You didn't tell him, did—"

"No! No, Jane! I didn't tell Nick Wrightman you're in the middle of a cornfield in the middle of nowhere doing God knows what, but you're missing the point. I can't keep you from getting fired forever, and quite frankly"—he stops, like he's afraid to finish the sentence—"I'm a little hurt that you won't tell *me* what the hell's going on."

Seconds roll by, highlighting my ability to disappoint those I love.

"Sid," I finally say in a tone close to a plea, "have you ever had to leave someone behind?"

"Come on, Jane—"

"No, answer me, Sid. Have you ever been on a proverbial sinking ship and had to leave someone behind who needed you, who was your responsibility, who was"—my voice fails me, breaks like a little girl's—"who feels like she's a part of you?" The silence saves me for a moment. "I'm not leaving her, Sid."

The silence is now oppressive.

"Goddamn it, Jane." But something shifts, and I hear Sid inhale, one of those deep breaths that represents a realization, like he's accepting something that he knows is the absolute worst idea in the world. But he's doing it for me. Because he's my friend.

"I promise I'll have something for you to print by the morning, Sid, and—"

"I know you will, or else we're both fired. And figure this mess out, Jane. Whatever it is. Whoever she is. I will handle Frank and I will handle Nick and I will handle all the other goddamn messes that are surely transpiring as we speak."

I tell him what he deserves, what he's taught me to say. "Thank you, Sid. It's not enough, but thank—"

I hear him smile. "Stop. You had me at—"

"No more movie lines, you said!" I laugh. "'Cliché,' 'pedestrian,' you said!"

"I actually said no more movie lines for you, not me. I get to do what I want. I'm the boss. Try to remember that, would you?"

I resist calling him Mister Tibbs, and I don't make him guess who's coming to dinner because I'm sure I'll eat Mother's corn casserole from the container, alone, in Dad's chair tonight. So I settle for "Yes, sir…with love."

He tries to hide his laugh, but I hear it. Loud and clear.

"Hey, Jane?" I let three beats go by because I know whatever he's about to say is going to make me cry. "Whatever it is, you can do this. You can fix her. You're the strongest bitch I know."

Lots of witty retorts surface, float through the air like wispy clouds of possibility, but the lump lodged in my throat prevents me from speaking, so I pretend to lose the signal and fade away until all I hear is the Iowa air whipping through the truck, calling me toward her.

"Badge," Nurse Ratched barks at me, barely looking up from the nurse's desk.

I start to pat myself down, searching for an ID badge that doesn't exist, because Kate Snelling doesn't exist. "Shoot! I must have dropped it—"

"Kate!" I hear from down the hall. I remind myself that I am Kate, and turn around, hoping my wig is in place and none of my blond hair is escaping. It's Rob Anderson, who tells the nurse to let me through.

She musters up a half shrug. "Your call, Chief."

Rob skips greetings and bursts out, "She moved." I stop breathing for a moment, soaking up what he's said, soaking up the facts that Bliss moved and also that the saddest man I've ever met has a smile on his face.

I start moving toward Bliss's room, my heart racing, and I fire off questions. "When? What happened?" I say, walking past a giant picture window with Jack and Mary Willow standing proud in the distance.

"Last night," he says, keeping up with my pace. "There were a flurry of movements, five in a row. I did what you said, kept trying out words: first, her name lots and lots of times, but then I tried her boyfriend's name, Mitch, and she moved her right index finger. He's on his way down here. Maybe it will—"

"Hasn't he been here yet?" I ask, moving toward Bliss's bed.

"Says he hates hospitals," Rob says, sounding unconvinced, but then adds, "Only been dating a few weeks; hardly a solid romance."

Rob Anderson doesn't realize he's pacing from the bed to the window and back. I watch him for a while, listen to him talk more in five minutes than he did in an hour yesterday. Odds. Possibilities. Best-case scenarios. *Doctors say it's a good sign.* Today, hope follows him around like a new companion.

"Uh, hello?" we hear a voice call from outside the hospital door, followed by a quiet knock. Mitch Blackman, the boyfriend, all six-foot-three quarterback and all-American, walks in. He glances at Bliss and then walks past her bed and stands over by the window.

"Mitch, this is Kate Snelling. She's a therapist for…patients like Bliss," Rob says, switching his focus from Bliss to Mitch.

When I shake Mitch's hand, a feeling I can't place emerges, and I let go before he does. "I'm so sorry, Mitch."

"Thanks," he says, watching Bliss from across the room. "So she moved last night?"

"Just a finger," Rob says, "and just for a sec, but it's something."

"Yeah, totally. It's something. Better than nothing, right?" Mitch fiddles with his Chicago Cubs ball cap. "So no talking yet?"

Rob shakes his head, stares at Mitch until he begins to bite his thumbnail. "You seem on edge, Mitch, wanna take a seat?" Just like that, Rob Anderson, doting father, becomes Chief Anderson, a cop built to scour the world for suspect activity.

"Nah, I'm fine… Me and hospitals just don't—"

"Right." Rob looks out the window for a moment, then says, "You know, Mitch, tell me again, if you would, what time you said you dropped Bliss off at home, because I've played it over in my head a hundred times…why Bliss would leave the comfort of her home and decide to go out walking in the pitch-black." He turns back to Mitch now. "All alone."

So many reasons to get out of this room. No wonder this poor kid is freaking out. Rob Anderson would freak me out even if I wasn't guilty. "Mr. Anderson, I can leave, if you guys need to—"

"Nonsense, Kate. Stay." Rob smiles. "Just a friendly conversation, right, Mitch?"

"Sure," Mitch says, standing taller now, eyes scanning, looking toward the door like he could use an exit. "Like I said, Chief—"

"Call me Rob, Mitch." Rob stops, stares at Bliss, then back at Mitch. "We're all friends here, right?"

"Like I said, sir…Rob," Mitch says, slightly panicked, now talking with large, athletic hand gestures. "I dropped Bliss off at nine fifteen, sir, right at your doorstep like you told me to because you were at the station. I remember the porch light on the right was flickering, and"—now Mitch's hands are flying in a frenzy, and his face is contorted into a tense grimace—"and I watched her." He looks over to Bliss's bed. "I watched Bliss take the key from under the sunflower front rug, put it in the door, and walk inside. Sir."

Something in Rob Anderson shifts, and he returns to being

Dad, focusing all attention on Bliss again. "All right, son," Rob says quietly, like he's finished some impromptu investigation, then adds, "Sorry."

I smile at Mitch Blackman, not a boy, but not yet a man, certainly not the one responsible for the crime. He's somewhere between crying and punching a hole in the wall.

"I'm gonna take off," he manages. "If she says anything," he stammers, "call me. Please?"

The finality of the hospital door shutting hangs in the air, an uninvited guest that threatens the small hope left here. I break the silence. "Well, that was—"

"I'm an asshole."

He sits in the chair next to Bliss, his elbows resting on his knees. In my head, I tell him he was just doing his job, but then I tell him to get his shit together because the real criminal is standing right in front of him. Nobody in Crocker County has a haircut like this. A blunt bang, really? And I've worn variations of the same outfit for three days now. What kind of cop are you? *When you finally arrest me,* I want to say, *I am not going to look at your face; the thought of disappointing you is already making me want to puke.*

I can't say any of that, so instead I say, "You might be an asshole, but you're a hell of a dad."

He turns, a half smile trying hard to come to fruition but competing with doubt. "I'm off my game," he says, followed by a breathless and apologetic, "I am so damn tired." He closes his eyes, breathes in deep. "People guilty of something usually volunteer too many details…and he was doing that…and I thought maybe he was lying about how she got home…" He hangs his head and sighs. "I just had him scared to death."

I look at Bliss, then back at Rob, trying to weigh out equal emotions for both of them. "Hey, Rob?"

"Yeah?" he says, head still hanging low.

"I have something… It's worth a shot." I take out my phone and walk toward him. "I heard she's a *Breakfast at Tiffany's* fan."

He looks up, doesn't try to help me, doesn't try to stop me. I hit play, and after five plucks of a guitar, he smiles, looking like he's swallowing away an emotion that is in some deep crevasse between happiness and regret. Audrey Hepburn as Holly Golightly starts to sing Johnny Mercer's lyrics to "Moon River," and I take Rob's hand, get him out of the chair, over to Bliss's side. Together, side by side, we hold the phone close to her.

When we get through a few bars, Rob smooths back a swath of Bliss's silky blond hair.

Where are you, Bliss Anderson? Come back, Bliss.

Rob and I stare at Bliss's hand, chipped purple nail polish and all, resting on the baby-pink hospital blanket. Even though we want it to move, to let us know she's coming back, it remains still, and Rob's hand squeezes mine so hard I want to wince. But I don't dare.

Tonight, I will rewatch *Breakfast at Tiffany's* and try to save my job by sending Sid a pithy review. I will beat him to his own question. Why a classic? I will then follow my rhetorical question with the truth: modern viewers need a timeless reminder that no matter who we are, we belong. Holly Golightly is annoying, but Paul loves her anyway, despite her many flaws, maybe even because of them. So I will enlighten Sid. I will find solidarity with Holly, another real phony, and together we'll search for our Tiffany's—that place that makes us all want to give a thing a name, call somewhere home. Belong.

Rob Anderson breathes in and out, in sync with Bliss, watching his only child live her life somewhere without him.

We want the same thing, I want to say to him. *Something wonderful waits for us*, I want to say. But I just sit with him, with Bliss, and float away to "Moon River," just the three of us, not a care in the world.

CHAPTER THIRTY

I HAVE TO GIVE SID something if I want to stay here and keep my job at the same time, but I can't bring myself to watch Bliss's *Breakfast at Tiffany's* tonight, here in Mom and Dad's living room. Plus, something I can't pinpoint is calling me.

This time I'm called to True View, True City's drive-in theater on the outskirts of town. The mere thought of it conjures up the iconic final scene in *Field of Dreams*. The spotlit cornfield-turned-baseball field makes me smile and think of what Dad would say if he returned from the afterlife to have a catch with me. *They've positioned the baseball diamond all wrong, and the way lights are pointing is not very efficient, and why the devil does my back still hurt if I'm a goddamned ghost?*

I don't know what will be playing there tonight, but whatever the film is, no matter how ancient, it will, no doubt, be justified by some sort of theme, as if it were True City's idea in the first place, instead of someone else's scraps. One has to admire that spirit of adaptability, an evolutionary must for a midwesterner.

My usual, preferred review-writing utensil, a felt-tip pen, doesn't seem right tonight, too permanent for open-ended possibilities, so on the way to the drive-in I stop at Strickner's Mercantile.

When I pull up on Main Street, I park between two empty cars, engines running, a typical sight in small-town Iowa. The only time one's running car would be messed with here is if a friendly passerby needed to move it for a snow plow or an extra-wide combine during harvest. With each step toward the front entrance, I think of Mother, holding my hand as a little girl, off to Strickner's for Care Bear stickers, a new kite, or a free watermelon Jolly Rancher from Miss Twila at the front register.

The same little bell on the door welcomes me as I enter the store, but not before Miss Twila, sporting gray hair now but with her same warm smile, greets me with a hug. Hugs are something I usually cut short, but today I lean into this one, taking the last moments of it to pretend it is another time.

"Janie Willow," she says, making no effort to escape my extra-long embrace, "all grown up."

"Good to see you, Miss Twila," I manage, but for some reason it catches in my throat, and my eyes well up, imagining my mother standing here with us.

"Los Angeles, huh?" she says when I finally let her go. "Well, good for you, Janie." The subtext here is even though the rest of True City thinks I'm an uppity traitor, Miss Twila has the good manners to pretend she thinks otherwise in my presence. "You make movies out there, is that right?"

I smile and shake my head. "Oh, I don't make movies; I just write about them."

She looks disappointed, the look on her face revealing a truth we can both agree with: writing about art instead of making the art is like describing the harvest instead of growing the damn corn.

"Well, you were always clever, Janie Willow." She pauses, takes a deep breath, and we both know what's coming. "I'm so very sorry about your folks."

"Thank you, Twila."

But before I can say any more, Twila is off, bolting down aisle three with a purposeful and practical gait. "Let me grab you what you came for, darlin'," she hollers back.

What I came for? Did I tell her?

While I wait, I notice a young mother in line at the register, fumbling to find her wallet while jostling her baby from side to side. When I go to hold her purse for her, she hands me her baby girl instead. For a moment, I think, My God, I could be Buffalo Bill the serial killer, but then I remember I'm in Iowa.

The mother is muttering something, but all I hear are the little baby sounds coming from this perfect, tiny mouth. When she lays her head on my shoulder, I relax and gently place my hand on her back for support. I breathe in her baby smell, and just as I start to pretend that she is mine, that I am somehow worthy of such a miracle, the mother takes her back.

"Thanks," she says, leaving me childless. "Darn wallet's in the car. Left it there after paying Lanie's 4-H dues earlier. Tell Twila I'll be right back."

I reach for my wallet. "No worries. I got this. No biggie."

"Nonsense, the both of you," Twila says, returning. "I'll put it on your tab, Mrs. Jensen." She hands me a pack of perfectly sharpened pencils. "And here ya go, Janie. Just what you need for all that writin'."

Before I can ponder if I had mentioned this earlier, before I can ponder how exactly people here seem to know what I need before I do, she puts my pencils on a tab that doesn't exist and places something in my hand.

"Watermelon, right?" Twila says with a wink, and I stumble back out onto Main Street.

When I pull into True View, I see a sign announcing tonight's main feature: *Castaway*. An ocean in the middle of a cornfield.

This is going to take some persuasion on my part, convincing Sid that reviewing a has-been movie is somehow relevant to my readers. But it is. *Castaway* is one of those films that seems to change every time you see it, not because the film has changed, but because you have changed. It's like *The Old Man and the Sea*. You can read it at various stages of life, but it will be a different book each time, depending on your current demons and dreams. I will tell Sid this, and when I'm finished, he will think reviewing this film was his idea to begin with.

I place my notebook and new pencils on the passenger's seat, ready for work, but something tells me this review is going to write itself, that I am already understanding why it is this movie, this night, that my island was LA, and now I am back from the dead, returning to a home, a life that has moved on without me. Neither place is mine now; the island was just a temporary place to make me forget who I was, and home is just a heartland purgatory. I'm supposed to be the progressive one, LA's cutting edge, but somehow the people here, with their movie time warps and their affinity for yesterday, are light-years ahead of me.

I roll down the windows, let in the rich, Iowa air, and let the starlight illuminate just enough to make me see. That it's not the meatloaf, it's not a watermelon Jolly Rancher, and it's not a volleyball named Wilson that breaks our heart. It's the loss it represents. It's two souls drifting away, flying beyond the clouds, beyond the moon, beyond my reach. It's a smiling young girl, happiness personified, needing to find her way back home. It's a lost corn queen trying to remember the kingdom she left behind.

Real life sneaks in for a moment, like Sid somehow knows I'm on the brink of drifting away. What the hell will Sid think of my reviewing a has-been movie? I can hear it already. What's next, Jane? *Ferris Bueller's Day Off? St. Elmo's Fire? Back to the Future?*

But I let it all pour over me, let the two most powerful conduits of human emotion—music and story—swirl together in one beautiful thing called *film*. I let the magic on the screen breathe in and out of real life, the gentle lapping of ocean waves becoming one with the breeze rustling through the cornfields that surround me, that have always surrounded me.

The music swells, somehow captures the bittersweetness that is life, the chance at love intertwined with the stabbing pain of loss, of things that can never, ever be the same. Each part of the orchestral score, each separate string providing both a bass and treble, an underbelly of sadness with hope dancing in for a few solo notes, reminding us of the power of desire, the power of one.

By the light of the moon on the big screen, by the light of the moon right here in this cornfield, all of us watch in wonder, with heavy hearts, as Wilson drifts farther and farther away. Then as the moonlight reflects both on the black ocean water and the tops of cornstalks, the soundtrack crescendos into a full-bellied overture of what we all feel—too small in a big world, lost when something we love is taken from us.

The smell of popcorn wafts past my window, and the cool night air reminds me where I am. I am watching a movie in the middle of a cornfield in True City, Iowa. But that's not really where I am. I am swimming toward her, wading through oceans and cornfields of regret to bring her back.

CHAPTER THIRTY-ONE

INT. THE MIDDLE—TODAY

           BLISS (V.O.)

Why are people trying to talk to
me? Why do they keep saying my
name? Bliss? Bliss? Bliss? It's
like they think something's wrong
with me. Sometimes it goes on for
minutes. Don't they know we're
supposed to keep quiet? *The Show*
is about to start. I try to tell
them with my eyes, you know, that
everything is okay, but they still
sound weird, all muffled and panicked at the same time.

FADE IN: Auditorium, BLISS sitting in the

front row with the other girls. Award-show
music plays, and a giant spotlight dances
around the auditorium.

RED-DRESS GIRL
(whispers and makes *L* on forehead)
You're going to lose.

GREEN-DRESS GIRL
(smiling and giving a thumbs-up)
You got this, Bliss.

GREEN-DRESS GIRL's peacock on her dress comes to
life and spreads its feathers.

GREEN-DRESS GIRL
(winking, stroking the feathers)
All eyes on you, Blissy.

BLISS
(quietly)
I am excited for *The Show*, but
I am getting tired again, just
trying to keep…my…eyes…open.

WOMAN (O.S.)
(urgently)
Open your eyes, Bliss! Do not fall
asleep, baby.

A monarch butterfly suddenly lands on BLISS's hand. She examines it, and it flies away. The scent of hollyhocks floods the room, and one by one, hollyhocks sprout up, the first one, baby pink, grows out of the seat in front of BLISS, then one more pops out of the stage in front of her. It grows and grows and grows until it winds around the podium, explodes into the air, and shoots up toward the ceiling like it's trying to see what's on the other side.

                    BLISS
            (dreamily, sleepily)
    Who are you? Where are you? You
    sound far away, yet so close.

                WOMAN (O.S.)
    It was my job to look after you,
    and I let you down.

                    BLISS
    Are you an angel?

                WOMAN (O.S.)
    No.

                    (pause)
    I don't know.

BLISS

Are you coming to *The Show*?

WOMAN (O.S.)
(sadly)

I can't. I live somewhere different from you, but you can't come
here, Bliss. You belong there.

BLISS
(disappointed)

Okay.

(pause)

What is *The Show*, anyway? Is it a
competition or…just a show?

WOMAN (O.S.)
(voice trailing off)

It's the biggest mystery of all,
Bliss…

The auditorium grows dark, and a booming voice
announces that *The Show* is beginning. All spot-
lights converge on the podium where AUDREY HEPBURN
stands, waiting for the raucous applause to cease.

AUDREY HEPBURN

Our first nominee is happiness,

personified. She is a wonderful
actress, her shining role being
Marian Paroo from *The Music Man*,
a beautiful parallel to the fictional River City and homage to
her small hometown of True City,
Iowa.

BLISS
(to GREEN-DRESS GIRL)
True City! I remember now. That's
where I'm from!

AUDREY HEPBURN
She is an unlikely star from an
unlikely place.

(smiles)
I've always said that nothing is
impossible. The word itself says
I'm possible!

The audience erupts in applause.

AUDREY HEPBURN
(warmly)
Bliss Anderson, this is your life…

The lights go completely dark except for a giant

screen in the front of the auditorium. The first
image is a large silver gift box being unwrapped,
its shiny yellow ribbon falling in slow motion
like an undulating wave. Time reverses, demon-
strated by an out-of-focus camera view. An image
comes into focus. It is BLISS as a baby. Her
father holds her, rocks her back and forth. His
smile is too big for his face.

                    BLISS
                (whispering)
        Daddy.

A WOMAN touches BLISS's tiny face. Tears of joy
stream down the WOMAN's face.

                    BLISS
                (wistful)
        Mom? That's my mom.

                    (pause)
        I had a mom.

                WOMAN (O.S.)
                (crying)
        I'm so sorry, Bliss. I'm so sorry,
        sweetheart.

BLISS looks up; the ceiling is covered in

hollyhocks and the auditorium is teeming with monarch butterflies.

CUT TO:

BLISS is a toddler, running, playing with GREEN-DRESS GIRL, putting their faces through an *American Gothic* parody cutout.

BLISS

(looking at GREEN-DRESS GIRL)

That's you.

(quietly)

That's us.

GREEN-DRESS GIRL nods, smiles.

CUT TO:

BLISS, now maybe twelve, fills the screen with her long legs and long, blond hair blowing in the Iowa summer wind. The scene changes to BLISS with her hair up in a bun, in her mother's too-big black dress, pearls, and sunglasses. She recites a line from *Breakfast at Tiffany's* into the mirror.

AUDREY HEPBURN blows BLISS a kiss from the podium.

CUT TO:

A coffin appears on the screen, and the audience goes silent. A teenaged, crying BLISS is draped over the coffin.

> **WOMAN (O.S.)**
> (audibly crying)
> Oh, Bliss.

> **BLISS**
> (looks up toward the WOMAN's voice)
> That's you. You're my mom.

> (eyes tear up)

CUT TO:

A laughing BLISS, slightly older now, is with a boy. They flirt. BLISS pushes him away.

BLISS suddenly hears a new sound, not what's playing on the screen before her, not her mother's voice from above, and not the audience, but something else. This is from far, far away, not The Middle. This is from the Other Place.

> **OTHER-PLACE NOISE (O.S.)**
> (whispers in ear)
> Mitch.

BLISS looks around the auditorium for the voice, but knows it's far away.

> **OTHER-PLACE NOISE (O.S.)**
> (again)
> Mitch.

BLISS looks at her finger, moves it up and down, not knowing why.

CUT TO:

BLISS and the boy are stars of the big screen for a moment, but then the screen goes black. The auditorium listens in the darkness, on the edges of their seats. There is a scuffle. BLISS and the boy argue.

> **BLISS**
> (mouths, looking at the screen)
> Stop it!

CUT TO:

The screen fills with a blacktop road at night.

BLISS is breathing hard, walking fast, crying. The audience reacts in a collective murmur.

> OTHER-PLACE NOISE (O.S.)
> ("Moon River" plays)
> It's worth a shot. I heard she's a
> *Breakfast at Tiffany's* fan.

BLISS remains still, listening intently. The audience members are now frozen in time, their faces eternally captured with various expressions, while BLISS spins into a panoramic view of the whole auditorium.

> BLISS
> (spinning)
> Getting. So. Tired.

> (dreamily listening to "Moon River")

CHAPTER THIRTY-TWO

1995

J WAITED UNTIL NOBODY COULD see me, which wasn't hard, because nobody really saw me for a while after it happened. For weeks after that last trip to the corn maze, I'd made it an art form, flying under the radar of the nosiest people on Earth: my parents, my neighbors, my conscience. I waited until Mom and Dad had gone to town for the Elks' fundraiser meeting, and I waited until the Browns, one farm over, had turned on their porch lights, the signal for supper.

Finding my way to the willow was easy. I could've done it blindfolded. First, I walked out the front door, past the tire swing, past the barn, past the first corncrib, took a left at the second corncrib, took a right, walked ten paces until I reached the dirt path that led to it. Fabled to be one of the oldest willow trees in all of Iowa, it seemed the tree itself knew this, knew that despite its whimsical name, its grandeur made it king.

When I was little, I would find myself on my favorite branch, an outstretched arm enclosed by a wall of droopy leaves that wept down around me, creating my very own tree room. It wasn't only by chance that a majestic willow tree had planted itself on our Willow family property. My grandfather, who apparently had a ripe sense of humor, thought the Willow farm should most certainly have a willow tree and planted it when he was a young boy. They are known to take root easily, eager to grow, so with my grandfather's nurturing, it was well on its way to tree stardom.

From my favorite bough, a special vantage point, I used to peer out through the curtain-wall of leaves and observe thousands of acres—the Browns' six-hundred acres, the Andersons' pale-yellow farmhouse, the Hennings' weathered red barn—and I would imagine the tree's roots stretching for miles, reaching in intricate patterns toward every farmhouse, every barn, every ounce of life it could find.

"It's a good one this week," Mom would say, placing the newspaper down on a gingham blanket along with the picnic treats, and the two of us would sit in the giant willow's shade.

"Is it *Kramer vs. Kramer* or *Manhattan*?" I always knew what movies were out. The Willow household got two channels, channels four and nine, my primary source for movie trailers. I also knew that my Pauline Kael, my mentor—my "other mother" as Mother sometimes called her when she was feeling jealous—published a weekly film review in the *Des Moines Register*. Other girls my age read magazines like *Cricket* or, if they had older sisters, *Teen Beat*, but I preferred the musings of the always-fabulous and always-right Pauline.

Why I had taken to film criticism at the ripe age of ten was

never entirely clear. Maybe I took after Dad, the ultimate revision-
ist, reimagining each film with smarter dialogue, a better ending.
Or maybe at the heart of every midwesterner, young or old, lay
a deep desire to pass judgment. Or perhaps it was the fact that I
was an only child looking for an imaginary sibling in the form of a
sassy, sometimes brutally caustic forty-year-old writer.

Either way, I hung on her every word, often contemplating
what Ms. Kael would say about my everyday life. *That oatmeal lacks
a certain something, leaves me wanting, and not in a good way*, I would
imagine her saying. Or *You call that a bike? It's an embarrassment—
the gauche tassels, the overly patriotic paint job, the new-fangled handlebars
that reek of innovation gone wrong.*

"*Manhattan*." Mom knew she could not compete with Pauline
Kael, the object of my affection, so she embraced her. "You know,
she's really on fire this week. Said some choice things about Woody
Allen and said the film was full of some real 'characters.'"

Mother and I took turns reading the review, laughing at Ms.
Kael's not-so-subtle sarcasm, and spent the afternoons under our
massive willow in the midst of an idyllic dream of a childhood
that I was too young to recognize as such. Life so good, it played
without my knowing it was a movie in progress.

So on that day, when I'd returned to the same willow tree to
bury a part of myself, it seemed I was burying two mothers, two
daughters. I slipped off my backpack, took out the tiny patch of
blanket I'd torn from the blanket I made for her, the same sad little
patch-of-a-star that now haunted me. Even when it was hidden
under my bed, I felt its presence. I felt her presence, and it was too
much to bear, knowing she was somewhere. Without me.

I picked up the shovel I'd left at the base of the tree two days

earlier when I also left a pile of Dad's sawdust. Iowa's cold fall tem-
peratures made it difficult to dig in half-frozen ground, but Dad
had taught me that the sawdust would help it thaw. The sun began
to retreat behind the golden stalks of corn lining the horizon. The
tree was now a giant, black silhouette, surrounded by yellow and
red leaves that covered the ground like a blanket of fire. I swiped
away the leaves and dug a small hole right underneath my favorite
bough, the one I long ago used to hoist myself up. I placed the
little patch of blanket in the hole, piled the cold Iowa soil back on
top until the one lonely star disappeared.

CHAPTER THIRTY-THREE

*J*ANIE! THANKS FOR DOING this," Connor says, waiting for me in front of the True City Community Theater.

"Anything for your mom, Connor," I say, looking around like a nervous fugitive who is standing next door to the police station. Main Street is fairly empty today, but Rob's pickup is parked right in front of the Cop Shop, and my half-assed trucker-hat disguise will not suffice if Rob sees me.

I whisk Connor inside the theater and we are greeted by Mr. Linart. "Well, I'll be buggered! You came back, Janie!" He flies around the stage, passing out scripts. "I've got me Marion now, but Harold Hill's out sick. I'll have to be an actor today."

The stage and set are a mess, a symbolic reminder of everyone's current status—a perpetual state of limbo until Bliss awakens. Different set pieces from signature scenes are strewn all about the stage. There is an unfinished wooden footbridge jutting out from the stage floor, and right where the unfulfilled footbridge ends abruptly, two-by-fours exposing its vulnerable innards, stands a tall bookshelf filled to the brim with what appears to be Mr. Linart's personal library—including several volumes of Shakespeare and a worn copy of *The Catcher in the Rye* with curling Post-it Notes sticking out of it.

"Miss Marion!" Mr. Linart directs me toward the half footbridge, and when I mistakenly go on the opposite side of the bookshelf, he yells in anger, "No, no, no, not there!" He is in the middle of throwing up his hands when he says, "Wait. On second thought, stay there." He makes a camera with his hands and frames me hiding behind the bookshelf. "It's bloody genius! Perfect dramatic irony!"

Harold Hill and Marion Paroo separated by their Shakespearean wall.

Mr. Linart is directing Connor to join the other horns in the orchestra pit and all of the actors to hide backstage when we all hear the front theater door open. I can't see from behind the bookshelf, but I immediately know who it is. The deafening silence among the actors and crew give him away.

"Hey, Chief!" Mr. Linart says, sounding uncomfortable as I hear Rob walk toward the stage.

A nervous Mr. Linart tries to salvage the situation. "Here to check on our progress? You can tell Bliss we're getting everything in place"—he stops, lost in the hopelessness of it all—"for when she comes back."

Rob doesn't respond, and thank God, he doesn't see me behind the wall. I hear footsteps travel up the small steps leading up to the stage, and then they stop. Seconds, minutes, lifetimes go by while we all wait for Rob Anderson to say something, but he doesn't. How could he? How could he tell us all that he tried to walk by the theater door without walking in, but when he heard the music, the horns warming up, the actors practicing vocals, he was drawn inside where he could pretend that everything was okay.

Mr. Linart can't take the tension, and blurts, "So what do you want, Chief?"

The horns are silent in their pit, the actors all quietly hiding behind True City's clouds and storefronts, and I am frozen behind my literary wall of shame. I am not dressed as Kate Snelling, but as Jane Willow, and Jane Willow and Rob Anderson cannot be introduced.

"What do I want?" Rob laughs, and in a sad, dreamy confession says, "I want to be Harold Hill." We all know why. Harold Hill is in the business of miracles.

Nobody moves. We swim around in the despair of it all until Mr. Linart surprises us all by doing the only possible thing that could make anything right. "Here," he says, handing Rob the script, "you're Harold Hill."

Mr. Linart guides Rob over to the other side of my wall and places him directly in front of the bookshelf, with nothing but *The Tempest* between us.

I make deals with the gods. *Please, whatever you do, don't let Mr. Linart slip up and call me Janie—or, worse yet, make me speak and give myself away.*

Through a crack of space between books I see Mr. Linart point to a line on Rob's script, but then disaster strikes. Some sort of crash, a scream, then a giggle. "What a load of cobblers!" Mr. Linart lets out and begins to storm away toward the orchestra pit. The rest of the musicians practice "Till There Was You," but Rob and I have to leave River City behind us.

We are stuck on two different sides of an unmoving wall in the heart of True City.

"Well, don't just stand there!" Mr. Linart yells back at me because he can't yell at Rob the grieving father. "Break a bloody leg and do something, anything, until I sort out whatever mess they've made down there!"

But all I can think about is how Rob looked when he woke up from falling asleep in the chair next to Bliss, that one fleeting moment when he'd forgotten the tragedy of his life, and he glanced at me with hope in his eyes, the corners of his mouth turned upward, ready for joy. I would trade everything I have to see that again. I would walk away, straight into oblivion, to lift the pain from this beautiful man.

God, I am a disaster on a cinematic scale. I have done the impossible. I have actually made an abysmal situation, a truly messed-up-beyond-belief scenario, infinitely worse. I am falling for a man that I can never have, never deserve. Rob Anderson is the unlikely perspective I've been lacking. Rob Anderson is the lens I lost years ago, and the world never looked so good. Too bad it's not mine to take.

Here I am, on the verge of blowing my cover, but all I care about is getting through to Rob Anderson, somehow telling him that the mystery woman behind this wall is crazy about him. I glance down at the stage floor and see one pink, lonely Sweethearts candy, no doubt one of Connor's that he dropped sometime on set.

There it is. Crystal clear. *Don't think, Jane Willow. Just sing what's in your heart.* So I begin a song I sang in my fourth-grade talent show.

"Let me call you sweetheart, I'm in love with you" comes out shaky at first but then finds its legs. There is enough background noise on the set that nobody stops to listen, so it's just Rob and me.

"Let me hear you whisper that you love me too." I sound so sincere when I sing this, I surprise even myself, and I'm sure he can hear my heart thumping. I hear Rob's feet shift a bit.

When I sing "Keep the love-light glowing in your eyes so true," I lose it. The word *true* falls apart at the end, and I clear my throat to disguise my almost-blubber. All of the emotion of the last few weeks unloads and reduces me to the desperate woman that I am.

I hear Mr. Linart, coming back toward us. "Crikey!" he says, "Corn Queen can sing!"

Through the small gap in between books I see Rob's face soften, and his eyes tell me he wants to see this secret, singing sweetheart in person. I actually wonder if he's hoping it's me behind this wall. In my lunacy, I swear I hear someone finish the song with a whisper. "Let me call you sweetheart. I'm in love with you too."

Before he can get to me, before I can continue the ruinous streak I'm on, I slip out behind River City's cardboard pool-hall window and dash past Winthrop Paroo crouching backstage, wondering where his sister is going.

Connor's brass and woodwinds swell, disillusioned with the hope of a reprise, and I crash through the theater's back exit door while the soundtrack plays on.

CHAPTER THIRTY-FOUR

"Y OU NEED A BREAK, Rob," I say in the hospital room two hours after secretly singing to him on stage. I tuck my fake black hair behind my ear. "You're exhausted, and you could use a shower."

"Don't hold back, storyteller." He runs his hands through his unkempt hair and then vulnerability sweeps over him. "Going home sounds—"

"Lonely. I know. That's why you're not going to stay there."

I wonder if he's thinking about Marian Paroo, and I feel a pang of jealousy. Even though I am Marian Paroo.

Batshit crazy. That's what this all is. Bat. Shit. Crazy.

This poor man does need a break, and I need to find something to write about for Sid. I could review a James Bond film from Dad's personal collection, but I'd already gone the classic route once. "Come on," I say, and grab his hand, "it's my professional opinion that you should go home, clean up, and I'll come get you." I tuck Bliss's blanket under her. "We're going to the movies."

"But what if she—"

"I already talked with the nurse. She'll call us if Bliss as much as flutters an eye. Besides, when Bliss wakes up—and she will wake up—you don't want to look like a pile of shit. Teenagers are all about appearances."

"I should talk to your boss about your language," Rob says, an almost-smile creeping in.

"He already knows," I assure him. "Let's go."

When I get to Rob's house, I'm surprised to see the chief of police lives on a farm. "It was my parents' farm." He opens the porch's screen door and invites me in. "They both passed a while back, but I promised them I'd keep it up."

So he is as good a son as he is a father. The last good man. Right here in Iowa. I imagine my parents knew him and knew this. I try not to think about what he will say when he finds out who I am. What I am. What I've done.

He glances over at the entry side table that holds frame after frame of Bliss, from baby pictures to grade school pictures, and one recent one featuring a mouthful of braces. "Told her the farm is hers if she wanted it someday, and she rolled her eyes." He smiles. "When she was little, she wanted to live here forever, but now she can't wait to leave."

Sounds familiar.

We both end up looking at the biggest picture on the table—a brown-eyed woman with long, brown hair pinned up on one side with two pink hollyhocks. She is mid-laugh, unaware of the picture being taken, a sneak-peek snapshot of a fulfilled woman.

When our eyes meet, he says, "That's Molly," with a finality that sucks the air out of the room.

Bliss's mother. Beautiful. Happy. Gone. I can't take my eyes off her.

"Kate?" he says twice because I've forgotten that's my name. "Just gotta do one last thing."

While he turns to walk down the hallway, I look at his kitchen tabletop. In between a pile of mail and some keys is a small leather journal. I wait until he's down the hallway before I open it up to see it's full of poems. His poems. Scribbled in pencil, sometimes pen. All brief. All in third person. I quickly close it, commit one to memory.

Next to the journal I see last week's *Des Moines Register* open to my review column. "What a Schmidt Hole" stares back at me along with Cinegirl's caricature. I turn them both upside down.

I glance over at the DVD cases piled up at the bottom of his entertainment center. Underneath the Indiana Jones trilogy, *The Empire Strikes Back*, *Star Wars*, and *Return of the Jedi*, near a math textbook, is *Breakfast at Tiffany's* stacked on top of something. On closer inspection, I see that it's the screenplay, its pages curled up from wear. On the top right-hand side of the cover showing Audrey in her signature black dress and pearls, it reads *Property of Bliss Anderson*, and I don't doubt it. Rob had told me she'd memorized every line of dialogue and sometimes pretended life was one big screenplay by saying stage directions out loud. *Dusts the bookshelf with aggression*, she'd say while doing her chores, followed by actual, aggressive dusting, and then she'd ask, *Was it good? Was it believable?*

Another DVD case is peeking out, barely, behind a stack of

books just tall enough to hide it. I scoot them to the right enough to see the title, and when I do, warmth rushes through me, starting in my feet, working its way up toward my neck. I take it out to hold it in my hand, stare at the smiling faces on the cover, wonder what all that feels like.

"It's no Fellini," Rob says, reentering the room and reaching for his coat, "but it's a personal favorite of mine." He looks at me for an extra beat, a few seconds longer than he has to, and I lean into the little piece of him he's given me.

Me too.

I gently place the movie back where it belongs and try to figure out how not to look like a snoop.

"You can come if you want," he says and walks toward the front door.

I follow him outside past a corncrib and barn, where we end up at an old John Deere tractor. He climbs up in one smooth, experienced move and extends his hand. This isn't the first time I've been on a tractor, but it's the only time I can recall when I've wanted to be.

"If I don't run her at least once a week, she won't start next time I need her."

His use of the feminine pronoun makes me surprisingly jealous of this tractor, and a flush comes over me. Now I'm nestled tight behind him on a big, green metal seat, and my hands float aimlessly around, trying to land on his waist without seeming too forward.

So we ride. The only sound is the hiccupping and spewing of the tractor, and although he could be asking me a thousand warranted questions—where am I from, how did I get into this line of work, do I have a boyfriend—he doesn't say a word. We ride in silence, taking in the endless cornfields, limitless landscape, a respite from hopelessness.

The tractor lurches forward, forces me to grab him tighter. "What's your favorite flower?" he finally asks in between tractor noises. When I don't say anything for a moment, he adds, "You can tell a lot about a woman by knowing her favorite flower." I can hear he's smiling, trying to make it seem less like he's flirting and more like legitimate small talk.

I think of Molly Anderson and her hollyhocks.

"Lilacs," I tell him.

He wastes no time asking for a reason. "Why?"

This is where I normally weave a lie, divert attention from truths that will make me vulnerable, but today I want to tell Rob Anderson the truth. This is a small, small thing, but he deserves some truth from me. "My mother's favorite flower"—I catch my breath about that—"and"—I smile wide, exposing the underbelly of my exposed heart—"they are the flower of new love."

He nods his head slightly. We ride, comfortable in saying nothing, which says everything.

He lets the tractor slow down, then come to a complete stop. He turns to me, gives me a look I've never seen from him—a long, knowing stare that seems to honor the solidarity we share in bringing Bliss back from wherever she is.

With no noise now except the wind blowing through the cornstalks, I break the silence. "What do you want?" I smile, feeling a bit like Sid and I are exchanging movie lines again, except this is not Sid. This is a man who could make me want to never get off this damn tractor. Channeling my best Jimmy Stewart, I say, "Want the moon? Let me throw a lasso around it, pull it down for you."

He smiles. "No moon yet," he says, looking up at the early evening sky. "Just a tired, tired sun."

"Right," I say, stalling, because he places his hand on my shoulder and scoots me closer to him until there isn't any tractor seat between us. Any adult accomplishment I've achieved evaporates in the crisp air, and I am reduced to the Janie I was with Joey, overanalyzing my facial expressions, where my hands are, my accelerated breathing.

I strengthen my grip on his waist and hang on to Rob Anderson, part-time farmer, full-time father, all-time great Renaissance man who can read you your rights and mention Federico Fellini in the same sentence. He moves his hand from my shoulder to my cheek, leans in and kisses me with the confidence of a man who knows exactly how to kiss a girl in the middle of a cornfield. I breathe in his warmth, let our bodies melt into each other for a moment, and close my eyes. Every look he's given me since I've met him, every word, every brush of his hands moves through me, a new-love electricity, that universal voltage of a first kiss.

When I open my eyes, I see his real smile, the fresh-aired kind, untainted by the sadness that awaits him back in the hospital room. He turns back around, starts up the tractor. Now thoroughly warmed up, she ignites with ease, makes her way through row after row of corn. I hang on to Rob Anderson, richest man in True City. I tuck this away while we ride through the endless cornfield and watch the sun retire, a reminder of what has passed.

We show up at True View in Rob's pickup truck, a less conspicuous choice than his police truck. We don't want questions tonight, because we don't have any answers. Darkness creeps in, and here we sit, two lost souls, one incognito, the other in his Sunday jeans.

Tonight's feature is *Groundhog Day*, and when I see Bill Murray, I feel at home, flashing back to my *Stripes* almost-monologue at the Corn Festival. Rows and rows of cars and pickup trucks, most caked with a day's hard work, are lined up to forget the day. Rob adjusts the radio as the opening sequence begins.

It takes me eight minutes to realize three things.

One: This movie is a stroke of genius. How could I have never written a review of it before, and how many other films have I not given their due? In my head, I formulate draft one of the review I'll send Sid, which features how deftly the oft-ruined theme of second chances is handled here, how right Dad was about the power of revision.

Two: I am Bill Murray's Phil Connors. He is suspicious of happiness, even when it stares him down, day after day, and he is a grade-A asshole on all accounts.

Three: If I had to pick one day to relive over and over again, I would pick this one, with one major revision—Bliss would wake up.

"What stories have you told her?" Rob says while staring, defeated, through the mud-splattered windshield. "That's what you do, right? Tell stories?"

"I've still got a lot of stories."

"What happens when you run out?"

Both of us stare straight ahead, watch Bill Murray and Andi MacDowell dance in a gazebo as slow, fat snow falls.

In the background above the drive-in screen, a falling star streaks across the black sky. I look at Rob, still staring straight ahead at dancing, happy people, larger than life, and I realize he missed the falling star. But this is his star, his shot at a wish, and since I can't have a second chance, I use my wish on him.

Listen to me, star—this one's for Rob Anderson. Give this man what he needs. Make Bliss wake up, and let him find love again. With someone worthy of him.

Bill Murray delivers his last bit of dialogue, tells us that it's finally happened, that today has become tomorrow.

The credits begin to roll, and Rob and I are forced to let this day come to an end, with nothing but a very uncertain tomorrow in our future. I look to the sky one last time, wait for the unlikely event of another shooting star, my own cosmic second chance, but all I see is a sky full of the brightest stars I've ever seen.

CHAPTER THIRTY-FIVE

*R*OB ANDERSON SITS NEXT to a still Bliss while the warm, hopeful sun dares to pour through the hospital-room window.

"Hey, Rob," I say, peeking my head through the cracked hospital door, and search for signs, anything that will tell me if he regrets kissing me last night. I walk through the door, walk over to where he is slumped, defeated, in the chair next to Bliss's bed. Something has happened. The way he looks between slow blinks, the way his hands, strong and capable, gently touch Bliss's face, send a chill through my weary body. I look at him and feel outrageous things, like how I want to ride on the tractor again with him saying nothing at all. How I want to drink coffee with him early in the morning, before the sunlight shines a harsh light on impossible dreams, and I want to save Bliss and somehow be a part of this broken family. When I look at him again, I see True City's chief of police, the man who will soon arrest me for hit and run. Just yesterday, he told me, told Kate, that he was making his case and wouldn't stop until he found out who hurt his Bliss. I believe him, because I can feel it already. Rob Anderson is the good man who will never forgive me for this lying charade.

"Statistically speaking…" he says to me, to the universe, as he stares out the window at the parking lot below. The unfinished sentence trails out of him, lingers in the sterile hospital air as an audible manifestation of one man's rock bottom. "Statistically speaking," he repeats, just like the doctors must have, "her chances of regaining consciousness are now very slim. It's day twenty-one," he whispers. "Three weeks." He shuts his eyes, some sort of brief respite from a moment too heavy to bear all at once. "Time's up," he says, his voice breaking now.

Chances are slim. Chances. Where are you, Dad? Where are you, Harold Hill?

Rob could see the confusion in my eyes. But she was showing progress. But she was getting better. But she was coming back to life.

He regurgitates what the doctor must have said. "This happens sometimes. A coma patient will have a short burst of activity, often all in one day, almost like some godforsaken, cosmic last hurrah, often signaling the end," he says, staring at the shiny, buffed floor, a mirror for his dismal reflection. "And then, just like that…" But he is unable to speak anymore.

I wondered why the doctor had been less than enthusiastic when Bliss had shown us a flurry of activity. He knew what we didn't, what we weren't willing to see. His job is to consider numbers, facts, statistics. That is to say, she is not his Bliss.

The doctor walks in, clinging to his clipboard, moving slower than usual, probably postponing what he has to say with each exaggerated step. He looks as sad as a doctor can look. "Good morning," he says, the declaration sounding ridiculous to all of us, including him. He walks to Bliss, shines a light in her eye, pokes her arm with some sharp-looking tool, and as if he knows what's going to happen—nothing—he abandons the routine, stops, takes a big breath.

"Don't say 'statistically speaking,'" Rob says, adding, "She's not a statistic." He pauses. "She's all I have left." I want to tell him that's not true—he has me. And he still has her; he just doesn't know it yet. She will wake up.

The doctor raises his chin, pulls back his shoulders, looks like he's trying to remember taking notes on this in medical school, some unit of study on grieving in which you learn how to tell a father his only child is going to die. "This is a very difficult prognosis to deliver." He transfers his clipboard from one hand to another, giving him another two seconds before having to deliver the final blow. "Her pupils are unresponsive…and she's not responding to painful stimuli anymore. It's my job to tell you that, statistically, when these things happen"—he quickly adds *historically* like it's somehow better—"historically, only 4 percent of coma patients recover consciousness after three weeks."

The doctor looks to me. "You're the therapist, right?" When I nod, he adds, "She can attest to the same…data." With the agility of a trained bad-news deliverer, he cuts his losses, prepares to move on to the next patient on his rounds. "I recommend getting a good night's sleep and considering…tomorrow…making a decision."

Nobody is having trouble filling in the doctor's words after he walks out the door, but I am the only one who isn't accepting them.

I start in, tucking Bliss's hair behind her ear and smoothing her blanket. "That's just one person's opinion, Rob. Doctors are wrong all the time—"

"Why do you care so much?" He's now resorted to staring at his hands, folded in a half-abandoned prayer formation. "I'm serious." He takes off in a new, angrier direction. "How dare you tell me how to feel? You walked in here out of nowhere… You know nothing about me…or Bliss." He turns his head now, like he can't bear to look at me. "Take your paycheck. Go home. This can't be the first patient you couldn't save."

His words shoot through me, send a sharp pain to my center. Does he really mean what he's saying? Does he want me to leave? I look away and catch my breath. The reality is that I truly don't know why I care so much. It now goes beyond the accident, beyond my feeling responsible. When I look at her, I want her to have the life I never can. I want to be her Harold Hill, help her realize her dreams, help her *Believe so*, even in the darkest of times. I want to revive my own forgotten dreams, will my dreams onto hers.

So why do I care? There is no way to answer his question. There is no way to explain that I cannot give up on her, that I am responsible not only for her pain, but for something far beyond that, something that inexplicably feels like her happiness.

"She's going to wake up," I say, standing by her side. "I just have to find the right words to—"

"The right fucking words?" Rob Anderson explodes out of the chair. "What the hell is wrong with you? She's gone! My baby girl is gone!" he cries, and with anger that has to go somewhere, he walks to the hospital door and punches it. "God…damn it," he says, cradling his crumpled fist.

"Oh my God." I run to him, perusing the damage. "I'll get some ice," I say, but before I can get out the door, I run into someone coming in.

"Charlotte!" I say as she walks in with Janelle and Connor. Panicked, I back up into the room, trying to pretend I'm not hiding behind the pink curtain dividing Bliss's room from the adjoining one.

She stares first at Rob and his throbbing hand, then back at me. I am now resigned to my whole world unraveling—me going to jail directly and losing Charlotte, again, and Bliss drifting, uncontested, into oblivion.

Charlotte's face contorts into a scrunched-up confusion. "Janie?" she whispers, walking over to me.

"Kate," I say, my eyes wide and pleading. "Kate Snelling." I extend my hand. "I'm here from the, uh, National Institute for In-Transition"—I sigh—"Coma Patients."

"Mom?" Janelle says, daggers back. "What's she doing here?"

"Let's go out into the hall, um..." Charlotte searches for my fake name.

"Kate," I say, closing my eyes for a chance to swim in the blackness that is this nightmare.

"Okay, Kate," she forces out, raised eyebrows now pointing toward the door. "Let's go out here, and I can introduce you to my daughter, a good friend of Bliss's."

Rob, elevating his hand, jumps into the tension. "Do you two know each other?"

"No," both Charlotte and I say.

"Totally," Janelle snarls.

"I, uh, met her a couple of days ago when you stepped out, Rob, but I just...forgot her name."

Rob takes turns staring at the two of us. "I'm...gonna...go get some ice," he says and heads toward the door.

When Rob leaves, Connor stands paralyzed, staring at Bliss, and Janelle, already wiping her eyes, walks over to the bed. "Hey, Blissy."

Charlotte spits out questions in loud, incredulous whispers. "Why are you wearing a wig? What are you doing here? How did Rob hurt his hand? Has Bliss moved at all today or talked or—"

"No," I say, touching my fake hair. "She hasn't shown any response for two days, but she's going to wake up; it's just a matter of time."

Charlotte looks into my eyes the way a lifelong friend can and sees me in all my deceitful glory. She softens, waits for her oldest friend to tell her the truth. "You don't even know Bliss. What's going on, Janie?"

Connor, Janelle, and Charlotte all stare at me, the stranger standing before them. "I…I did something unforgivable, and I'm trying to make it right."

"Janie? You're freaking me out!" Charlotte says, but she's interrupted by a knock on the hospital door.

"Sorry to interrupt," the nurse says and scurries in, carrying a new IV bag.

"It's okay," Charlotte says, staring at her two solemn, red-faced children. "We were just leaving." Charlotte looks at me. "When you want to tell me what's going on"—she pauses, then adds "Kate" in a tone so sad I want to throw myself out the hospital-room window—"you know where to find me." She collects her children, stops in front of the door, her back turned on me for once. "You always have."

I stand in the middle of the room, feeling more alone than I have in eighteen lonely years.

"Ms. Snelling?" The nurse stops what she's doing, stares at me with a nurturing concern that I both admire and detest. "Gettin' pretty tense in here."

"What gave it away?" I say, still standing on my island of shame.

"Let's see," she says, hanging Bliss's IV bag on a small hook. "A grieving father's injured fist, a coma patient who hasn't so much as moved a finger in three days, and some serious tension between you and that red-headed lady."

She finishes her tasks and orders me to sit down. I am tired. She is convincing. So I sit.

"Look, I don't know much, but after watching you here for the last three weeks, I know one thing for sure—this girl means a hell of a lot more to you than just a patient on your list, and I'm not asking questions; you obviously have your reasons." She walks closer to me. "I just want to say that I admire what you tried to do."

We both stare at Bliss, breathing in and out, wherever she is.

"And it's none of my business, but..." She folds her hands like she's trying to will herself not to say any more. "But I see the way Mr. Anderson looks at you, and, well..."

I turn to her, my silence asking her to tell me something, anything that doesn't sound like how much he hates me, or should hate me.

She unfolds her hands, puts them in her uniform pockets. "It's like a little of the grief disappears from his face when you're in the room." She smiles. "Those lilacs... He asked me to bring them from my yard, because he said you like them. This whole town's seen him go through a lot: first, his wife, now Bliss." She stops, one eyebrow raised in a hopeful arch. "We're all rootin' for him, you know, that he'll find love again." Her face is soft but serious. "He's a good man."

The lilacs are bursting out of an old mason jar, and their scent fills the room with memories of Mother. *Be nice.*

"Have you ever wanted to will someone back to life?" I ask nicely.

I expect her answer to be every patient she's ever lost, or her mother, or some favorite aunt, but instead she nods, says, "It's not a some*one*, per se." Her eyes filled with tears now.

"I'm sorry," I say. "I didn't mean to—"

"No, it's okay." She blinks away her tears. "It's so silly. I know she was just a dog." She laughs. "I must sound crazy, crying about a dead dog."

"No, not at all. She was part of your family. Family is important," I say, trying to control my own emotions as I think of my parents, my only family, gone forever. I take this kind woman's hand. "I'm so sorry. When did you lose your…"

"Allie," she says. "Short for Alabaster. Prettiest white Akita I've ever seen." She takes a deep breath. "Happened three weeks ago. Was my fault. I let her out after nine…way later than I usually do. That damn blacktop is a deathtrap after nightfall." Her voice breaks. "She got hit by a car. Same night as Bliss, just a half mile farther down the road. What are the odds?"

And then my knees buckle and I need to sit down. Images from that night flood my foggy brain. The shadow moving across the road. My vision distracted by grief. The flash of white. Speak. Find the words. Ask her. "Who… Where do you live?"

"I'm Melinda," she says. "Melinda Stephens. Been staying with my folks since my divorce."

The Stephens' farm. Blacktop road. After nine o'clock.

Give me a sign, Universe. That was what I'd said. That was what I'd asked for, to find out what I was here for.

I still don't have an answer for that, but I am one step closer to the truth.

"I gotta go." I give Melinda the most apologetic hug I can give. "I'm so sorry," I say, and I mean it. "Tell Rob I'll be back," I say, gathering my things before giving Bliss one last kiss on her forehead.

"Wait for me," I whisper to her. "I'm coming back for you."

I jump in Dad's truck, drive home in a blur, run through the front door, out to the garage, and lift back the tarp covering the Aston Martin. When I'd covered the car three weeks ago, I'd been too devastated, too afraid to look closely at the damage because that meant looking closely at what I'd done. But here it is now, evidence waiting patiently for me to find the courage to look for its truth.

The tarp flies back, revealing the front bumper, and the dent I vaguely remember seeing is still there, but there is something else—barely visible, but there. I crouch down, glide my trembling hand over the bottom edge of my California license plate until I feel it. Lodged between the left side of the license-plate frame and the underbelly of the chrome bumper is a perfect little tuft of silky white fur.

Chapter Thirty-Six

INT. THE MIDDLE—TODAY

FADE IN: Auditorium

BLISS watches her life play out on the big screen. The crowded audience watches with her and eats popcorn. The screen shows BLISS and her boyfriend MITCH in his truck parked on a dark gravel road.

> **BLISS**
> (breathless)
> Can we slow down?

> **MITCH**
> (kisses her harder)
> Shh. You love it and you know it.

BLISS
(louder)
Please, Mitch. It's not that I
don't want to do it…just not yet.
It's only been a few weeks and…

MITCH
(drunk and agitated)
What the hell, Bliss! We had fun
at the party… I like you… Why are
you being so lame?

BLISS
(lowers head)
Why are you being such a dick?

MITCH
(grabbing her)
You don't mean that, baby.

BLISS
(trying to push him away)
Just stop it, Mitch.

MITCH
(reaching under her skirt)
I can think of plenty of girls who
would just love to…

BLISS
(disgusted, reaches for
the door handle)
I'd rather walk home, thank you.

MITCH
(angrier now)
Come on, Bliss!

(anger turns to worry)
I'm in deep shit if you walk home
in the dark.

BLISS
(walking with a purpose down
the side of the road)
Go home, Mitch. Have a good time.
You'll make a better date for
yourself than me.

MITCH
(accelerating, talking through
the open passenger-door window)
Goddamn it, Bliss. Get back in
the truck! I'm serious! None of
this ever happened, do you understand me? Not the party, not this
bullshit in the truck, not you running back home like a crazy bitch.

Now get back in the car, and we'll
get our stories straight. I'm not
getting in trouble over this.

The audience watches in horror as the big screen
shows BLISS running faster down the road and
a panicked MITCH accelerate one last time, and
swerve, out of control, toward BLISS.

BLISS gets out of her seat, the only person
standing in the auditorium. She stares at the
big screen, then lowers her head for a moment, a
sort of realization of where she is, where she
isn't.

> **BLISS**
> (looks back up, talks to the screen)
> I remember now.

> **GREEN-DRESS GIRL**
> (stands up next to her,
> takes her hand)
> I'm so sorry, Blissy.

> (she turns into a peacock
> and flies away)

> **BLISS**
> Wait! Where are you going?

(whispers)
You're going home, aren't you,
Janelle?

BLISS's life continues to play out for the auditorium, her world, to see. BLISS watches herself
squint at the bright headlights of MITCH'S red
Ford truck as it barrels down the road. When the
truck gets a few yards from BLISS, MITCH slows
and keeps his distance. But not for long. MITCH
angrily gestures for her to get in the truck,
getting angrier when she doesn't, and suddenly
loses control. The truck veers first to the left
and then to the right, hitting BLISS.

The audience lets out a collective shriek as BLISS's
body hurls through the starry Iowa night in slow
motion, like an astronaut hurtling through space.

BLISS leaves her seat, walks down the aisle, up
the steps to the stage, past AUDREY HEPBURN, who
looks at her with a sorry sadness. BLISS touches
the giant screen, the image of her body lying
lifeless in the ditch. She places her hand on her
now-throbbing head.

                    BLISS
        (looks up, past the ceiling)
        I don't want to go back.

WOMAN (O.S.)

No, Bliss! You need to wake up!
It's time to go home.

BLISS

(sleepy)

I'm so tired. I just want to sleep.
And go with you.

(barely audible)

There's nothing to go back for.

WOMAN (O.S.)

Bliss!

BLISS

(hears something)

Do you hear that?

OTHER-PLACE NOISE (O.S.)

Statistically speaking…

BLISS

(tired, confused)

Who is that? Who's saying that?

(shielding her eyes)

Where is that light coming from?

OTHER-PLACE NOISE (O.S.)

My baby girl is gone!

BLISS

(drifting in and out of sleep)

Dad?

WOMAN (O.S.)

(distant)

I have to go now. I'm so sorry, Bliss. Don't fall asleep, Bliss.

(crying)

Go home to Dad.

Suddenly, all of the hollyhocks retreat, growing backward, up the auditorium walls, up and out, bursting through the ceiling. It breaks apart, exposing what's above, a heavenly sky. Hundreds of monarch butterflies, in mass exodus, fly away together toward the celestial clouds.

BLISS

(eyelids heavy)

Bye, Mommy.

WOMAN (O.S.)

(a distant whisper)

I love you, Bliss. You're everything I ever wanted.

BLISS crumples into a heap on the stage, her dress
enveloping her in a blanket of yellow chiffon as
she collapses and, finally, shuts her eyes.

AUDREY HEPBURN
Ladies and gentlemen, Bliss Anderson.

The audience claps as closing credits of BLISS's
life—parents, friends, teachers—scroll in perfect cadence down the screen.

AUDREY HEPBURN sings "Moon River" into the podium
microphone, reminding us just how far away it is.

An orchestra erupts, swells with the emotion of
a whole auditorium.

The audience mouths what they already know. So
much life to be lived.

CHAPTER THIRTY-SEVEN

*R*OB ANDERSON SITS NEXT to Bliss's hospital bed, clinging to dwindling hope and some sort of box.

"Hey." I walk to him, to them. I want to feel better that I didn't put her in this hospital bed, but I don't. I want her to wake up more than ever. When I get her to wake up, I will find out who did this.

He doesn't look up, yet I somehow know he's comforted by my being here. I wonder how I'll convince Rob that Bliss isn't finished here yet, that she has so much more living to do, and she deserves our believing in her. I am startled by my own thoughts. How I imagine us together, him asking me questions about my LA life, me bringing him lunch at the station, but this daydream of a fantasy doesn't work without Bliss, without our Bliss to watch grow and live.

He reaches into the box sitting on his lap and pulls out a fist-sized rock with the word *Daddy* written on it in purple marker. "She made this for me on Father's Day when she was seven," he says, taking turns staring at it, then at Bliss, looking more still than ever. "I was her rock," he says, choking on the words. "That's what she used to say."

I watch Rob Anderson, Bliss's rock, shatter into a million pieces. He lets out a gasp, an audible giving up, and places the box of keepsakes on the tiled floor.

I touch his shoulder, a reminder that I feel his pain, but I cannot comfort him more than that. Not now. Not when so much work needs to be done. I walk to her, whisper to her. "Where are you, Bliss?" I say. "It's time to come back."

She is so still that I have to watch her chest to see if she's breathing.

"Time is running out, Bliss." When I say this, Rob shakes his head at my naive use of the present tense. "We're running out of time, Bliss," I say again, louder.

"Stop, Kate." Rob doesn't sound angry anymore, just defeated, and the kind of broken that sucks the air out of a room. "The doctor came in twenty minutes ago. Wants to know what I want to do."

When I hear this, something in me breaks. Layer upon layer of defensive protection, eighteen years in the making, is stripped away in this place, in this moment, and I am raw with vulnerability and desperation. Right here, right now, I officially want to trade my life for hers. Make her wake up. Take whatever you want. My career. My last chance at happiness. My life.

"Did you hear me, Kate? The doctor wants…" His voice trails away, and I push it toward the darkness in the room where I can't reach it.

I don't look at him. Instead, I focus on her. "Bliss, I have a story for you. There once was a happy, precocious, full-of-life girl who—"

"Stop, Kate."

"—grew up in a beautiful land surrounded by majestic walls of corn and the brightest stars in all the world. She loved her mother and father so much that it hurt to even think of it. When she was little, she never imagined leaving, but when she got older—"

"Kate." He says my name not as a question this time, but as an answer, like he's figured out I'm not talking about Bliss anymore.

"—she made new, pretend dreams, because her old dreams, the broken ones that had to be buried deep in the black Iowa soil, were too painful to think about, and then eventually, after she'd already lost a lifetime more than she could imagine, she lost everything."

I wipe my wet face with my sleeve.

"Kate?" Rob looks at me. "You okay?" he says, seeing a glimpse of Janie Willow.

"And then she met someone she didn't even know she needed. Someone young and hopeful, who deserves to be happy. And if you wake up"—I try to see through my blurry vision—"then maybe she can forgive herself for…"

"Kate?"

"Wake up!" I cry at the still-sleeping Bliss.

"Kate! That's enough."

The stillness in the room highlights the horrible truth: she is not going to wake up.

My chest tightens with the love I want to give, with the very idea of her smiling, laughing, running toward her future. My legs weaken, and my whole body turns numb as I slump onto the bed with her.

She is not going to wake up. I have lost both of them. In one lifetime. She is not going to wake up.

I force myself to tell the truth. "I thought I could do it, Rob" comes out as a whisper, and I turn my face so he won't see me. "I thought I could save her. I'm so sorry."

He walks over to the bed, puts his arm around me, and for a long time, we are silent, just breathing with her, in and out.

In and out.

In and out.

All we can do is wait.

We look at her left big toe painted with bright-purple polish, now starting to grow out, peeking out from underneath the end of the blanket.

"Right before the accident, she asked me how tall she would get, when she was fully grown." He smiles. "Because taller actresses get more parts than shorter ones."

I sniff away sadness for Rob's sake and smile. "How tall was... her mom?"

"Not very," he says, "but that's irrelevant."

My eyes ask the obvious question.

"Molly couldn't carry a child... She'd always known it, but all she ever wanted was to be a mother, so when Bliss came along, even though we were so young..."

"Came along?"

"Yeah. We adopted her when she was just eleven months old. Right after we were married."

A soft lump forms in my throat.

"I don't really believe in fate, but Molly did... She knew Bliss was supposed to be ours."

"How?" I manage. "How did you get her?"

"Regular adoption takes months, years sometimes, so when a friend of my mother's told us there was an unwanted baby here in town—we were living in Davenport at the time—we hired a lawyer, who worked it out with the people at the state office and then went to meet her. Frank and Rita Stephens had been taking care of her temporarily." His face lights up when he says, "It was love at first sight," but then he sobers. "Bliss asked if she could meet her biological mother for her eighteenth birthday... one more thing she'll miss."

He is talking, but I am underwater, drowning, and his words are simply muffled utterings. I hear the words *corn* and *maze* and *found in a canvas bag* as I flounder and the room begins to spin. I come up for air and hear him clearer.

"This is all she had when they found her." Rob reaches into the box on the floor, pulls out my blanket of stars.

I walk over to him, take the blanket, breathe it in. The yester-year scents swirling in it send me sinking, farther and farther, as I free-fall backward into a sea of memories. I float down slowly, and I see her up above me, all alone.

Leave the darkness behind. Move toward the light.

Go get her.

This time, go get her.

I push against the weight of the water and swim through it, going up, up, up until I break through the surface, and suddenly I am in the corn maze and she is there and I take her home.

"Kate! Can you hear me?" Rob says, his arms around me, holding me up. "You fainted. I caught you on the way down."

"Rob." I lift my head and take his face in my hands. Without thinking, I kiss him like he needs reviving, but maybe it's me who needs it. "It's going to be okay." I take off my wig, let my long, blond hair fall to my shoulders. I dare to smile even though he looks paralyzed with shock. "Just trust me, Rob."

I take his hand, and we go to her. "Bliss, listen to me. I lost you once, but I'm not losing you again." *Breathe. Breathe.* "Eighteen years ago..." *Breathe. Breathe.* "I loved you so much...but I couldn't..." *Breathe. Breathe.*

"Oh my God." Rob turns to me. "Who—"

"Bliss, listen to me," I say, touching her face. "I need you to wake up."

"Who are you?" Rob stammers. "How did you...?"

I study her eyelids, frozen and still, and know it is time to say the words that I never thought I'd get to say, the words that are all we have left.

"Bliss, I'm..." *Breathe. Breathe.* "Eighteen years ago, I gave birth to you, and I've loved you ever since." My tears fall to her face, and I gently wipe them with the palm of my hand. "That is to say, I'm your mother."

"Wait," Rob says, looking at the wig on the floor. "Who... What's..."

She makes no sign of movement, so I take her hand in mine and lean into her silence.

Suddenly I am there again—in my bathtub, screaming for her to enter this world—and I don't have to search hard for the words that make it happen. Three words. Three words prompt her birth.

It's just us.

Nobody else can fix this.

It's just us.

Now here we are, needing another birth, another entering into this world, and I hang on these three words like a Corn Queen hangs on the hope of rain.

"It's just us," I tell her. *We can do this. Again.* "I am your mother, and I am telling you we can do this." *Wake up. Nobody else can help us. Wake up, Bliss. I'm home now. I get it. I know why I'm here. I know why I'm home. I'd asked for a sign, and I got it. I got my Bliss. The universe gave me a reason to stay. The world outside now seems like a world I don't want to be in without you.*

I place the blanket on her and tell the truth. "I made this for you because…you are my star." I cry. "It's just us."

BLISS
(groggy)
I fell asleep, but something woke
me up. I think I'm supposed to
wake up.

AUDREY HEPBURN
I know.

(she smiles)
You've won! You've won, Bliss!

BLISS
(gets up, stands in middle of stage)
What did I win?

                    AUDREY HEPBURN
                 (with the wisdom of a
                  legendary film icon)
            A second chance.

                        BLISS
            Chance? At what?

                    AUDREY HEPBURN
                        (nods)
            At the great *Show of Life*.

              (walks off-stage, waves goodbye)
            Enjoy *The Show*, Bliss.

An endless red carpet unrolls. AUDREY HEPBURN
follows it toward the horizon. BLISS starts down
the red carpet, follows AUDREY toward a horizon
from which she knows she can't return.

                        BLISS
               (moving toward the horizon,
                despite AUDREY waving her back)
            So…tired.

                OTHER-PLACE VOICES (O.S.)
            It's just us.

BLISS
(repeats the words)
It's just us.

OTHER-PLACE VOICES (O.S.)
I am your mother, and I am telling
you we can do this.

BLISS
(confused)
Mom's gone. Who is this?

OTHER-PLACE VOICES (O.S.)
I made this for you because…you
are my star.

BLISS takes a moment, thinks about what the voice
has said, thinks about who exactly could say such
words. A firestorm of electricity shoots through
her brain, then races through her body. This is her
death scene and come-back-to-life scene all at once.
There's a lot at stake. She lifts her chin slightly,
acknowledges the poor lighting, wonders what music
will be added here in post-production, but then she
forgets all that. Remembers she has a mother.

She smiles, waves goodbye to AUDREY HEPBURN, and
turns toward home.

BLISS

(wakes up)

CHAPTER THIRTY-EIGHT

*Y*OU FOUND ME," I hear a quiet voice say.

My hand instinctively covers my heart, beating hard with purpose. This voice is not Rob's. This voice is tired and groggy and the sweetest voice I've ever heard. I force myself to watch her lips, to see if they move. They do.

"I knew… I knew you'd come back for me someday," she says, eyes now open to reveal a color blue that looked like home.

Bliss.

My daughter.

"Bliss!" I say, flooding the hospital blanket with tears, taking her hand.

"Baby girl, you're back!" Rob says, taking the other hand, touching her face.

Bliss smiles. "I'm so sorry, Daddy." She looks at me. "We have the same hair."

Rob wipes his eyes and looks at me. "Thank you…whoever you are."

"Willow," I say, extending my shaking hand. "Janie Willow."

The three of us—Bliss waking up in her bed, Rob on one side, me on the other—form a continuous circle of energy with our linked hands.

That night on the blacktop flashes before me. If I didn't hit Bliss, then who did?

Rob and I wait and watch. We wait for Bliss to show us she's ready for the question. Together, after three hours of easing her back into the world she'd abruptly left, Rob asks the question that needs asking.

"What happened, Bliss?" he asks in a soft voice, trying not to upset her.

She exhales in preparation and, after a few seconds, whispers "Mitch" and then again, this time louder. "Mitch."

The details drop like quiet little bombs.

A dark gravel road. Told him to stop. Started to walk home. Truck roared toward me. Left me by the side of the road.

The truth of it pollutes the room: he was afraid he'd lose his college scholarship.

Upon hearing the news, Rob Anderson, True City's chief of police and Bliss's loving father, flies out of the room with arresting speed.

While Rob apprehends Mitch Blackman, I stare at Bliss's peaceful countenance and reluctantly decide to let her rest, even though I want to make up for a lifetime of missed memories.

I dial Charlotte's number, because I need to be the one to tell her. Good news is best delivered by a best friend. So are secrets.

"Char?" I say, trying to steady my voice.

"Janie?" There is a pause, and I consider her possible questions. *Where are you? Why were you in Bliss's hospital room dressed in a disguise?* But the loudest question rings out clear in deafening silence. *Why did you lie to me?*

"Yeah, it's me...Janie," I say, letting the name, my name, announce itself as a piece of me returns, and I somehow feel whole after all these years.

Hallowed be thy name. Forgive me my trespasses. Forgive us our trespasses.

"She's back, Char," I manage. "Bliss is awake."

Silence.

She cries into the phone for a few seconds, followed by, "Janelle! Connor! Get down here!"

Footsteps tramping down stairs. Screaming. Cries of joy.

"Char?"

"Yeah" sneaks out between sobs.

"Are you sitting down?"

"Yeah," Charlotte answers, but I hear the weariness in her voice.

I wait a beat, because I have already waited too long. I say a silent goodbye to the woman, the girl, who bore the burden of this secret for so long.

So I confess to Charlotte the sin that consumed Janie Willow.

I tell my best friend that eighteen years ago I had a baby girl. I tell her that she was made of light and pure happiness and all things perfect, and I abandoned her in the Nelsons' corn maze.

I tell her that somehow, after losing her, I have her back now, and how will I ever be able to repay the universe for this gift?

I wait for my choir director friend to say *amen* or something equally godly, but instead, she speaks as a new Charlotte, reborn in the glow of hope. "The universe doesn't charge for the hope of tomorrow, Janie, just as long as you don't squander today."

We both digest that, and my gut tells me it's as much about her as me. Together, in silence, we sing a thousand hallelujahs for yesterday, for today, and for the second chances that await us both tomorrow.

Love is patient, they say. *Out of the ashes*, they say. *Fire before rebirth*, they say.

Yep.

CHAPTER THIRTY-NINE

J DON'T LEAVE HER SIDE for the next three days. I watch her sleep. I watch her breathe. I watch the way her eyes light up when she tells me about her puffy red snowsuit and her first memory of snow, and when in kindergarten she was Tinkerbell for Halloween and gave all her classmates the ability to fly. *Of all the babies in all the world, I got the best one.*

The world stops so I can breathe her in, then it starts again, spins with intent, in honor of what the future holds. That is to say, the world stops for love.

She is awake. She is fine. She is mine.

It is time. My life isn't really real until he knows about it, so I pick up the phone.

"Sid," I say to the man who took care of me during my lost years, who taught me to do the hard work, to sometimes edit with care instead of delete with abandon.

"Jane." I hear so much in his voice. Relief. Restrained impatience. Acceptance.

The two of us sit in silence for a moment, so far apart, so together.

He saves me like he always does, speaking first because he can tell I'm on the verge of vulnerability. "Your little *Groundhog Day* piece was a hit. Maybe you should write from the middle of a cornfield more often."

"I'm considering it."

He leaves this alone, pretends I never said it, because he hopes I don't mean it. We both know that Cinegirl will go on. I am Cinegirl, wherever I end up, but we both know there has been a shift. Sid presses on like editors must. "You and Phil Connors have a lot in common."

"Is that so?"

"Hello…emotionally unavailable." Sid laughs. "You're arrogant, charming, and shockingly unwilling to change."

"Aw. You think I'm charming?"

Sid lets a moment of silence pass by before he reveals something he seems to fear and hope simultaneously. "You could use a good, old-fashioned time loop and an endless Groundhog Day from which to start anew."

I know exactly how I'd like that day to go.

"So did you do it?" he asks after a heavy pause. Doubt, or maybe fear, oozes from the outskirts of his question, and I can tell he's unsure of what my answer will be. "Did you do what you needed to do?" He takes another pause, for himself as much as me. "Did you fix what needed to be fixed?"

Sid is the closest version of my father I'll ever get—the one person who knows about the soft inside I keep under wraps; that alone could turn me into a blubbering mess, but there is something in the way he asks, the way he is rooting for me that makes me take pause. I want to say yes: what needed to be fixed is fixed, she is okay, and as it turns out, she is the only thing that could possibly have fixed me.

"Well?"

"I've been given"—I try to swallow the words, but they deserve better—"a gift, Sid." A cry-gasp escapes without my consent. "Can you fucking believe it, Sid? Me!"

"There it is."

"Jesus, don't give me shit about cursing right now, Sid. This is my goddamned close-up. Against all odds, I am the lead in a story so unbelievably beautiful I'd have to write a scathing review of it just to maintain my reputation as an unsentimental critic."

"Done yet?"

"Yes," I say, then revise. "No. Sid, I have a..." The words just stop. I know the rest of the sentence, hear it in my head, but the words won't come out. Instead, they dance around like they know better. And they do. No words can possibly do her justice. "Sid, I have someone I want you to meet."

He takes a beat, then says, "Always wanted to visit Iowa."

"Really?"

"Nah."

He hears me laugh, but the tears I keep to myself. So here we are, Sid and I, in our third act, not yet ready for the closing credits to scroll by, yet hesitant to see the next scene. True cinephiles know that most beginnings are really just endings in disguise. I wonder if it's happening to him right now too—the movie reel of our minds playing those movie endings that make us all feel a little bit more alive—big *Cuckoo's Nest* Chief freeing himself, freeing us, by crashing through the mental hospital window, Truman leaving his fabricated world and taking his first steps into the beautiful unknown, Butch and Sundance going out in style, the only way they know how.

"So…"

"So…"

We both know we've got to stop this sentimental train wreck, yet I can't bring myself to do it.

"Look," I say, "it's not like we're riding off into the sunset just yet, Sid. We have a whole career before we live happily—"

He hangs up before I can deliver the line that we both know comes next, the cliché of a line that fairy tales dare to repeat at will, that critics like me laugh off the page, and that Hollywood is downright addicted to.

"Damn you, Sid," I say to no one, but what I really mean is *Thank you, Sid. Thank you for everything.*

Music cue.

Fin.

Credits roll.

EPILOGUE

Six Weeks Later
True City Community Theater

𝓗 AROLD HILL HAS WAITED for her. Of course he has. *Believe so.* All of them —Mr. Linart, Connor, the whole cast and crew, all of True City—have waited while Bliss slept, dreaming dreams that none of us will ever know, and now, Harold Hill and Marion Paroo will take the stage together. True City's Main Street is alive and bustling with people waiting to see the miracle of a girl who was willed back to life, the same girl who will now act out the story of a con man, a librarian, and a small-town miracle that was no miracle at all.

I wear for the first time the black silk gown I'd bought for the hope of walking the red carpet with Mom and Dad. Sidney had it sent it to me, no questions asked, which is quite a miracle in itself. Even though it's too formal for the occasion and will prompt comments about putting on airs, about catching a cold, about "What would Jack and Mary think?" I don't care, because Mom and Dad wouldn't care. It's yet another chance to right a wrong, to revise a missed opportunity. That is to say, it's our red carpet do-over. They would be so proud of Bliss, and they would sit with me, front row, smiling at her on stage just like they smiled at me while I sang and danced until it rained.

It is true that I look ridiculous with Mom's country-blue winter coat over my gown, but nobody seems to notice any more than they'd notice a parka over church clothes or a snowsuit over a Halloween costume. In my left pocket, I have two butterscotch candies. *Pick one out, kid; the butterscotch ones are good.* In my right pocket, I have the patch I cut from Bliss's blanket of stars. I imagine the years it spent under our willow tree, wondering if it would ever see the light. So tonight I embody us all—Mom, Dad, Sid and all things Hollywood, and my Bliss.

On the sidewalk outside the theater, I see Melinda Stephens walking her new, white Akita puppy that was given to her— anonymously, of course. It sure feels good making things right.

I walk in the theater's main doors, carrying a dozen roses that I'll give Bliss when she bows later and the crowd cheers for a performance beyond her years. I am nervous. This makes giving a critic's acceptance speech seem like a Saturday matinee. But we have practiced. Every line. Every facial expression. Every gesture. We've got this. She's got this.

I am still nervous. Guess this is how it is for mothers.

Charlotte sits next to me, wearing her new holiday sweater that she claims she found in the back of her closet. But I know better. Midwesterners always downplay a celebration, even when they find themselves engulfed in the very fanfare they've designed.

Next to her sits Julia, her high-flying lover, dressed in a black chiffon skirt pulled over her black leotard, and as the overhead stage lights bounce off the tiny little sequins in Julia's skirt, I am struck by the wonder of it all—the will of life, the will of love, and the inevitable show that must go on.

Janelle sits to my left and in a fit of excitement—for the show, for her best friend, Bliss, for the holiday spirit that makes people stop being assholes for a minute—she grabs my hand and gives it a little squeeze. So, in turn, I grab Charlotte's hand to form an undeniable trifecta of family, friendship, and a childhood not forgotten. Audrey Hepburn starts to strum "Moon River" somewhere in the recesses of my mind, telling me what the future holds, but my heart is heavy with the world Charlotte and I have already seen together in this lifetime. She is my forever friend. Nothing could be more right.

Well, it could be a little more right. I look for Rob, who is meeting us here because he is coming straight from the station. He will arrive in uniform, so handsome that he looks like he's merely playing a cop in a movie, and he will arrive on time, because he's a good father. He will by now have read the letter I left for him earlier—the letter in which I tried to do the right thing.

It really is the right thing to do, but this time, the critic hates being right, and I suddenly wish I hadn't written it at all. I wish I hadn't told him that he's the only man I've ever known who can shoot a gun and write a poem in the same day. I wish I hadn't told him that the last two months have been the best days of my life, that when I'm with him I have no words. I wish I hadn't told him that it's unfair to assume that he'll love me back, because the alternative would mean saying no to this perfect family that was thrust upon us, and maybe he was just playing along because it might be the best for Bliss. Maybe I was being selfish wanting it all. I wish I wouldn't have given him the ultimatum of showing up at my door tonight when he brings Bliss by after the show. I wish I wouldn't have said any of it now, because if he doesn't show up, for Bliss and I that means *it's just us* again, and while that is enough, God knows it is, it's not quite the complete *us* I imagine in my dreams.

In the letter's closing, after revising several horrible, nerve-induced lines like *We'll always have the tractor* and *Frankly, I do give a damn*, I settled for the truth. *I love you.* And then I recalled the line of poetry I'd seen in his journal. *When love shows up like an afternoon thunderstorm, give it shelter.*

As the show is about to begin and I hear Connor warming up his trombone, I feel a tap on my shoulder. When I turn around, I see a familiar face, the same face I saw when I pulled up to the outskirts of True City several weeks ago. He is cleaner, but it is he, the farmer who greeted me back home, gave his heartfelt condolences for my parents, and who insisted on calling me Janie like he knew who I was. How could I not have recognized him? Was it my LA-induced vanity that erased my ability to remember people, or had there simply been too many years in between?

"Mr. Stephens," I say, taking his hand. "When I saw you a while back, I... I'm sorry I didn't remember you."

"No apology necessary, Janie. It's been a long time." He holds on to my hand a little longer, like he's got something to say, and he does. "So many memories. You and your folks at the coffee shop; you, the Corn Queen who made it rain; and all your trips to the corn maze. Especially your last one."

I stop breathing for a moment. Pieces of the puzzle come to

me frame by frame. Mr. Stephens's farm was the adjoining land next to the Nelsons' corn maze. He saw me. He saw me on that fateful day.

Ours eyes lock in a type of solidarity most people can never understand. "I saw you when I was doing fieldwork that late afternoon, didn't think anything of it, but when I heard the news about the baby being left there, well, I put it all together."

"And you never told." All the crowd noise falls away; everything falls away.

"Wasn't my place." He smiles, squeezes my hand a little tighter. "But after you left, I made sure your folks got to know her. Fixed it up so your dad was her Elks sponsor. She swung on your tire swing, and when she was older, he made her watch James Bond movies with him. That's why she wants to be an actress, you know." He laughs. "You can blame your dad for that." He stops for a moment. "He missed you a lot. But Bliss took your spot for a long while there."

I think I see his eyes moisten, but it's hard to see through my own right now. "They knew her, Janie. They just didn't know she was their granddaughter. Thought you might want to know that," he says, and then, like it was no big thing, he brings absolution, redemption, right here in True City. "They'd be proud, Janie. Of both of you."

He turns back around, like it was nothing, like he's not the pillar of integrity that he is, because anything else would be less than humble. He chose respecting my privacy over a much easier path, and I am dizzy with what *Do unto others* looks like in real life. I've never been more proud to call this place home.

I am still reeling when the curtain opens. Still reeling after the

"Rock Island" train opener, the "Iowa Stubborn" number, and the "Ya Got Trouble" scene, so by the time I see Bliss enter the stage and sing "Goodnight, My Someone," just like Mom sang to me, the world melts away.

Bliss's voice carries throughout the theater, but I imagine she's singing to me.

It's just us.

Her soft, blond hair falls in little ringlets around her face, and for a moment, I am looking at myself. She is looking out the set's fake window at fake stars, but everything about her is real. When the song swells, she tilts her head slightly, and our eyes meet right as she sings.

She is real.

Soon, Harold Hill will peek his head out from behind the curtain, ready to peddle his personal brand of hope, trying to convince them the impossible is possible.

And we will all believe it.

"Miss you, ambassadors," I say and blow a kiss to the sky.

Harold Hill is ready for the next scene, and so am I.

❧

I am sitting in Mom's recliner, eating the last portion of her heavenly corn casserole from the deep freezer, and I am surrounded by humility.

The last time I was in my LA screening room, a lifetime ago, I watched a grieving James Bond caress the love of his life and refuse to say goodbye. *We have all the time in the world.* My darkness, my world, impenetrable then, even on the brightest of days.

We don't have all the time in the world. There is darkness. There will always be darkness.

But light finds a way.

I think of the first line of *Hole of Schmidt*, and it is suddenly illuminating. "You're digging a hole to nowhere." It's a metaphor. I get it now, Nick. Gary Schmidt sees a young girl from Sierra Leone on a late-night documentary highlighting the extreme poverty there, and he begins a quest in her honor. One man risks everything for a girl he's never met. He attempts the impossible: to rewrite her story.

I owe Nick Wrightman a phone call, and a revision.

I take off my bracelet that, for years, had been both my punishment and my salvation. *She is happy* were the words I'd had engraved underneath, the secret part of the bracelet that touched my skin every day, always. Until today. Today I will take it off. She is now my reminder that love exists, in the flesh. Tomorrow I will bury this bracelet, bury After Jane, bury what was lost under the willow tree.

When Sid sent me my gown, I had him send me something else, something I've neglected for too long, and I see the perfect place for it. I take the framed poster out of its mailing box and hang it above the fireplace. Just thinking of the ringing bell and the stars talking to each other will keep me company. Jimmy Stewart's getting out of this town. He's gonna see the world right in front of him. This is what Mom and Dad wanted for me all along.

How could I have not seen it before? Movies don't create magic, they reflect it. We are the real magic—our families, our friendships, our audacity to find hope amid dismal circumstances.

Outside, snow blankets the land. Christmas will be here soon.

She will be here soon. Maybe they will be here soon. There will be a knock, and it will reverberate through the big wooden front door Dad fixed a dozen times, and the sound will travel through Mom's kitchen, through Dad's den, through the living room. It will breathe new life into this old house.

When I open the door, Bliss will smile and say, *What did you think? Did you totally love it? Mr. Linart said we were really, really, really good. I mean, for opening night, you know. Thanks for practicing my lines with me; it totally helped so much. And what do you think? Do you totally think I can really do this? That I'm good enough to do this? I mean, you should know, right? This is totally your world, right? So, do you think I could be a real...?* And she will take a break here from her excessive adverbs, from her excitement, but not her rhetorical questions, and bare her soul a little. *Do you think I could be a real actor? What do you think?*

I will say *Believe so.*

She will know what that means—that she will be whatever she wants to be, and I will be there every step of the way.

So many movies, so little time.

Outside, the world's brightest stars light up the sky. Mom and Dad are somewhere out there, making me hope we are indeed all star stuff. Thank you. Thank you for somehow, some way, luring me home.

And Rob? We are two wanderers, waiting to see if our endings coincide in a land called True City.

There is a knock at the door, and I swear I smell the faint scent of lilacs, and I think, just maybe, that I hear two voices.

No matter what lies on the other side of that door, I have a daughter. I have to keep looking forward, keep looking up.

That is to say, so much depends on the stars.

Fade to black.

THE END

READING GROUP GUIDE

1. How accurately do you feel the two settings in this novel (Los Angeles and the rural Midwest) were portrayed? Have you been to either location? Which place do you most identify with: the West Coast or the Midwest?

2. Would you live in Jane's hometown? What did you like about it? What did you dislike?

3. Jane's shameful secret from her past prevents her from returning home and therefore keeps her from her family. How realistic is the concept that shame could shape someone's life to that extent? Is guilt something that is an especially midwestern trait or more of a universal one?

4. Jane is both physically and emotionally marked by her home. To what degree does where you grew up make you who you are? How have you been shaped by your own home?

5. How many movies referenced in this novel did you recognize? Did it make you want to see any of them for the first time or revisit some of the classic favorites? What are your favorite movies and why? Jane often associates particular films with people she knows. Do you ever think of friends or family members by such an association?

6. Jane is the most memorable Corn Queen in Crocker County. In your hometown, were there any legendary characters? What role did you play?

7. Charlotte Davis puts her utter desperation on display with her meatloaf hotline. What is the most humiliating job you've ever had?

8. When Jane sees her mother's corn casseroles stacked up like "little corpses" in the deep freezer, waiting for when her only daughter might make a visit, it is a defining moment for her. What defining moments have brought you to a crossroads in your life? What did you do?

9. Jane has many flaws as a character. What do you think were her greatest sins? Her most redeeming acts? Do you have empathy for the way she handles her struggles, or were you disturbed by the choices she made to try to reconcile them?

10. The notion of second chances is paramount in this novel. Do you believe in second chances, or are they the stuff of movies and Hollywood endings?

11. How does Jane change or evolve throughout this story? What can be learned from her journey?

12. What was your favorite or most memorable passage in the book? Why did it make an impression?

13. At the end of the book, who do you envision at the door? What does the future hold for Jane, Rob, and Bliss? What future do you think Jane deserves?

A Conversation
with the Author

Why did you make Jane a movie critic?

Okay, this is funny. (And when I say "funny," I mean "tragically embarrassing as a writer.") Originally, Jane was a food critic. I spent a *long* time scouring fancy cookbooks, watching ridiculous amounts of every cooking show imaginable, and when my keen-eyed but brutally honest husband read the first chapter of my original story, he said, "Babe, this food stuff is forced. You're not a foodie. You own five Crock-Pots. You love movies. Write about movies." And voilà, Jane was a movie critic. Jane's original idol was Ruth Reichl, food critic extraordinaire, who was then replaced by Pauline Kael, film critic extraordinaire. The scene when Jane gets advice from the spirit of Pauline Kael always reminded me of that scene when Clarence gets mentored by the spirit of Elvis in Quentin Tarantino's *True Romance*. But I digress. Regarding the food research, I now know weird things about foie gras, balut, and various bisque soups. Ultimately, my husband is right; I'm not a foodie. My friends out here in the west think my penchant for

Midwest casseroles and my various Pinterest Crock-Pot boards are pretty funny. Don't get me started on how little ketchup they eat out here. It's all salsa, all the time. Whatever.

How much of your own Midwest experience/real-life experience is present in this novel?

There's always a hint of the writer in every book, but in this particular book, there's a lot. Since this book is essentially a love letter to Iowa, my imaginary world was based on my childhood, and so much of it was unearthed from the recesses of my memory while writing. The two grain silos named after Jane's parents were, in fact, based on two grain silos in Albert City, Iowa. In the 1970s, they were the two biggest silos in the country, and for some reason unknown to me, they were named Big Bertha and Fat Albert, and the naming of grain silos seemed as normal to my Iowan natives as it might for people who name boats, I guess.

The fictional town of True City was a combination of the little town I grew up in (Truesdale, Iowa, population 72!) and the town where I went to school (Albert City, Iowa, population 800).

My mom loves musicals and made us watch *The Sound of Music* every year; my dad, like Jane's, has a flair for precise language and would remind us that "only meat can be done, tasks are finished" on a weekly basis. He also was the manager of our grain elevator (maybe that's why I have a soft spot for grain silos), and on the weekends, my mother, my six siblings, and I played in my father's band, Maynard and the Moonlighters, where I got to mingle with many of the types of people that I based Mr. Stephens on—the kinds of people who, at the end of the day, did the right thing and said nothing of it.

Where did the inspiration for this story come from?

A few years ago, on my way home from school (I teach middle school English), I heard a slight thump while driving. In retrospect, it was probably something inconsequential like a rock on the highway or maybe even just the way the car reacted to a bump in the road, but at the time, my initial reaction was a series of emotions alternating between panic and denial. Did I hit something? You're just tired; it was nothing. Oh my God, what if it was a kitten? Why would a kitten be on the highway? I even pulled the car over to peruse the area and make sure I didn't see anything. Then, as I resumed my drive home, I was struck with this: Is it normal to have those kinds of thoughts (zero to prison) in reaction to a small incident like that? Do other people see headlines in their heads— LOCAL TEACHER CHARGED WITH HIT-AND-RUN INVOLVING SMALL ANIMAL IN FRONT OF DAIRY QUEEN—or is this, perhaps, strictly a midwesterner's reaction? Does where we come from shape who we are? Are midwesterners somehow programmed for guilt? By the time I got home, a story had formed about a woman, transplanted in the west, who returns to her Midwest home to face her sins and after being involved in a hit-and-run accident has to make things right.

When do you find time to write?

As a mother of two children, along with a full-time teaching job, I have to get very creative to find time to write. I wrote my first two books on maternity leave—babies sleep a lot—and for a while I was a little terrified that I wouldn't be able to write a book without gestating, like those two acts of creation couldn't be separated. But since our family was beautifully complete with our two boys, I decided I'd have to figure it out. So I accepted that I'd never have the luxury of uninterrupted hours of time like you see in the movies—pontificating writers, well-groomed, wearing smart scarves and sitting at grown-up-looking desks. As my boys grew older and busier with school functions and sports events, I began writing on receipts, napkins, or random scraps of paper at the bottom of my purse. (I've kept a fair amount of these to remind me of this period in my life when novels were written in between soccer games and trips to the grocery store.) The idea for my next book came while listening to a fascinating news story on the radio, and I jotted down a title and the first line of the book on the back of a Target receipt. And for me, most of the real act of writing, the important stuff, doesn't happen at the computer. I have to work it all out in my head before I start typing. It's actually very exciting yet unsettling, the first stages of a book coming to life. There are all these little pieces you know are important, but they just don't seem to go together. I'm not satisfied until I figure out the puzzle. At night, as I'm falling asleep (nobody is asking me to check homework or make them a sandwich at this hour), I rearrange ideas, figure out how it's all connected, and then, in the morning, sometimes, if I'm really, really lucky, some of the pieces (and oftentimes actual lines) have been sorted. So, I guess my writing office is often in my car as I take advantage of stolen moments at stoplights or as I'm falling asleep. (Not sleeping in my car. In an actual bed.) And truthfully, my husband helps me carve out time to write by being the best dad in the world. This is a luxury I am grateful for every single day.

Did you do any research for this particular novel?

I researched the medical aspects of being in a coma and also various film critics, but the most interesting research I did was on teens who hide their pregnancies. I wanted to make sure that Janie hiding a pregnancy was plausible, and sadly, not only is it, but it is more common than you might think. I knew Janie was going to give birth on her own, and when researching the plausibility of this, I stumbled upon a news story about a teenage girl in the 1980s who hid her pregnancy, gave birth in her bedroom, and, knowing she couldn't care for this child, left her in a Burger King bathroom to safely be found. Ironically, the baby was adopted and grew up just miles away from the birth mother without her knowing it. Years later, when the now-grown baby, who had children of her own, wanted to meet her birth mother, they had a lovely reunion on television. It really solidified my feelings about the possibility of second chances, even in motherhood. Especially in motherhood.

Did you set out to make us laugh or cry?

Oh, both! It is really important to me as a writer—and as a reader, actually—that a story is both funny but also very tender at moments. I tend to read things that have a balance between these two. In my own stories, I strive for 70 percent funny, 30 percent gut-wrenchingly sad. (The English major in me just glanced at that again to make sure the math added up.) But the third emotion I am always interested in is shame.

I'm really intrigued by shame. Who doesn't have personal experience with shame? It's different from embarrassment. It's when embarrassment and guilt collide. This is the stuff of a midwesterner's nightmares. *I did something super dumb and it's my fault. Ugh.* I really do lean into those awkward moments on the page, draw them out to spotlight those times that remind me of when I've said something ridiculous or horrible and the whole room has stopped to observe the train wreck.

Do you have an ideal reader in mind when you're writing?

Well, the smart, writerly answer is no. Of course not. Writing with others' opinions in mind taints the authenticity of what you're trying to say. But that's for the cool kids—those writers I imagine who never second-guess their work. I find myself second-guessing quite a bit, especially in later drafts, after the glow of "I think this might be good" has worn off. I don't know if I have an ideal reader in mind, but I definitely have voices that pop up. My husband tends to secretly want everything I write to sound like a hard-boiled Raymond Chandler novel. I happen to know this. So I often think of that when my narration gets a bit too chatty and I need to stick to action and dialogue. Often, though, I think of what authors I admire would say. Would Maria Semple laugh at *any* of this? Would Lorrie Moore be bored with how literal this sentence is? Celeste Ng would never overwrite like I just did. That type of stuff. It's maddening.

When did you know you wanted to be a writer?

The first story I can remember writing was a one-page story that I wrote during my brother David's wrestling meet. I think I was six or seven. It was about a pumpkin who was sad because nobody chose him from the pumpkin patch. When my mother read it, she made me feel like I was the only little girl who could pull off such a feat, writing a story. Her praise deemed me a writer and, therefore, I think, deep down, I defined myself as such. When I became a teacher, I never forgot that—how to tread lightly when someone shows you their heart and soul on the page, and to be very loud when telling someone they have talent. Later, at the University of Iowa, I fell in love with the short story, and a profound moment for me was buying my first Lorrie Moore book at Prairie Lights in Iowa City. From the first sentence, I knew that, for me, this is what a writer sounded like. And that's what I wanted to be.

ACKNOWLEDGMENTS

Thank you to my agent, Stephanie Rostan, for your wisdom and patience. Your believing in this book is everything. Everything. Go ahead and humbly continue to tell me that it is all your pleasure, that championing books is what you do, but I will be grateful to you forever.

Thank you to the amazing team at Sourcebooks and to my dream editor, Shana Drehs. This book ending up with you was a cosmic gift. What are the odds that a story about finding one's way back home somehow found a midwestern publisher with an editor who grew up a few cornfields away from me? Shana, you made this book better, and I am grateful for not only your phenomenal skill, but also your immense kindness.

To John, my smart and witty husband, the father of my children, my in-house editor. Only you and I know the myriad ways in which you saved this book. I love you and am grateful for your brutal but important critiques. Believe so.

Thank you to my boys, Hardy and Hatcher, the loves of my life. You are the reason I write.

Meg Getty, you live inside this book. There isn't a chapter you didn't help revise (repeatedly!), and words cannot express my gratitude for your smart and honest feedback. Thank you for still loving this book on the fiftieth read. The Lost Queen is here. This is all happening. Start the car.

Amanda Arant, your thorough and thoughtful commentary on this novel was invaluable. You made me think about so many things in new ways, and I am eternally grateful for your amazing insight as a reader. And thank you also to those who provided feedback on early drafts: Heidi, Josh, Mena, Adam, Lorna, Ashlee, Danielle, Lin, Diana, Randy, Leah, Grace, Matt, Stephanie, and Dana.

Thank you to both my Leiknes and Zipf families for your support over many, many years. Dad, you gave me your love of words. Mom, thank you for telling me I was a writer when I was just a little girl. Work hard, be nice. You taught me that.

Thank you to every teacher I've ever had. Dreams so often begin with great teachers.

Thank you to all the students I've had the pleasure of teaching over the years. We learn from one another. Never stop writing.

Finally, thank you to Iowa and all of the fine people who I grew up with there. What a childhood we had.

ABOUT THE AUTHOR

Photo © Zoe Shorten

Elizabeth Leiknes grew up in rural Iowa and can make thirty-seven dishes featuring corn. She graduated from the University of Iowa before receiving her master's in writing from the University of Nevada, Reno. Her previous two novels received Starred Reviews from *Kirkus Reviews* and *Booklist*. She lives with her husband and two children near Lake Tahoe, Nevada.